A BOY'S CRY

Andrew Beckford

www.aabeckford.com

© 2011 Petcaii Publishing

www.aabeckford.com

ISBN: 978-0-9569819-1-2

ACKNOWLEDGEMENTS

To Jessica Hall, who has helped to edit the manuscript of A Boy's Cry, with enthusiasm and her invaluable assistance with this book in more ways than one; for which I will always be grateful.

As someone who has taught for so long, I have developed some mixed emotions about the profession, teaching which has become a part and parcel of my private life. I have subsequently grown to defend it as a profession, especially when I know that it can mean life or death for every child. It was therefore not surprising that I responded to a column once written by Trevor Kavanagh. I was taken aback when he replied to my email. From there on, there were a few pleasant exchanges of emails. I would like to say that from our correspondence came the completion of my first book and likewise this book. I would like to therefore express my gratitude for the wisdom that he had shared with me and the motivation he had given me.

I have been most touched by charities that I know are working flat out to prevent the cruelty of children, and one of them is NSPCC. I wish to dedicate this book to them and hope that somehow, the scenarios I have shown here, though not in as much depth as I would have loved to, will make a difference in someone's life. I intend to work flat out with NSPCC because I know that their job is worth every second of their time. When I see a young adult on the road trying to pitch for committed sponsor and that young adult recognized me as a teacher from her school, I am just overwhelmed with pride that someone like that is prepared to take the insults and rejection for such a worthy cause. I dedicate this book to people like her because people like her will prevent another baby P, Victoria Climbie and Khyra Ishaq whose lives were snuffed out by child abuse and neglect. I pray that with the downward economic crisis that everyone will be vigilant and strong in playing their part in preventing such shameful disregard for human lives. My brother, Michael Jureidini has inspired me more than ever with this book and therefore, I also dedicate this book to him.

Most of all, I thank Jehovah God for giving me the inspiration, strength and courage to persevere through my writings, and ultimately, allowing me to complete this book.

Last, but by no means least; I wish to thank my work colleague, Lorraine Salmon who has had an equal interest in the welfare of children and who has made a significant contribution to the corrections of this book.

It is important for me to highlight the fact that A Boy's Cry and its themes, setting and characters are in its majority imaginary. References to persons and places are fictitious throughout.

Chapter 1

Jade was fifteen and lived in an unusually quiet street off Jamaica Avenue, New York City. Her petite body and innocent appearance was enough cause for her mother to be very protective.

"Jade!" Doreen shouted. "Jade, you get your backside in this house, now!" Jade was sitting on the column of the gate.

"But, Mom, I was only getting some fresh air!"

"Fresh air my ass," Doreen snapped. "More like getting a look at Joseph, who you know has been watching you. Besides, what will Mr. Bailey think of us when he sees you behaving that way?"

"Mom, Mr. Bailey always minds his business. He's a decent man, but everyone knows that he lives off of the state," Jade called back, drumming her heels against the gatepost.

"Watch what you say, young lady. You know that the man has the mind of a twelve year old, but his Christian values remain intact." Mr. Bailey was the Jacksons' neighbor, a shy, introverted man. Although rarely seen in public, his childlike demeanor gave most people the impression of a quiet twelve year old boy trapped in the body of a forty two year old man.

"My only concern is you and that new guy across the street," Doreen warned her daughter. Joseph had moved in with his father two months ago. "Look at my face. Do I look as if I were born yesterday?"

Two days was, however, enough for him to know her well. On that very first day he had set eyes upon Jade, the chemistry was instant. Joseph never wasted time to introduce himself to her, it was short, but long enough to make his point. A salient point of returning to meet the most beautiful girl his eyes had ever seen.

"Listen, Mom, I don't know what you're on about, I don't even know who Joseph is," Jade protested. That was, however, a lie, as Jade and Joseph had been seeing each other secretly since the day he had moved in. No one, however, had a clue as they had both been careful.

"You listen, girl, don't you lie to me now. You know that the Lord does not condone lies. Besides, no daughter of mine is going to sit on a gatepost all afternoon. My daughter will grow up to be a lady!"

"Hey, honey, where my babies at?" a man's voice interrupted them.

"Oh, Lord have mercy, your father's home and the table ain't even set yet," Doreen exclaimed. Like her three daughters, she doted on Douglas.

Jade rolled her eyes as she hopped down from the gate. "He has to understand, Ma, its summer break! You stay at home, clean the house, wash the clothes, and take care of us. Dad can't be having it his way all the time."

"Hush your mouth, how dare you talk about your father like that!"

"Sorry, Mom, I was just trying to help!" Jade sulked as she returned to the house to begin setting out cutlery.

"Give us a kiss, sugar plum," Douglas ordered as he lovingly wrapped his firm hands around Doreen's waist.

"Stop it, Doug!" Doreen protested, trying to squirm away. "We ain't teenagers any more. The first time you were like this, I was only seventeen and look what happened!"

"We got a beautiful daughter and we called her Nadine," Douglas answered as he caught her lips, giving her a slow but steady kiss.

"Stop it, Doug, Jade's watching." Doreen giggled.

Douglas shrugged, unconcerned. "She's no baby anymore."

"Thank you, Dad. I know I can always depend on you!" Jade laughed as she finished setting up the table. The plates, cutlery, and mats were all in place, ready for the usual family meal.

"Well, while we are on that subject, you let her know that a boyfriend should be the last thing on her mind. I think she has a crush on the new kid on the block," Doreen informed her husband.

"You mean Joseph?" Doug asked.

"Yes, same one."

"That's interesting because I just invited them both here on the 13th for the barbeque," Douglas revealed. Doreen's eyes met Jade's and if the blush on the girl's face failed to reveal her nervousness, her trembling lips surely gave it away. Doreen made no comment, she only hoped that Joseph didn't return her daughter's feelings. It would be simple to help Jade get over a simple rejection, but a relationship, Doreen feared, would only restart that vicious cycle of her own life.

"Mmm, that smells good," Douglas rhapsodized. Doreen had served his favorite, spaghetti Bolognese. The kitchen door opened, and Nadine and Crystal Jackson tumbled into the room.

"Damn, did you smell that food, girls? You must have smelled it to be here on the dot of serving time," Douglas said. They giggled as they quickly took their places on the left hand side of the table. Jade took her place on the right as she had done since she was three.

"I'll say grace," Nadine offered. She was the eldest; nineteen, feisty, and confident. Her size had done little to diminish her elephant-sized ego.

"May the Lord bless the hand that prepared this meal, and may His grace and kindness extend to the less fortunate. Amen." The Jacksons were outwardly a close-knit family; their relaxed, teasing manner around each other was the envy of many others on the block. Little did they know, the happy exterior was nothing but a façade. Masked beneath it was a hideous reality.

The phone rang and Douglas jumped as if he had been expecting the call.

"I'll get that," he muttered, rising quickly from the table. Doreen followed his movement suspiciously. Doug never answered the phone, especially when he was at dinner.

"Hello?"

"Douglas, I want that two hundred I loaned you a month ago."

"Listen, I'm having dinner with my family. Just give me until next payday, OK? That's only two weeks," Douglas begged.

"OK then. No later, or I'll be coming to see you." The line went dead. Doug hung up the receiver, and took a moment to compose himself before he returned to the table. Everything was going to be OK. It didn't matter that one of them had slipped and contacted him at home; it was only one. He could handle it.

The girls were left to clean up the mess. They were glad to do so, they were good girls. Besides, it was the least they could do. They lived in a beautiful cul-de-sac in a three bedroom house, and although Nadine complained that Springfield Gardens wasn't exactly her ideal location, she was grateful that Emmanuel, her boyfriend, was allowed to sleep over whenever and however he chose. The other girls didn't like what they thought of as Nadine's 'special treatment', but they learned to live with it, and the sisters managed to share their single bedroom in relative harmony.

Doreen followed Doug upstairs. "Douglas, I am your wife and I know when something is wrong with my husband. Now, tell me what's going on," she demanded.

"Nothing's wrong, honey," Doug told her, working to keep his voice calm.

"So, you expect me to believe that your sudden determination to answer the phone before anyone else is nothing?" She paused, waiting for a reply, but none was forthcoming. "Oh my God!" she exclaimed, her hand flying to her mouth. "You are having an affair!"

"Girls, did you hear that?" Jade asked. They had been drying the dishes, but all three froze in place at their mother's frantic shout from overhead.

"They're having a fight," Nadine murmured.

"I never heard them yell like that before," Crystal said, looking anxiously at the ceiling.

"I have to know what's going on." Distraught, Jade ran out of the kitchen and upstairs before either of the others could prevent her. The bedroom door was ajar and she burst in on her parents.

"What's going on? Mom? Dad?" She looked from one to the other, her face flushed.

"Nothing, honey, just a slight disagreement," Douglas attempted to reassure his youngest daughter.

"Slight?" Doreen screeched. "He is having an affair!"

"Nonsense," Douglas protested vehemently.

"Dad, we're a family, remember?" Jade wailed. Nadine followed her into the room.

"OK, Dad, if what Mom is saying is nonsense, then why you don't tell us what is going on?" she asked reasonably, putting her arm around her sister.

"OK, if you must know..." Douglas hesitated.

"Go on, spit it out, or has the cat got your tongue? Who is she?" Doreen demanded on tenterhooks.

Douglas spoke reluctantly, staring down at his feet. "I owe some money. Two hundred each, to five different people. Now they want it back."

"That's *it?*" Doreen asked in disbelief. "You goddamn liar!"

"Mom, stop it, please! I think he's telling the truth," Jade pleaded.

Douglas threw up his hands. "Fine, you want to call the man back? Check up on me?" He pulled a card from his back pocket and thrust it at his wife. Doreen snatched it from him and pushed past Nadine, hurrying downstairs. She dialed the number with trembling fingers.

"Hello?"

The man on the other end sounded annoyed. "Who the hell is this?"

"This is Mrs. Jackson. Did you just call my husband?" she demanded.

"As a matter of fact, I did. Tell that man to give me my two hundred dollars, you hear?"

"You'll get it tomorrow. Don't you ever call here again!" Doreen banged down the receiver. Despite her anger at Douglas' foolishness, she was secretly relieved. The idea of sharing her husband with another woman was unthinkable to her, anything else, she could deal with.

However, Doreen failed to recognize the full scope of the problem. Douglas had been humiliated by his wife's discovery of his debt. She gave him the thousand dollars with strict instructions to distribute it amongst his creditors, and as he became sullen and silent in the days that followed, she wrote it off as a man's wounded pride. She did not once stop to consider the question of how a newly appointed bank manager could get into such debt.

"Sorry, darling, I am really sorry for losing trust in you, I just could never stand losing you," Doreen groveled.

He coyly hugged her, biting his lips as he faced the opposite side of her shoulders, looking confused. It was not the way he had planned his life. He hoped it to be a nightmare and he just wanted this time to be a blotch that would pass, he was just not strong to face anything stronger than this.

"Let us forget this incident, I should have said what had happened, but my pride had gotten the better of me," he admitted as he stroked her shoulder length hair backward.

At that point, the rest of the girls gathered around them hugging them in a circle as if to show the strength of the family. They, too, wanted to forget all about this.

It was in moments like those that the day had passed by so quickly, so by the time the day of the barbeque came around, Doreen had almost forgotten about the incident. She hoped that a day together as a family would shake Douglas out of his foul mood and help to restore their happiness together. Douglas was a typical, ambitious man, short, about 5' 4" tall, but his strong persona made up for all the social miscarriages; so much so that his decisions or intentions were never questioned. One had to be Doreen to understand the man behind the flesh. She understood his insecurities. He had vowed to himself never to be poor again.

Douglas had come from a dirt poor family and had promised himself not to ever return to such a lifestyle. He would rather be found six feet under before he lived a day without knowing if a meal would be on the table any day, wondering how to wear the same torn pants without it being noticed, and worst of all, seeing the third rugged old man leaving his mother's room doing the last act of shame; zipping up his pants. Doreen and his children were all he had and she knew that, but the irony of his actions were too much, enough to leave even Doreen short sighted of what was to follow.

Chapter 2

Too excited to sleep, Jade was out of bed by seven in the morning on the day of the barbeque and going through her clothes. After trying on and discarding half a dozen different outfits, she finally settled on her polka-dot vest and miniskirt. Her older sister found her in the kitchen eating breakfast.

"Well, well, someone's up early," Nadine teased. Everyone knew of Joseph by then and the crush that Jade had on him, although, they had no idea about their relationship.

"What is that supposed to mean?" Jade asked defensively.

"Nothing at all, I'm not saying a word." Nadine put on the coffee, grinning. Jade pulled a face.

Nadine watched as Jade fidgeted around looking like someone who had lost their shadow.

"I think that I will need to go to the shops early, we will need some more goods for the barbeque," said Jade.

"Like what?" asked Nadine.

"Ahm…the barbeque ketchup?" she said, sounding unsure.

Nadine knew of the rumor within the family, but she never would have imagined in a million years that Jade or Joseph, for that matter, would have moved so fast. The actions of Jade however roused suspicion, she was just not the type to take it up on herself to do anything for anyone, even if it were for her own dying mother; she was the most selfish person Nadine had known. She even thought that if there were a competition, Jade would have won the coveted trophy for being selfish. She itched to know where Jade had gone, she had to know.

Nadine knew something alright. It was her who had the vantage point of looking from the window of her room from the dark grey curtain that same day Jade had supposedly gone to the shops.

She pried for more than an hour with her hands moving the curtains slightly from its window, just enough for her to see and no one else to see her. She made sure that the lights were off, but if only she could lip read from her strategic point.

It was, however, enough when she saw Jade making the first move of kissing Joseph on his cheeks.

"Slut." She inadvertently cursed as she continued watching in the most uncomfortable poise.

At one point, Joseph looked up directly to the window and it was as if their eyes had made four. She wondered if she had moved the curtains before he could see its movements or if he really had seen her despite the dark room. She took another peek, but still like true teenage lovers, they were engrossed into each other, so she was convinced that she was not caught.

She watched for awhile until she just could not watch anymore. That fifteen minutes on the return of Jade was perhaps the longest suspension for Nadine.

She heard the opening of the door and excitement took over her medium sized body. She pondered on how to deal with the situation. *Should I pretend not to know anything or should I come outright to her?* she continued pondering. She decided on the former.

Her main task was now to pretend that she never saw, she had to convince herself that she knew nothing of their liaison.

"Hi, Jade?"

"Hi, Nadine." replied Jade, looking innocent, yet, smitten all over.

"So, where is the ketchup?" asked Nadine.

"They never had any, at least not the one that we need," she replied with a straight face.

"So, did you not stop anywhere else to get what we needed?"

"No, you will know later," Jade said.

It was clear to Nadine that Jade knew that she was onto something. The suspension was, however, eating her piece by piece, but it kept the day an interesting one; besides, the ball would be rolling not long from now she thought.

However, the day, for Jade, seemed to crawl by as she helped her mother and sisters get everything ready.

When the doorbell rang, she was out of her chair in a second and darting through the house to open it, beaming her best hostess smile.

"Hi, Mr. Redford, Joseph, please come in." She blushed.

"With pleasure. I hope we're not too early?" Jerome Redford smiled down at her as he took off his coat.

"Oh, no, sir, you're just on time," Jade assured him. There was a moment of silence as her eyes drifted toward his son.

"So, where is your mom,

where is your dad, and the rest of the invitees?" Jerome asked politely.

"Oh!" Jade remembered her manners.

"I'm sorry, let me take your coats. You're the first to arrive and the rest of the family is out back. Please, go ahead and join them." She waved them down the hall and as they passed her on the way out to the garden, Jade couldn't resist the opportunity to give Joseph an appreciative once-over from behind. *Mmm, nice ass,* she thought, and as her gaze rose, she realized he had turned around and was watching her. Their eyes locked, and Jade felt her face flame with embarrassment at having been caught staring. Then, Joseph smiled at her, his entire face lighting up as he did, and she felt her shyness melt away as if it had never been. It was if they had never met before.

"Uh, Joseph?" He raised his eyebrows questioningly. "Would you like to help me greet the rest of our guests?" Her palms were sweating; she laced her fingers tightly together.

"Sure, why not? Your house, your rules, right?" Joseph started back down the hall. Behind him, Jerome chuckled.

"Son, before you disappear with Jade, it is only good manners to come introduce yourself to our hosts," he pointed out good-naturedly.

Joseph looked sheepish. "Yeah, sorry, Dad. I'll be back in a minute, Jade, OK?" He smiled at her again and followed Jerome outside. Jade took the opportunity to dart into the bathroom to rinse her hands. The doorbell rang a second time, and she hurried to get it, wiping her hands on a towel. Her grandparents smiled at her from the threshold.

"Oh my, which one of you is this now? Is this Nadine?" Mrs. Jones asked.

Jade giggled. "No, Gramma, I'm Jade, your favorite."

"Oh dear, never mind me, I swear the dementia is kicking in." Mrs. Jones laughed. "Stand up straight, let me have a good look at my favorite granddaughter then." Jade obliged, but her thoughts were elsewhere.

"Gramma, Mom and Dad have been talking about you all day. They can't wait to see you. Why don't we go and find them?" she suggested innocently. Her grandmother kissed her forehead and followed her through the house.

Doreen and Douglas stood hand in hand in animated conversation with Jerome and his son while the girls tended to the sausage and the chicken on the small hibachi barbecue. Doreen's face lit up when she saw her parents.

"Dad, Ma!" she screamed with delight as she rushed to their side. Nadine and Crystal followed to be hugged and kissed in turn. It was the perfect opportunity for Joseph to sneak away, although he did not go unnoticed by Jade's sisters. "Smart ass guy," Nadine commented.

"What?" Doreen asked.

"Nothing, Mom." Nadine glanced ruefully at Crystal, both of them piqued at the lost opportunity to meet the young man who might one day become their brother-in-law.

Joseph slipped into the den where Jade was waiting, sitting on the edge of a worn, but comfortable, couch. This was in keeping with the rest of the decor – varnished floorboards scattered with slightly faded rag rugs that had been made by Jade's grandmother, small knick knacks on the shelves [mostly dogs; the favorite seemed to be German shepherds], and Doug's La-Z-Boy recliner in front of the television.

Joseph went to sit beside Jade on the couch. "I'm sorry I was so long. I'm being a very bad house guest," he apologized.

Jade smiled. "Don't worry about it, I know what they're like. They'd keep anyone talking for days."

"Well, you know them best. Hey, you've got such a beautiful smile. You get that from your Mom," Joseph complimented her. Jade blushed.

"Thanks... thank you. And, you, uh, have the most beautiful eyes." She glanced shyly up at him. Joseph grinned back at her, aware enough of his good looks to use them to his advantage, especially knowing Jade liked him. His height and his chiseled features were bonus enough, but it was his eyes that drew the most attention; wide and deep brown with lashes almost as thick as a girls. Jade's admiration for him was evident, and Joseph planned to use it to his advantage.

"I think I should tell you, I'm sixteen now. You?"

"I am fifteen. I will be sixteen a week on Wednesday," Jade told him, playing absently with the hem of her skirt.

"Interesting, that makes you a Leo. I am a Virgo." Joseph shifted closer to her. They were both very much aware that the rest of the party would be very unlikely to interrupt. From the music and laughter emanating from the back yard, they were having much too good a time to wonder where the two young people were. Joseph took advantage of their privacy to put his arm around Jade, the fingertips of his free hand touching her arm slightly. Jade shivered at the contact. "You have the smoothest skin I have ever felt," Joseph murmured.

"And, how many have you felt in your time?" Jade asked sharply.

"No-one's but yours, so that means you have the smoothest skin ever," he assured her smoothly. Jade gazed into his eyes wonderingly, thinking again how beautiful they were, how deep.

The doorbell shook her out of her reverie. With a longing look at Joseph, she got up and went reluctantly to let in their next guests, Mr. and Mrs. Chambers and their two children, seven-year-old twins. Jade greeted them politely, suddenly aware of her demeanor. Mr. Chambers was the priest at the local church, it would hardly do to let him catch her mooning over Joseph. She made light conversation as she took their coats, trying not to let her excitement at Joseph's apparent reciprocation of her feelings show. Joseph watched her through the open door, disappointed at the interruption. He felt very strongly that in Jade he had found something very much worth having.

Nadine came in the back door, followed by Crystal. "Hi, Reverend Chambers, Mrs. Chambers. Would you like to follow Crystal out back? My parents will be pleased to see you." As they moved away, Nadine turned to Joseph. "Why don't you go on with them and get a drink, Joseph?" she asked, glancing pointedly at her sister.

"Uh, sure," Joseph agreed immediately, following her gaze. Jade looked stricken. Nadine studied her for a moment, and then sighed.

"As a matter of fact, stay." Nadine sat on the couch tugging Jade down beside her while Joseph sat in the recliner facing them. Nadine took her sister's hands.

"Jade, I know how you feel about this young man. That's great. I'm real happy for you." She turned her gaze on Joseph, who looked back at her uncertainly. "What I want to know is how he feels about you. Are you serious about her, or is she just an amusement to you for a little while?"

Jade groaned and covered her face with her hands. "Nadine! Quit embarrassing me! You're acting like Mom!"

Joseph smiled. "Jade, it's fine. I wouldn't expect any less. Your sister's just looking out for you." He turned to Nadine. "It's a little early, of course, but I've admired and been seeing Jade since I moved here. She's a beautiful girl. And, I know her personality is just as lovely as her face." Jade stared at him, her eyes shining. Joseph reached across and took her hand as he added, "I want to get to know her fully. I want to be a part of her life. I would never, ever hurt her." The sincerity in his tone was such that Nadine was charmed completely. She beamed at him, quite forgetting the reason she had for confronting him in the first place.

"Oh, honey, that is just the sweetest thing I ever heard!" She squeezed his hand where it rested on Jade's. "Jade, you shouldn't tell Mom and Dad just yet, though. Give yourselves time to work things out between you before you bring them into it, OK?" She hugged her sister tightly, delighted at her luck. Joseph and Jade headed back through to the yard to join the party, leaving Nadine sitting on the couch smiling to herself as she thought about Cinderella stories and princes. It seemed that had happened for her youngest sister. Crystal poked her head around the door.

"What is the matter? Your mood sure changed since talking to Jade and Joseph," she said, alight with curiosity.

"You should have been here a while ago. Jade's made a great catch. He's a fish worth keeping in the net, for sure!" She pulled her sister into a hug, both girls giggling with delight.

The party was in full swing. Eighteen people mingled and chatted together in the backyard against the background music of Millie Small and the Beatles. Douglas and Doreen seemed to have forgotten all arguments, smooching, laughing, and enjoying each other's company. Then, the door bell rang. Those not fully immersed in the party atmosphere might have noticed a different edge to the sound; one that was demanding and even angry. Jerome, being a little tipsy from one too many beers, rose to his feet unsteadily. "I'll get it, I'll get it," he proclaimed grandly, heading toward the front door as if it were his own house. To the rest of the company, it seemed like a lifetime passed before he made it indoors. He walked freely as the spirit had seemingly taken its toll. He was not drunk, but tipsy, that was for sure. Jerome was at the door, but what transpired thereafter, no one knows. No one could ever forget that loud bang that greeted him, followed with the everlasting scream. It was the weirdest scream, like the sound of a whale with a pain too hard to describe, yet, it lasted for just a moment.

The gunshots split the party's atmosphere like a knife. Everyone froze in place like a game of musical statues, all eyes turning toward the house.

Joseph was the first to break the sudden paralysis. He ran for the front door, followed closely by Douglas and Mr. Chambers. They found him on his knees on the doorstep, cradling his father's head in his lap.

Jerome was white as a sheet, his mouth opening and closing like a fish out of water. His shirt was drenched with blood, shockingly bright in the afternoon sunlight. Of the shooter, there was no sign.

Joseph looked up at them, his eyes dazed. "My dad's been shot," he told them, his voice strangely calm. Jerome grabbed blindly at his son's shirt, leaving a bloody stain across the breast like a brand. He was trying to say something, but none of them could tell what it was. Joseph stared down into his father's face and just like that, his eerie calm vanished. "Help me! *Someone, help, for God's sake!*" he screamed over and over, tears pouring down his face. Behind him, the other guests were crowding forward, some panicking, some sobbing, some silent in deep shock, but they could have been on the other side of the Hudson for all the attention the boy gave them. Joseph clutched his father frantically, feeling his world fracture at the seams and fall apart around him, like so much of a broken glass.

Chapter 3

By the time the emergency services had arrived, the street was filled with people in dressing gowns and slippers, watching as the area outside the Jackson house was cordoned off and the investigative team began the search for any scrap of evidence. It was amazing how tragedy could transform a quiet neighborhood into a bustling one in hours. The residents gathered in small gossiping knots, straining to pick up any information. In cases like those, the community bond could become stronger or weaker, but it was clear that they were strong and united. Joseph and Jade were possibly the best demonstration of that as he clung tightly to her hands, and she did her best to comfort him.

"Joseph, we need to go to the hospital," Jade pleaded. He sat beside her in stunned silence, staring down at their interlocked fingers as if he had never seen such a thing before. "Honey, your dad needs you now more than ever. I'll come with you."

Joseph barely seemed to hear her. He kept repeating to himself in a dull monotone, "Why him? Why us? *Why me?"*

"Joseph?" They both looked up at the interruption, and Joseph seemed to stir a little at the sight of his Uncle Barry, who lived a few blocks away on Kingston Avenue. The police had called to tell him what had happened, and Barry had dropped everything to get to his nephew.

"Uncle Barry!" Joseph launched himself into the older man's arms. Barry held him tightly, steering him into the back of his car. Jade, still hanging on to Joseph's free hand, went with them. Meanwhile, en-route to the hospital, the back of the ambulance was a hive of activity as the paramedics struggled to save Jerome, his life hanging in the balance as he wheezed into an oxygen mask.

"He'll be alright, Joseph, everything's going to be OK," Barry soothed him. The boy nodded distractedly, still so deeply shocked it seemed little of what his uncle was saying was getting through. Barry kept talking in the hope that the sound of his voice would provide some comfort. "You're going to stay with me until this is all over. You can't go home on your own, and the police might want to look around there, anyway. You don't wanna be there when they do that, kid. I already spoke to social services, they know you gonna be with me till your dad gets better."

"Your dad is strong, don't forget how he managed to get out of that lake, you pushed him in on the day he took you fishing, and it was for your birthday," Barry said as he went down memory lane, a tactic to soothe Joseph.

"I did not do that on purpose," said Joseph.

"Yeah, right, you could fool me, but don't you worry because you are safe with me and my brother will pull through," he reassured.

Joseph managed a weak smile, relieved that whatever else was happening, he would at least be taken care of.

Standing on the sidewalk outside the Jackson residence, Detective Mitchell Armstrong stood watching the forensics team in their white plastic suits collecting shell casings. It amused him faintly that they all looked the same; like a small army of futuristic recycled snowmen. The most they had been able to tell him so far was that they were handgun rounds. The rest would have to wait until the ballistics tests had been completed. Armstrong shook a cigarette from a soft pack of Marlboro Reds and lit up, frowning ponderously. In a neighborhood that quiet, the shooting made no sense. There were too many missing pieces.

"Detective!" Armstrong glanced over his shoulder. One of the uniformed officers was hurrying toward him from the Redford house. That, too, had been roped off for the forensics investigation. The beat cop handed him a plastic evidence bag containing a sheet of yellow legal paper.

Armstrong turned toward the nearest streetlamp, careful to hold his butt away from the bag. He read through the contents of the letter carefully, ignoring the young cop's impatient glances toward the crime scene.

Dearest' friend Jerome,

How long have we been friends? Almost 25 years now, and I had your back the whole time. And, this is how you repay me? You better think real hard before you decide to try and bring down my marriage or maybe it'll be a bullet you get in the back next time. I didn't waste 15 years of wedded bliss to have a shit like you trash my reputation.

"What do you think, boss?" The uniform was practically bouncing with eagerness. New guy for sure. "You want us to look into this? Pretty convincing stuff, right? We found it in the grocery cabinet stashed behind the Lucky Charms."

Armstrong gave him a withering look and handed him the evidence bag.

"I'm not interested in cereal. Give this back to the forensics guys for testing. Then, go help the team questioning the neighbors. Let me know when they find that getaway car." The rookie looked crestfallen, but turned away.

Pitching his half-smoked butt, Armstrong headed for the victim's house. The blackmail letter was an indication that something wasn't right in Redford's life, but he remained unconvinced. Something wasn't right there. The shooting bore the hallmarks of a sloppy, amateur job. All the witnesses so far questioned had agreed that the gunman had opened fire as soon as Jerome Redford had opened the Jackson's front door, and Armstrong had to wonder if they hadn't quite literally jumped the gun. If, in fact, Redford had not been the intended target at all.

"Sir!" The rookie, who had stopped to listen to his

radio, now wheeled and scampered back toward Armstrong for the entire world like a good retriever puppy. "Sir, they've found the getaway car. Burnt to a crisp, they said, but maybe..."

Armstrong ran for his car. Two hours after their arrival at the hospital, Joseph's smile had gone, especially when he was finally able to see once again the body of his father's face, pale and still, and old-looking under the harsh ambulance fluorescents, and icy terror once more encased his heart.

They hastened behind the emergency stretcher looking on with anguish at the seemingly lifeless body of Jerome being wheeled in with the oxygen mask covering half his face, the blood bag with the Pvc tube carefully inserted on his body. It was then that the realization had hit them as if they were totally deluded to the extent of his injuries.

They all waited, naturally feeling anxious and at the same time totally helpless. It seemed as if they were waiting for a million years. Jade comforted the teenager boy she had hoped to be her life time partner. She, herself, wondered how this had happened, but it was wise to say not a word as Joseph sat beside her fidgety as reality had sunk in. Barry had preferred to stand pacing at least six feet backwards and forwards.

Then suddenly, a young doctor in green scrubs walked into the relatives' room with the clipboard clutched to the side of his breast and looked with uncertainty toward Joseph to Barry. "I'm Dr. Lawrence," he said. He had a faint Southern accent. "I'm looking for Joseph Redford?" Joseph stared at him vacantly.

Barry moved to sit beside Joseph and put his arm around the boy's shoulders. He looked up at the doctor. "Sorry. He's a little out of it." He paused for a moment, struck by the absurdity of minding one's manners at a time like that. "I'm Barry, Jerome's brother. How is he? Will he be OK?"

The doctor sat down opposite them and stared down at his hands for a moment. Then, he looked at Barry and just like that, Barry knew the news wasn't good.

"I'm very sorry, we did everything we could. Jerome suffered gunshot wounds to both his right lung and abdomen. He suffered a massive traumatic haemothorax – blood in his lung – and his liver was damaged beyond repair." He looked at Joseph's pale, agonized face and winced. "I'm very sorry," he said again.

"Sorry about what?" Joseph's voice was unnaturally high. He turned to Barry, his expression one of heartbreaking bewilderment. "Uncle Barry? Where's Dad? *What's happening?*"

Barry held his shoulders. "Joey," he began, using the nickname from the boy's childhood, "he's telling us your dad has passed away."

Joseph began to shake his head slowly. His huge, brown eyes swimming with tears, never left Barry's gaze.

"Yes, son. I'm sorry, it's true. He's not coming back."

"No. *No!*" Joseph suddenly lunged at the doctor, seizing fistfuls of his shirt and shaking him. "He was alive in the ambulance! *I saw him!* What did you do?

Make him better, that's your job, make him better or... or I'll..." His voice trailed off as Barry wrapped his arms around him and gently pulled him away. Joseph struggled, but Barry hugged him closer.

Just like that, the fight went out of the boy. He went limp against his uncle's chest, sobbing. Barry looked up at Dr. Lawrence, seeing little more than blurred colors through his own tears. "Thank you," he murmured, and as the doctor quietly left them, Barry buried his face in Joseph's hair, rocking him as he cried.

Chapter 4

The burned out car was found in a ditch about five miles away from Jamaica Avenue. It would have been the best evidence going had it not been a common sixties model, stripped of its license plate and burned beyond all recognition. That left Detective Armstrong with a single lead to follow up: the blackmail letter

Two days later at eleven p.m., Detective Armstrong finally had a lead on the letter. Questioning of friends and colleagues of Jerome's had led Mitchell to Paul Anderson and Jim Davies. Armstrong flashed his badge at the doorman on duty at the Free Style Club. He was waved inside and followed by two plain clothes colleagues, who made his way through the milling crowd to the bar. He knew to be careful, even without the patrons eyeing them warily. Mitchell knew them. Generally, people of the most deviant persuasion view authority figures with distaste and distrust; not that he could blame them since they were often persecuted because of who they were. They would do anything that was criminal, so blackmailing was the least of their crimes. The bartender had slicked-back hair and an earring. He eyed the detectives uneasily as they approached. Armstrong beckoned him over.

"Evening. You know Jim Davies and Paul Anderson?"

The bartender glanced sideways at the patrons lining the bar and watching curiously. He leaned forward and spoke in a low voice. "Hey, man, I don't want no trouble."

Armstrong mirrored his stance and his tone. "Then, you better tell me where I can find them so their trouble doesn't become your trouble."

The bartender blanched. "Over in the far corner, by the bathrooms. The guys in the hats," he muttered. Armstrong gave him a big, cheesy grin and patted his cheek.

"Thanks, boyo." The three of them wove through to the small table, at which two men in tipped-back hats and cheap suits were drinking whiskey sours and talking urgently.

"Jim Davies and Paul Anderson?" They looked up, faces showing annoyance at the interruption. Annoyance rapidly became alarm as they realized who was talking to them. The taller of the two attempted to bluster it out.

"Who wants to know?"

"Detective Armstrong, NYPD," he said, showing his badge. "I'd like to speak to you about the murder of Jerome Redford," he said. As he spoke, the other detectives moved in swiftly and made sure that the men couldn't escape.

"What the hell's going on here? I've done nothing wrong. I want my lawyer, now!" Davies demanded. Paul Anderson kept quiet. He seemed to have a better idea of what was happening.

"Never said you did, just said I wanted a word. Now, we can do it here in front of everyone, or you can join me down at the station," Mitchell said. They said nothing for a minute, and then Davies spoke.

"Fine, take us to your station," he said. They were both escorted to the 43rd St. precinct where they were led to separate interrogation rooms, and Armstrong left Anderson to sweat while he worked on questioning Jim Davies.

"Where were you on August 13th at 6:45 p.m.?" Armstrong demanded.

"I was with my wife, Ingrid, and my two children playing *Scrabble*," Jim told him.

"Are you sure you weren't playing *Murder She Wrote* with Paul Anderson?" Armstrong asked, looking at his notes.

"A bit cheesy, Sir, but just what's that supposed to mean?" Jim asked, looking puzzled. At that point, Armstrong threw the letter in the evidence bag on the table in front of him. Jim stared at it as if he had never seen it before. "I don't know who wrote that, but it sure ain't my handwriting. Are you trying to pin Jerome's murder on us?" He looked at the detective in disbelief. "You're looking in the wrong direction, man! We had nothing to do with this. This is bullshit!"

"And, how the hell you know of his name?"

"You are kidding me. Who the hell in this area

hasn't seen this on the news?" Anderson asked.

Further interrogation revealed that both men had airtight alibis. Paul admitted to writing the letter, but insisted that he had nothing to do with Jerome's murder. He explained that Jerome had discovered his plan to smuggling with Davies, and at that point, he knew that he should say not another word.

Jerome had had threatened to tell Paul's wife, but had agreed to keep quiet after Davies and Anderson had offered him two grand to keep his mouth shut. Armstrong interrogated them a further thirty minutes, and it just never add up. It was clear that there was a lot to the story, but even then it was just one of those dealings where Jerome was at the right place at the right time to hear enough so as to blackmail the men himself. Jerome had turned out to not be a saint himself but for all Armstrong's efforts, there was just not enough evidence for him to convict them, so there was no option but to release them both. They were not totally off the hook, though.

"Excuse me, gentlemen, and sorry for the inconvenience," apologized Armstrong

"And, so you should," said Jim. He suddenly decided to show his hidden confidence.

Three months had passed and still no one had been arrested. Armstrong admitted to Barry and Joseph that since they had no new leads, Jerome's murder was in danger of becoming an unsolved mystery. The case had been left open, however, and although many of Armstrong's department regarded it as a back-burner job, he continued to pursue it on his own time. By that time, Doreen and Douglas were back living in their home with the girls, and things were returning to normal. Joseph had become almost a part of the family. Like Nadine, Jade was permitted to have her boyfriend stay overnight since she was now sixteen. At first, Doreen had been opposed to that since Nadine had had to wait until she was eighteen, but in the end she agreed to make allowances for Jade as she trusted her to be sensible and mature.

One morning, Joseph arrived at the Jackson's residence at nine in the morning, which was earlier than usual. "My, my, you're up pretty early today," Crystal commented as she let him in.

"Well, I've finished my semester exams and Uncle Barry hasn't been around, so I decided to visit with my second family," Joseph replied charmingly. He was at High School and wanted to do a four year course at college, so his exams and lessons at High School meant a lot to him. He was currently on his second two-week break from his studies.

"Take good care of her." Crystal threw him a skeptical look.

"Why don't you leave the poor guy alone?" Doreen chided as she caught the tail end of the conversation. "We're all going to the Methodist convention, but Jade's not feeling so good, so she will need your company, Joseph." She beamed at him affectionately.

"Thank you, Mom, I'll look after her," he said as he followed the others out to the car where Douglas was waiting. Crystal was either being protective of her sister, or perhaps there was a pinch of jealously showing its ugly face. No one was sure. "Oh, Mom, about what time will you be back? I need to tell Uncle Barry so he knows what time to expect me home," Joseph asked, the picture of innocence.

"We're going all the way out to New Jersey, so you won't expect us back till about ten," Doreen told him. Joseph hid a smile, it was as if everything was falling into place for him. As the door closed behind Doreen, Jade came down the stairs.

"They're all gone, then?"

"Until ten," Joseph told her gleefully. She was supposedly ill with the flu so she was dressed in her night gown, and it was a loose night gown.

"Aren't you afraid of catching my virus?" she asked teasingly as he started to unfasten her gown.

"Speak to me like that again because I want to catch more than your virus," he replied as their body contact became more amorous. The noise she made was too loud for even Joseph as they played amongst themselves for that entire day. Whipped cream, strawberries, vanilla ice cream, and even a few enhancement pills were all a part of their experiments. It was their first time, so why not?

"Wow, it's so quiet," Douglas said as he turned the key to the door. They all came in, and being that it was so tidy, clean, and quiet, they preferred not to disturb Jade and Joseph. All but Crystal. She crept to the door of Jade's room and the fresh, but pungent, smell of the room awakened her suspicions; but she said nothing to anyone, reasoning that as the deed was done, there was just nothing else she could do.

That poignant memory remained fresh in Crystal's mind two months later. It was on the tenth day of January 1968 when Crystal noticed something different about Jade. Her greatest fear, she was certain, was about to turn into reality.

"Jade, you have gained some weight, especially to your stomach," Crystal said.

"I don't know what you're on about," Jade answered defensively.

"I've noticed how you been trying to tighten your waistband and the regular trips to the bathroom," Crystal pointed out. "Have you told Joseph? No, let's cut to the chase. Have you told Mom and Dad?" At that point, Jade broke down.

"Yes, I am pregnant, you know that this would kill Dad, not to mention Mom." She revealed her secret at last. Crystal seemed unnerved, but sympathetic nevertheless.

"What about Joseph, does he know?"

"He's back from college next week, I'll tell him then." Jade sat down and twisted her hands together nervously.

"OK, Dad didn't go to work today, in fact, everyone will be together at lunchtime. You should tell them then," Crystal advised.

"In front of Daddy and Nadine?" Jade asked with a quiver in her voice.

"Better now, honey, than later when your belly becomes too big to hide. Better now." Jade couldn't argue with her sister's logic.

Chapter 5

"Oh loving God, bless the hand which has prepared this food and we pray for the less fortunate." Nadine sat with her hands clasped as she said the grace. She was a happy young lady; she always was when her family was all together.

"So, Jade, Crystal told me that you've got something important to tell us. What is it?" Douglas inquired, reaching for the salad. Jade kept quiet, looking petrified.

"Come on, answer your dad, you're getting me worried now," Doreen said.

"I'm pregnant," Jade blurted out. Douglas choked on his mashed potato, but not to be outdone, Doreen started to cry. To say she was hysterical would have been an understatement.

"This is exactly what I warned about," argued Doreen.

"Calm down, I am sure that there is a mistake here. Are you sure that you are pregnant?" queried Douglas.

"I am, Dad," she answered with not another word. He looked in dismay; he was very protective of his daughter as his hope for her was for her to make a success of her life. She was natural with figures and so he had it all figured out that she would become a chartered accountant. She he thought was the one to stop the drought of mediocrity in the family, but all of that was, for him, impossible now.

"Mum, Dad, you have made it look as if I got a death sentence and that is not true," Jade defended herself.

"For all I care, I have washed my hands. I knew that this would have happened and look, you have not learnt from my own mistakes,"

The same cycle is to repeat itself again and again," lamented Doreen.

Problems, however, did not come in one or two for the Jackson family, they came in threes.

Things couldn't have been much worse. Douglas got up from the table and strode into the front hall, unable to look at his daughter. Leaning against the wall in an effort to calm himself, he spotted the day's mail on the hall table. There was a letter addressed to him lying on top, and he picked it up wearily and opened it.

To Douglas Jackson.

It is true that anyone with a double barreled name is trouble. My henchman missed you for Mr. Jerome Redford. The next time, the bullet won't miss you or your family. It is no longer $200, it is now $1000.

"Damn, this family is cursed!" Douglas whispered to himself, stumbling into the den to sit on the couch. This was enough for Douglas, something had to give, and it went. Suddenly, his chest tightened and a pain gripped him like a belt beyond his control, fastening tightly around his rib cage. He cried out in agony, collapsing to the floor, the letter falling from his spasming fingers. Everyone ran to his aid, but it was too late. Douglas' mouth and eyes were wide open. It was as if he had seen a deadly monster, but there was no movement from his body. His glassy, fish-like eyes stared straight ahead, seeing everything, and seeing nothing at all.

"HELP! HELP US!" Doreen shrieked. Everyone seemed helpless. Jade went to touch him, but Doreen pushed her away, her expression was so furious it almost seemed as if she would kill her daughter.

"Don't you dare! Don't you dare touch my husband! You murdered him! If it wasn't for you, he wouldn't have had this heart attack! I want you out of my house and I never want to see you again!"

The girls had never seen Doreen so determined and upset. They dared not say a word. The embarrassment of having the paramedics and the police on the scene again was totally unavoidable. Doreen was right, it was a heart attack. Douglas was pronounced dead immediately, and his body was taken away to the hospital morgue.

Doreen was inconsolable, certain as she was that Jade had put the stress on Douglas that had caused his death. But, that was nothing but speculation. Detective Armstrong was with the cops and with his eye for fine details, he saw the open letter between the crevices of the two settees.

"My, my, what have we got here?" He proceeded to read the letter. "I'll be damned! Come over here, fellas." He beckoned to his junior officers. "Take this letter to the lab now and check for finger prints." It was his last hope, a find that would certainly make his career. The order was issued.

"The coroner's report must get to my desk pronto, all his children and his wife must be interviewed. We need to determine if this man was being blackmailed," the detective commanded.

"This house must be haunted or they are just totally unlucky to have lightning strike at the same spot," he said to his assistant. The entire matter seemed inseparable, and it might just be his lucky strike. It was just a routine once more for everyone to be seen as a suspect, and now the entire neighborhood was to be watched and monitored, but had he knew what he was doing. He had no intention of making it a drawn out operation, this for him was a waste of time.

Two days later, Detective Armstrong got more than he had asked for on his desk. His assistant, David Jefferson, a twenty four year old Harvard graduate, brought him the paperwork; the coroner's report, Douglas' wife and children's interview transcripts, and a detailed report of Douglas' banking history.

The coroner's report came back positive for acute heart failure, but his banking history was more of a cause for concern. Detective Armstrong realized that there were discrepancies in the account statements. The check for $350 to the racecourse was the beginning in putting the jigsaw puzzle pieces together. It was, however, the money debited from Douglas' account that caught Armstrong's eyes. Douglas was not so stupid after all, his transactions were deliberate, it was as if he wanted to help them. Yes, Douglas, did not know his blackmailer/money launderer, but he had made arrangements to transfer money electronically, although, it was partly by force when the coward handed him the sort code and account number. If one did not know Douglas well enough, they would be certain to believe that the money was purposely unpaid in full. Armstrong realized that Douglas was a compulsive gambler, and that he must have had many enemies, one of them whom might have easily mistaken Jerome for Douglas. However, when he saw the results for the fingerprint tests on the envelope, he felt as if he had hit the jackpot. It seemed almost certain that his initial two suspects were back in the frame. However, on comparing the envelope prints with those of Davies and Anderson, there was no match. The detectives were not discouraged, however, they felt certain they were getting close with the new lead.

Jade, in the interim, had finally gotten in touch with Joseph. She didn't want to scare him off, so she resolved to play her cards very carefully.

"Darling, when will you be back?" Jade asked over the phone.

"I'll be back in two days, sorry for the short notice," Joseph told her.

"Oh no, that's good. By the way, I have been staying at Uncle Barry's," Jade said, trying to stay calm.

"What?" Joseph sounded confused.

"Yeah, I've been here five days now. Dad has died and we're all at different places until the investigations are over," she explained.

"I am sorry to hear that, but how did he die? And, how long will you be at Uncle Barry's?" Joseph asked, bewildered.

"It was a heart attack. I'll tell you the rest when you get here. I can't do it over the phone." Jade winced at the sound of her own voice. She sounded like an old wife.

"Damn, I know how you feel. Isn't it weird how not too long ago my dad died, and now yours?" Joseph asked sadly.

"There is a lot more to tell you, Joseph, but it can wait till you get home," Jade said again before breaking down while still on the receiver.

"What's wrong, honey? What's wrong?" Joseph asked, sounding concerned.

"My family has turned against me. They think I caused dad's heart attack," she sobbed.

"Calm down, Jade, calm down. I will get home sooner. But, why did they blame you? That's crazy!" Joseph demanded, confusion in his tone. Jade could not hold it in any longer.

"I'm pregnant," she mumbled. There was silence on Joseph's end for at least a minute.

"Pregnant?" he asked.

"Yes, I am having your baby."

"Does Uncle Barry know?"

"Yes."

"Oh, I am so dead now," Joseph groaned. "Tell you

what, I'm coming home now." Joseph hung up. Jade was literally frozen out of her own family. Barry was her rock to hold on to.

"Don't you worry, Jade. Joseph is a sensible lad, his family raised him well, he'll listen to sense when I talk to both of you together," he said reassuringly to Jade as she hung up the receiver. Uncle Barry knew his nephew well, and knew that before seven p.m., Joseph would be in the living room ready to live up to his responsibilities.

In the meantime, Doreen and her kids sat in the living room of Mrs. Pamela Jones, a devout Christian who lived alone in a four bedroom house. She believed that she was doing God's work by putting the family up for two weeks until they got the clear to move back into their home. After all, her husband had died of food poisoning some years previously, and the neighbors whispered that she had murdered him for his insurance money. She understood exactly what they were going through. She wished that everyone believed in her innocence, but Doreen and her children had always politely refused her dinner invitations. However, that night, they did not mind the cookies and tea that she had prepared for them.

"So, how long are we going to refuse to see Jade, Mom?" Crystal asked.

"Well, as long as I live," Doreen answered coldly.

"She has to be at the funeral," Nadine pointed out.

"Yes, but I will have nothing to say to her. Every one of you is to follow my lead. I warned her, and she caused such stress on your father, poor thing. I never even knew that he had a weak heart." She stressed her point in her desire to brainwash the others against Jade.

"Mom, I agree that she may have contributed to Dad's heart failure, but it is unfair for you to expect us to turn our backs on our sister." Nadine spoke firmly in Jade's defense.

"OK, have it your way, but as I live and breathe, I want nothing to do with her and her child. I can tell that this won't be her only mistake. She is not cut from the same cloth as the rest of you," Doreen lectured.

"Jade will learn from her mistake, and if she doesn't, then we will keep our distance." Nadine maintained her position as peace keeper among her sisters. Doreen had already made her own pact.

Just as Uncle Barry had predicted, Joseph arrived home that evening. He was fifteen minutes early. The setting was just fine, Barry sitting on his own with his arms spread like an eagle's wings on the arms of his chair. "OK, son, sit down beside Jade," Barry kindly requested. Joseph obliged. "Jade has something to tell you."

"She already did, and I will take care of my baby," Joseph promised.

"Is that it?" Barry demanded, looking upset.

"What else can I say?" Joseph asked defensively.

"Our family raised you to be responsible, and marrying your child's mother will prevent him or her from being a bastard," Barry shouted.

"I'm sorry, Uncle, but if I marry Jade then I wouldn't be responsible because it will happen against my will. But, taking care of my son or daughter is something I will do for life," Joseph insisted.

"I wouldn't want Joseph to do something he doesn't want to. As long as he supports and loves me, that's all I need," Jade assured him.

"Uncle Barry, I am responsible, so I will do what is right. I will set up house with Jade and when I can afford it and we are both ready, we will get married," Joseph said firmly. That brought a slight smile to Barry's face, but Jade beamed broad enough for them both.

"Well then, all's well that ends well," Uncle Barry said as he got them together for the meal he'd prepared. The roast beef and potato with plain rice was, in his opinion, good enough to celebrate the occasion. It was amazing to see how everyone completed the night as one big, happy family.

For some people, however, there was a lot more to be uncovered, and for Detective Armstrong, desire to crack the murder case only grew in intensity. He placed a phone call to Doreen at Mrs. Jones' house.

"Good morning, Mrs. Jones, this is Detective Armstrong from the NYPD. May I speak to Mrs. Doreen Jackson?"

"Of course," Mrs Jones said. It was nine in the morning and Doreen was still in bed; it was her day off from work. No longer a housewife, she had taken a job at the local dry cleaners to support her family, but it wasn't enough. She decided that eventually she would have to supplement her income with a second job.

"Hello, Detective Armstrong, how can I be of assistance to you?" Doreen asked, polite but wary.

"Well, if you can come to my office, I would be very much obliged. If you can have your girls accompany you, that would be fantastic," Armstrong said.

"Nadine has left already, but Crystal can be there with me, though."

"That will be fine."

"I shall see you shortly then," Doreen said before putting down the receiver. The house was only about two miles away from the precinct, and there was a bus every five minutes. They were dressed smartly, as they had planned to visit the mortuary to see Douglas before the funeral on the coming Saturday. Soon, they had arrived. David Jefferson greeted them and guided them to Armstrong's office.

"Crystal, would you please come with me?" David asked. That did not sound good. Doreen started to feel uneasy, as if they were suspects. Detective Armstrong entered his office with a lady, a stout but smartly turned-out woman. A young police officer was also present in the room. There were two recorders, one on the cabinet and one on the desk.

While that was happening in Armstrong's office, Crystal was in a similar situation, using the same procedures and questions. Doreen seemed agitated.

"What is this all about?" she asked anxiously.

"Just routine inquiries. We think we're near to discovering the circumstances that led your husband to his death, but we need your help," Armstrong explained soothingly. The interview strategy helped to relax her and so she became more open to his questions.

"Did your husband have many friends, people who came to visit him often?" Armstrong asked.

"As a matter of fact, no. He was not the friendly type, just a family man really," Doreen replied.

"Did anyone upset him on the day he died?"

"Yes, his daughter Jade announced her pregnancy to the family and this knocked him for six. She was his favorite, and her dad had high hopes for her," Doreen explained, wiping her eyes with her handkerchief.

"Did he have money problems with anyone?" Armstrong asked with his hands clasped to his chin. She paused at that question.

"Yes, it was in early August that we got a call. A man threatened Douglas and I. Douglas wouldn't say who it was until I called his bluff and accused him of an affair." She stopped in her tracks, as if she was finally putting the pieces together. "But, I gave him the money, it was a thousand dollars and I told him to divide it between the five people he owed money to. It was $200 each..." Doreen's voice trailed off as she realized Douglas probably hadn't paid off a single cent.

"This was the letter that sent him to the grave, Mrs. Jackson. We found it on the couch where he died." Armstrong calmly showed her the letter, which was in a transparent plastic bag. As she read it, Doreen shook her head in denial, but as she looked through his personal bank history, the tears flowed faster. She now knew that her Douglas had been a compulsive gambler and had used money that he couldn't possibly have had, even if he had won a big sum because it always went back to the trifects or quinella in hopes of bigger winnings.

Doreen was forced to sign the agreement allowing Detective Armstrong to scour through the family's calls. She had no choice, and so she signed away her family's privacy with her head hanging in shame.

"Thank you very much for your time, Mrs. Jackson," Armstrong said. Crystal was waiting for her mother, and arm in arm they left. Detective Armstrong punched the air victoriously, certain that it would lead him to the man they so desperately needed.

"Mom, we have nothing to be ashamed of. Hold your head up high. Dad had a weakness, but it wasn't our fault," Crystal tried to console her mother as they waited for the bus.

"And, it was said, a little child shall lead them. How true it is," Doreen murmured to herself.

"You owe Jade an apology," Crystal said pointedly.

"Let's not talk about that now. She helped to put him six feet under, I want nothing to do with her," Doreen said stubbornly. Her stiff-necked pride, it seemed, had got the better of her. Doreen walked quietly as she tried to have her own moment because what had really bugged her was that Detective Armstrong never put much emphasis on the five men she thought might have been involved in her husband's death. In fact, he once said a person, and so she was left in total wonder.

Chapter 6

Douglas' funeral was on the evening of the January 20th, 1968. Strangely, the mood was not the one of total gloom that would have been expected, the attendees seemed to be going through the motions. Jade was perhaps the most sorrowful as she sat away from the rest of the family, unable to speak to any of them until the graveside service.

Death Has No Sting was being sung by the family Doug's work colleagues who had come to pay their respects when Doreen approached Jade, Joseph, and Barry. Crystal watched in relief. Finally, she thought, her mother would explain the developments and make amends. After all, Joseph, with the help of Barry and an evening job he had filing at an office, had found a small apartment for he and Jade to live in with the baby when it was born. Everyone thought that, for the sake of the grandchild, Doreen's move to make amends was the only sensible way forward.

"You have a nerve showing your face here," Doreen hissed in Jade's ear. Joseph and Barry were in earshot. The veins were standing out in Doreen's neck with the extent of her fury while Jade attempted to maintain an air of indifference. Crystal realized what was happening, she knew her mother well enough to expect that. She joined them in time to hear Doreen's vicious last few words to her daughter. "Killing him wasn't enough, you want him to turn in his grave as well, you want him never to rest in peace?"

"Stop that, Mom, stop it," Crystal reprimanded Doreen. The older woman ignored her. "Damn it, Mother, you and I both know that Dad was a gambler and that at least ten men were trying to kill him! That's what gave him a heart attack!" Crystal shouted. It was a wrong move because that statement alone struck a nerve with more than one party. Barry was the first to look at Doreen with hate. Joseph was too shocked to say a word.

"Are you telling me that the bullet that my brother got was meant for Douglas instead?" Barry demanded with fire in his eyes. The audience was frozen in silence. What was meant to be a loving memorial had turned into a total farce.

"Come on, Joseph, we are going home." Jade started to follow. "No, Jade, you are best staying at the flat on your own tonight. Let us see how much your dim gambling family cares," Barry said spitefully. At last, Doreen was faced with reality. She didn't say a word, but her vengeful feelings were there in her eyes and until she could see someone else to blame, Jade was still her prime target. Jade walked away, but Crystal followed her.

"I will stay with you tonight, Jade," she offered.

"I'll be fine," Jade answered.

"No, stress can lead to a miscarriage, I learned that in school and none of my sisters will have a miscarriage," a determined Crystal warned.

"I take back every single word!" Joseph shouted as he slammed the door behind him. Barry had entered ahead of him. He turned to Joseph and looked at him perplexedly. "I can't face her any more, Uncle. Every time I see her, I'll be wondering why did her family cause my father's death," he said.

"Joseph, that family will also give you a child. You can't desert her."

"Uncle, I'm going to go to Canada and study medicine there."

"So, I take it you're planning to stay with your Aunt Vida?" Barry asked.

"Yes, until I can get back on my feet," he answered.

"And, what of Jade and the baby?" Barry asked.

"I will take care of them, but I need the space now, can't you understand?"

"OK, I do. In fact, I will join you. We have had enough drama and maybe it is time for a change of environment."

Two weeks later, Doreen had moved back to her home yet again. That time, she was all alone. Nadine had moved out to settle in the hustle and bustle of a skyscraper in Manhattan. Rumor had it that she had found refuge in a relationship with an architect by the name of Clive. The family, for her, had become too dysfunctional and while she kept her devotion to Doreen, she kept her distance from them.

The insurance payment that Doreen had received from Doug's death could only stretch so far, and so she continued at the local dry cleaners and got a secretarial job to supplement her income. Soon, nothing mattered, even when she learned from Detective Armstrong that the illegal loan shark was her next door neighbor, Mr. Bailey, the same quiet and harmless man whose praises she had once sung. In fact, he had been the last person anyone would have suspected, and with good reason. He seemed so meek, it was almost impossible to believe that he was a killer. It had been his voice that she had not recognized on the phone, and really, who would? No one ever really heard him speak. She had thought him a boy trapped in a man's body, but he certainly had the mind of a forty two year old to run an empire from his home that no one would ever have imagined.

Armstrong believed that he behaved like a mysterious vampire, keeping in during the days and going out at night, meeting his main henchman, one who went under several different names, but was discovered from his fingerprint matched to be one man, Christopher Bailey.

The Jacksons had been living next door to a calculated, psychotic criminal who had his own henchman and operated another office at an isolated and neglected warehouse one a hundred and fifty yards away. In the spare time afforded him by his reclusive lifestyle, he was able to assume the identities of ten different men. The murder weapon found at the warehouse matched the bullets that had killed Jerome.

Everyone was stunned, and it had surely placed a strain on trust in the neighborhood. With everyone in the neighborhood on watch, it meant everyone was under constant observation.

Doreen became a recluse, attending only to her jobs and herself. Every cent of the two hundred thousand dollars they recovered from Mr. Bailey had to be returned. He was sentenced to thirty years for unregistered illegal loan activity, and he was also charged with fraud, claiming false disability benefits, stealing from the state, and most importantly, first-degree murder.

Chapter 7

Jade was now eight months pregnant. She wasn't feeling well and more than ever, she wanted Joseph to be by her side. He had moved out of their flat and was staying with his Uncle Barry, or so she thought. Crystal's company, while helpful, was not reassuring enough for Jade, and rightly so.

Eventually, tired of hearing nothing, she called Barry. The man who answered the phone was unfamiliar.

"Hi, is this Barry?" she asked.

"No, this isn't. Barry has moved away. I am the new occupant of the house." Jade's heart sank. She was struck dumb for a moment. "Hello?" the voice on the other end asked.

"I'm sorry, but do you have any idea where Barry and his nephew might have gone?" Jade's hand was clenched tightly around the receiver, her knuckles turning white with strain.

"Oh gosh, I could not say where they are now, but from what the agent told me, the previous owners have immigrated to Canada," the man explained. Jade was too flustered at that point to say another word. She placed the receiver down and then slumped down to the ground where she started to cry.

"We will manage, we will do it alone," Jade made an oath to herself. But, deep down in her heart, she prayed that Joseph had not forsaken her or his child. After all, he had promised in front of Barry never to forsake her or their child. However, a month later after the boy was born in the delivery room, she had to accept that her oath was all she had to keep going. Not one other person was beside her. The midwife handed her the baby and she just about managed a smile.

"So, what's the baby's name?" the midwife, a woman by the name of Susan, asked.

"Anthony," Jade replied dully.

"Anthony, that's lovely. Is there a middle name?" Susan asked.

"Joseph Redford, Anthony Joseph Redford," Jade said bitterly.

"He's a strong boy and you must look after him with love," Susan told her. Jade sensed that she had picked up on her lack of enthusiasm.

"Yes, I will." She handed the baby to the midwife. As she lay in the bed deep in thought, she remembered Anthony's cute face and the innocent cry he made as she had cuddled him, but now she was a single mother, and she had to fend for her newborn son and for herself. She had to find herself a job. Luckily for Jade, she had perfected the art of shorthand. She surmised that getting a secretarial job was her best option to support Anthony and herself. "It's me and you, baby, just me and you," Jade muttered, and she was right. Doreen had scorned her very existence. If she had anyone at all it was Crystal, and even her company was becoming scarce.

Three years had passed and Jade's shorthand skills proved to be a valuable commodity for Moat's Store Limited, a prospective book store in New York. She kept to herself, shunning the company of her colleagues, and immersed herself in her work.

During the days, Anthony was taken care of by a lady he affectionately called Ma, and even at three years old he was able to reflect on the aspects of his life that did not seem normal. He was very intelligent, but so much had happened within his three years that it began to affect him outwardly. Anthony couldn't identify anything specific except that his mother had him spend all his time in the care of another woman. Ma was an old lady, about sixty five, but she loved children. It was just a pity that Anthony was only one of the many she was paid to look after. When Jade dropped him off with Ma in the mornings, it was Anthony's least favorite time of day.

"Ma, I do not know what I would do without you," Jade said as she left Anthony in her care. However, Anthony wouldn't have it. He clutched his tiny fingers onto her skirt and screamed.

"I want my mommy, I want my mommy." He knew something with the arrangement was wrong, but he was powerless to do anything about it. He was a captive of his mother's choices, and of society.

1971 was a rough year to be living in. It was a time when the struggle to afford anything was dismal.

Drugs – cocaine, ganja, and even heroin - were widely available in the streets and back alleys of New York. Financial security was a major issue for Jade, and with money growing tighter as each day passed, her primary concern was how to make ends meet.

Friday, the third of March, was a good day for Jade. It was the day the stock take was done, and for her, that meant extra cash in hand. She gladly went to work that morning looking professional and pleasant. What she did not expect as she entered the storeroom was to see a short man helping the supervising team. He was an inventory accountant from the Manhattan branch. His frequent glances at her didn't escape her notice, but she tried successfully to ignore him until he approached her. His badge read 'Area Manager'.

"Hi, I could not help but notice how good a worker you are," he said.

"Right. It's a good opening line, though, I'll give you that much," Jade said cynically.

"No, I mean it! Anyway, what department do you work for?"

"I'm Jade, and I work as the main clerk for this branch. You?" she asked.

"I apologize, I should have introduced myself. I'm Nate, and as the badge says, I am the manager for the entire area."

Jade had great taste in men and the ability to see their best points, but in Nate's case, looks were not one of them. Nate was determined, and he saw an opportunity not to be missed. "In fifteen minutes, we will go upstairs to the mezzanine. I think there are sufficient people on the ground floor," he said with authority. Jade nodded. She had to comply, after all, he was her superior. Soon, he showed his position to be above her, and that stocktaking took approximately two hours.

The days turned into weeks, but strangely with no affection. It was a mutually beneficial relationship with the needs of each party being met by the other – money on the one hand and pretentious love on the other. The reality of the situation, however, hit Jade in the face when in June of 1971, she began being sick in the mornings and her stomach began to grow larger. She picked up the phone and hurriedly dialed Nate's number. "Darling, I think I am pregnant," she told him.

"That is good news, dear," Nate said. It was as if he was saying, 'Finally, it happened.' "So, you will now have to meet my family."

Jade had clocked him. She knew he was like a snake who knew exactly how to work his way in. The only thing that she had confidence in regarding her second pregnancy was that under no circumstances would Nate ignore his responsibilities as Joseph had. She also knew that his love for her, combined with his passive nature, made him weak. She had nothing to lose.

There was one thing that was becoming more evident, though, and that was Jade's lack of communication with Anthony. She saw him only for a short time after he returned from Ma's, and always after seven p.m. Soon, Anthony cried less, he had gotten used to her absence. Even during the weekends, his mother was replaced by Ma. Anthony started to become unruly, and one very rainy day he was left with Ma alone, the other children had not come for that weekend.

"Come on, my son, let me comb your hair," Ma coaxed Anthony. He didn't move a muscle. "You heard me, son, let me comb your hair."

Ma was lucky, he finally complied. And, she combed his thick, unkempt hair, but a stupid thought entered his head. He grabbed the comb from Ma and rammed its teeth into the old woman's plaited grey hair, and with the strength of a grown man, he pulled.

"Let go, let go!" Ma screamed. Anthony would not let go, though, his eyes looked as if he was possessed with a demon. "Let go, I said let go!" She began to cry, but when he let go, it was the worst thing he had ever done. He ran from her through the hot afternoon, and there she was behind him with her frail body, dragging her feet as she tried to equal his pace. What had caught Anthony's eye was unquestionably worrying. In the center of the kitchen was a lovely Austin dining suite, and on top of it rested a kitchen knife. Anthony was swift, and heaven only knew what got into his head, but he climbed onto the bench and then onto the table, and he clutched the knife in his small hands.

"My Lord, My Savior, help me now!" Ma wailed. She had never experienced that before, and from her brow perspiration of anxiety and fear dripped. Her one concern was for the safety of the child. "Give the knife to me, son, now be a good lad and give Ma that knife," she begged with her hair disheveled and falling around her terrified face. Anthony knelt on the table, preparing to climb down with the knife in his hand, and naturally any mother's instinct would have kicked in. Ma grabbed for the knife. The problem was that it was the blade that she had clutched just as Anthony pulled it from her grasp.

"Oh my God, what is going on here?" a female voice screamed. It was Annette, Ma's daughter. She was just in time to see Ma's bleeding hand with one finger hanging from its tendon. Annette knew what she was doing. She had the cloth wrapped around the wound, and she applied pressure while keeping the knife carefully away from the child. Soon, the emergency service was at hand and administered emergency treatment to Ma's injury. However, the situation became much more serious when Ma's blood pressure reached a deadly 180 over 150.

It was the first time Jade had reached the care center so early.

"Take your son now," Annette told her, her voice deadly calm.

"What is it, what has happened?" Jade demanded, bewildered.

"You just pray to God that my mother lives through this ordeal because if she does not, she will not be around to stop me from doing what I have in mind!" Annette snarled. The ambulance was on its way, carrying a disheveled and bleeding old lady called Ms. Joyce by so many; but to those closest to her, she was only Ma. She had the kindest heart that anyone could ever have imagined. It wasn't long before her family were gathered at her home, none of them expected her to live long.

"An ordeal like that would have killed me, and I'm only sixteen," Donovan, her grandson, said.

In the meantime, Jade got Anthony dressed and they walked home without saying a word. Anthony had looked in his mother's eyes, but he saw nothing, no emotion at all as she slipped his tiny hands through the sleeves. Then, she lifted him like a pile of belongings and left.

"Aunt, did you see that, it was as if that child didn't even belong to her, did you not notice?" Donovan exclaimed.

"Do not insult my intelligence, Donovan. I am a mother, too, remember!" Aunt Marie said. "If you had noticed, what does it have to do with us?" The phone rang and Marie ran to pick it up.

"Marie, it's me, Annette."

"Yes, how is mother?"

"She is doing well, thank the Lord," Annette said. "Her blood pressure is remarkably back to normal and the doctor said it was due to the shock."

"Thank You, God," Marie said.

"So, where is that stupid woman and her retarded son?" Annette demanded.

"Gone. I feel sorry for the son, though, you know. I watched them for twenty minutes as she changed his clothes and she said not one word to him," Marie replied.

"Not surprising."

"What was worse was that it was as if there was a

mutual understanding between the child and the mother not to communicate, but to hate. Sounds weird, but true," Marie lamented. "Even Donovan picked up on it."

"We won't be seeing them again, so they are not our problem now. Ma doesn't want to press charges, lucky for her," Annette told her resentfully. It was, indeed, lucky for Jade. She and her son heard nothing more from the woman or her family. However, Jade needed to find a replacement for Ma, and whoever she found was due for either a blessing or a curse.

Chapter 8

Jade was confused and desperate. She needed someone now more than ever before, so she rummaged through her drawer looking for a diary, a paper, a letter, note; anything with the number of a friend who could keep Anthony while she was at work. She diligently searched until she found a notepad tucked in the corner of a drawer in her nightgown, one that she hadn't worn in a while. On the notepad was Crystal's handwriting with her home number. Jade hesitated before dialing. The phone seemed to ring for hours on the other end, although, in reality it was probably only seconds before it was picked up.

"Hello?" a woman's voice answered.

"Hi, Crystal?" It had been so long since she had heard her sister's voice that Jade wasn't certain she recognized it.

"Yes, this is she. Who's speak...Pearls, Jade, is that you?" Crystal asked.

"Yes, it's me. I'm so sorry for not contacting you earlier."

"Not to worry, I have been busy myself," Crystal said. "So, how are you doing?"

"Not too bad, except that I am struggling with Anthony," Jade explained.

"I know, it must be hard with the dad not being around," Crystal commiserated.

"Well, I'm pregnant, expecting my second any time now. I haven't got anyone to keep Anthony at the moment, the neighbor has become tired of me now," Jade said uncomfortably.

"You have not really changed, have you, Pearls? Still so selfish and opportunistic. I bet I wouldn't have been hearing from you any time soon if you hadn't needed me to take your kid," Crystal demanded heatedly.

Jade kept her voice carefully level. "It's not like that, it's only for a while."

"OK, but only until you're over the delivery," Crystal finally agreed. Crystal was indeed the savior of the situation, and Anthony found great solace in his aunt. They chatted, played, and he started to show a unique intelligence that had never been seen before. He certainly had the knack to chat incessantly with Crystal and everyone else, except for when his mother came to the house to show off Marie, Anthony's sister, who had weighed a healthy eight pounds at birth, February 12th 1972.

"Oh, she is so cute," Crystal cooed as she looked into the pink pram. Anthony became curious as he gazed at his newborn sister with pride.

"She had everyone looking at her in the hospital. The midwives said that she was the most pleasant baby they had ever seen who barely cried," Jade said as she looked adoringly at her precious daughter.

"Jade, there is one thing. Anthony seems very withdrawn when he is with you. It is as if he is a different person, and he is only four. When you are not around, he is completely out of himself," Crystal said.

"That is Anthony for you, Jekyll and Hyde. He's playing smart. He knows very well that he has to behave well when he is around me." She pulled her muscles with her talk, but she never got the point that Crystal tried to convey. It was fear, an unhealthy fear of his mother that Crystal had correctly spotted, but she could not get it into Jade's thick skull.

"Anyway, I am sorry to disappoint you, but you will have to take Anthony with you because my boyfriend is moving in tomorrow and I do not feel it safe with him seeing or hearing things, if you know what I mean." Crystal chuckled. Jade giggled, but that was short lived when she realized the responsibility lay upon her again.

"Thanks, anyway, for your kindness. You have been the kindest of all the sisters to me," Jade said before hugging Crystal.

"That's alright, dear, I am sure you would have done the same for me," Crystal replied.

Jade was now twenty one. Her needs had changed, and she saw a new society evolving. War was becoming a greater reality with the Vietnam War at its peak. She was lucky, however, because Nate was there for her. From Crystal's home, it took her one hour to get home. The luxury of a taxi from Manhattan to Queens, Springfield Gardens was not as bad after all. The rent was becoming a burden to her, though.

As the taxi approached her new apartment residence, she noticed a short man dressed smartly in his pristine Hector Power blue slant pocket two piece and his pleated trousers. He looked bewildered as he seemed not to have expected Anthony with the group.

"Hi, darling, I thought Anthony would have been with his aunt for another two months," he greeted Jade quietly.

"She could not help it, and he is my son, after all," Jade snapped.

"Darling, can I have a quiet word when we get inside?" Nate asked as Jade fumbled for the correct key to the door. Anthony looked on quietly as he read every detail of the body language of his mother and Nate, whom he actually admitted. She entered the apartment, and there and then she tucked Marie quietly away, making sure she remained asleep. Anthony then ran to his room where he sat gazing into midair, thinking about something that would take ages; possibly even the whole day.

"Darling, I tried my best to support you and my daughter, but there is a problem," Nate said.

"And, what is that?" Jade asked.

"I give you enough money for your rent, for food and clothing, not to mention health bills," he continued.

"And, your point is?" she asked.

"I do not know how to say this, but I...I feel cheated. I feel as if I am maintaining another man's child, and I just cannot afford it!" He finally came out with it.

"You know that is not true!" Jade cried with tears running down her cheeks.

"Do not give me those alligator tears now because you know it is true." He held his ground.

"I work, too, and my money can stretch to look after my son, thank you!"

"And, who are you fooling?" Nate asked. "OK then, in that case, you will not mind if I tell you that as of today, my contribution will be reduced to a realistic amount to provide only for my daughter," Nate said. Jade froze, held her knuckles to her mouth, preventing herself from gaping.

"And, how much are we talking about?" she asked.

"Half," he sharply answered.

"You can't be serious, you give me only $300 a month, and you intend to halve that?" she gasped.

"Take me to court and it may be less. My brother would defend me very well," he challenged her. Jade knew she hadn't a leg to stand on. She also knew that he was being vindictive toward her for not committing to a relationship with him.

"If that is how you want it, that is fine, have it your way!" she said.

"Just one more thing, I will be there for my daughter as long as I live, and just remember one thing, if you hurt her in any way, you have hurt me. She must get all the love and attention she deserves," Nate warned before walking away without a smile.

Nate was no fool, he watched the relationship between Jade and Anthony, and saw fit to protect his daughter. The noose was getting tighter around Jade's neck because she knew that every penny spent on Anthony must be accounted for, so she was the sole supporter of Anthony and in her mind, that was no fear. After all, if Joseph was around, then the burden would have been off her. Although the oil crisis had ended by 1974, everyone was still feeling its effects. The increase in the price of cooking gas, the increase in the cost of electricity, even the price of bread had its knock on effect on Jade. Nate was stubborn, he stood his ground and made sure that Marie never suffered. He would buy the clothes, take her to the doctor himself, provide her with the health care, and then give Jade enough to sustain Marie alone. She could not cope until early one Wednesday morning, she met a pleasant lady at the bus stop.

"Lady, you look so depressed. What is the problem?" the mysterious, pleasant looking woman asked.

"Everything. I have two children, I have nowhere to keep them while in work, and the other problems are too burdensome for you to hear," Jade said.

"Forgive my poor manners, I am Gloria. I actually look after children, so there is one problem solved," Gloria explained.

"Really?" a gleeful Jade asked.

"Oh yes, I got a calling to look after children and that is what I do - at a small cost, of course," Gloria continued.

"And, how much is that?" Jade asked.

"$20 a week." she answered. "Per child."

"That is fine, you are like a savior to me, and to imagine that I met you at the bus station and usually ignore people who I think are being too personal or inquisitive!" Jade exclaimed

"Not to worry. Here is my address and phone number, feel free to call me any time," Gloria said. That was a relief for Jade, it was as if she had been given a million dollars right there and then.

Thursday morning could not come quickly enough as Jade got the children both ready and the bag packed with enough clothes for the rest of the week. They were all set. "Hello!" Jade shouted at the gate.

"Oh, hi!" The smiling face of the 5'2" woman answered as she guided Jade and the children indoors.

"What sweet children they are," Gloria said.

"Thank you."

"So, how old are they?" Gloria asked.

"They are six and three – Anthony here is six, and Marie is three years old," Jade answered. At first, Anthony was reluctant to leave his mother, but Gloria had her ways with children. Soon, he never realized that Jade had disappeared. She had made a deal with Gloria for a long term care. That meant that Anthony and Marie would not be with Gloria for only a day, but possibly for weeks.

One week had passed and Anthony had settled in well, so well that he started to call Gloria Mama. It was Marie who had become restless and anxious to see Jade again. It was not surprising, though, since Anthony had found a brother who protected him and played with him nonstop. That brother was Gabriel, Gloria's son. Gabriel was only six months younger than Anthony.

The weekend of the following week had arrived, and at about seven p.m. the dogs began barking furiously at something. Gloria looked out and saw Jade at the gate. The children were asleep. "Jade, where have you been?" Gloria inquired.

"I am very sorry, Gloria, but with overtime, I kept working very late and I was either too tired or it was too dangerous to go out alone after dark," Jade answered.

"Jade, it is not me, but the children I am worried about. They need to see you, that bond is very important to build," Gloria lectured. Jade, however, seemed immune to that talk. She had heard it somewhere else before. "OK, you owe me $40 Jade," Gloria reminded her.

"I am really sorry, but I have not gotten paid yet. I will get paid next week, if you could actually lend me $10 I would be so grateful," Jade said. Incredibly, Gloria did not even question or challenge anything.

"Wait a minute, let me see what I got." Gloria went indoors and one could hear as she went upstairs. It took her two minutes before she returned. "Again, it is for the children, Jade, that I am lending you this, so you owe me $50 now," Gloria said.

"Yes, Gloria."

"OK." Gloria went and woke the children. Marie was ecstatic beyond belief. She wanted to leave immediately. Anthony, however, began to cry. He didn't want to leave, but Jade was having none of it. "He can stay, I am fine with that," Gloria said.

"It is OK, I need him to come and get used to the new home," Jade replied.

"Oh, so you have moved then?" Gloria said.

"Yes, as a matter of fact, I live closer to Jamaica Avenue, only a couple of blocks from you," Jade said.

Jade eventually got her way, and Anthony and Marie had left for their new home. As usual, Anthony's countenance changed totally. He had a somber and depressed look, it was as if he never wanted to be around his mother. When he got into his new abode, he seemed less tense and more relaxed. It was probably the realization that they now lived just a couple of blocks away from Gloria that changed his unpleasant looks as he sauntered along the corridor, which led to the living room. As he walked along the corridor, he noticed a door was a mere partition to his new abode, and that his mother was renting half of a story house with a veranda leading to a pavement that ended at the gate after about ten yards. For some reason, his savant persona got the better of him, and he slowly put his right ear to the partition door. There, he heard movement, and so he was smart enough not to pull the handle of the door. The noise on the other side got his curiosity running even higher, and so, quietly and carefully, he comfortably positioned his body, and next, his ear to the door.

"What do you want now?" he heard a young man's voice finally. It made a difference to the shuffling he was hearing before, and he positioned himself again so that he could hear more. Unfortunately for him, Jade was standing over his small body, but he was too busy tuning into the happenings of his neighbor to notice until a thunderous whack across his ear sent him squealing like a pig in the abattoir.

"What the hell were you doing?" Jade shouted at Anthony. Anthony held onto his ear, still screaming. "Shut up, you bastard!" Jade shouted. Anthony tried to muffle his scream, but the aching ringing in his ear was too great. "What did you say, you stupid bastard!" Jade shouted as she rushed to Anthony, hitting him repeatedly over his head. Then, she saw her white stiletto heeled shoe. She grabbed it, but Anthony saw the danger and immediately ran outside. She chased after him. It was dark, about 8:30 p.m., but that did not prevent her chasing him. She was unable to catch up, so she put the shoe on the gravel, grabbed a handful, and madly threw it at him. Anthony saw a shed, and there he rested, confused and still in pain with his hands pressed to his left ear. It was the ear that had been exposed to that unexpected blow.

He stooped himself near the shed, trying to understand what he had done to deserve such an uneven share of punishment. In his small six year old brain, he just could not fathom it at all. Jade had locked the door and as Anthony stooped, he heard a cooing sound. He stood upright and just about managed to see at least half a dozen pigeons in the coop. He was so fascinated by the birds that momentarily the pain was forgotten, and his bitter experience was light years away.

In the meantime, Jade had Marie well cuddled. "Come on, dear, it is time for your wash," she gently said to Marie. Marie was then taken to the bathroom where she got a refreshing bath. Her back, chest, and even her face were well patted with baby powder. Jade made sure she was satisfied that Marie was well cared for before she went for Anthony.

"Come inside, Anthony!" she shouted. Anthony was, however, reluctant to enter. "Come on, child, and have your bath, and then a lovely glass of milk and a cookie!" Jade coaxed. It worked. He was hungry after all and so he entered, and what he saw of his mother was like she had become a different person. She looked like butter would not melt in her mouth, so much like an angel. Anthony was glad to see her looking like that because he so wanted her to be proud of him, to be loving and pleasing. He took the rag from her and walked by himself to the bathroom. He had learned how to wash himself well and so he took care to do so. Anthony saw the pajama belt on the inside of the door handle and so he dressed himself, and made his way to his mother. "Anthony!" Jade called.

"Yes, Mommy!" Anthony answered He followed the voice to the kitchen where he got his promised glass of milk and four tea biscuits.

"Now, look, son, things have changed. There is only one bedroom with one bed, and we all three will be on that one bed," she explained. "Things are different now, you understand?" Anthony looked over the glass at her and nodded. "Stop that," she reprimanded. "Yes or no, act as if you are intelligent."

"Yes, Mommy," Anthony politely answered. Anthony was a perceptive boy, and he realized that the situation was grim. He somehow felt better because he believed that the assault on him was not his fault, but due to Jade's vengeful frustration. It was not difficult as he went onto the bed with his head opposite the two women in his life. Jade took the duvet away, it was not necessary. The sheet was as white as snow and as she prepared the bed for the rest, Anthony was in his own world, he never even noticed Marie. Deep down he felt awkward, it was as if he never belonged. He was afraid that he might go on the bed at the wrong time, or get on the bed the wrong way. He never trusted his mother at all, and her straight face had him wondering 'what next?' Any excuse to hit him again, he thought.

"Come on, get on that bed now," Jade said. Fear had gripped Anthony too much to even think further. "Keep still on the bed," Jade said sternly to Anthony. Anthony stayed in space within his small corner until boredom had its own way, and he eventually slept, yet awake with his mother chasing him with an axe.

Then, a calm, peaceful sleep was well in place until it was disturbed by Jade. Like a horse with its hoof, Jade kicked Anthony to the floor. It was again unexpected, especially when Anthony was deeply asleep. He got onto the bed a second time, positioning himself away from Jade's feet, but another kick with double the strength of the first made him realize that it was intentional. Anthony felt his way to the kitchen in the dark where he found a spot, and there he sat dreaming of his freedom. That dream sent him to sleep so comfortably on the hard concrete floor. That weekend had become a nightmare, and Anthony could not wait for the Monday to be back in the loving, tender arms of Gloria, the only Mama he had come to know.

Chapter 9

4th July 1976

Monday again did not come too soon for Anthony, and he and Marie were well dressed and packed. It did not take long as they walked to Gloria's home, and for the first time they saw Mrs. Gloria Carlton with Mr. David Carlton. He was a tall, handsome, upright man who clearly had the same love and empathy for children that Gloria had. "So, you must be Jade," he said.

"Yes, Gloria told me how great you are." A shy, humble, and very naive tone could be heard from Jade. She looked so innocent and naive, and that was what caught Anthony's attention as he looked on. He could not understand how the vile and heartless woman he knew could be so calculating and manipulative. "I brought some of that thing I owe you, Gloria," Jade said.

"What are you on about?" Gloria asked. Jade took an envelope out and handed it to Gloria. Gloria looked, and in it she saw $40. It was like nothing to Gloria as she seemed to have one objective, and that was to care for the children.

"It was nice to meet you. I hope we do meet again, Jade," David said as he straightened his uniform, venturing to the gate. David was in the Marines, so it was not unusual for him to be absent from home for days, weeks, and even months.

"Wow, you are a lucky woman, Gloria," Jade said.

"Why?" Gloria asked.

"Well, to have such a wonderful husband," Jade said.

"Hands off," Gloria said with a giggle. "With these beautiful kids of yours, you are very lucky, too," Gloria said.

"It is just too much work," Jade said.

"Too much work? Look at Anthony, those beautiful brown eyes, his dimples, and that unmoved smile, what more could you ask for?" Gloria elaborated.

"Ahm," Jade said, only to be cut short.

"Not to mention, your daughter, very quiet, polite, bright, and a face that could eventually take her far, and you speak as if you are not lucky. God will smite you if you continue a talk like that, Jade," Gloria continued.

"Sorry, Gloria, but with being alone, it has not been easy," Jade said.

"Yeah, I meant to ask you, you have never mentioned either of their fathers," a puzzled looking Gloria said.

"Well, Anthony's dad is somewhere in Canada, but Anthony has never met him. Marie's dad has been around financially, but he makes sure what she gets can only stretch to her. He gives the money, but only to sustain her," Jade explained.

"Ah, I see," Gloria said. Gloria felt sad of the story, but tried not to show it. Her heart stretched even further to Anthony like it had never done before. Unbeknown to them, Anthony did not learn enough from eavesdropping, so he had his ears positioned from the living room which led to the veranda, listening to the end. That time, it was not the physical attack, but the emotional and psychological attack that hit him the hardest. He became more confused. In one part he felt great that he was so wanted by Gloria, someone who appreciated him, but at the same time, part of him felt rejected. Anger and resentment to a father he had never met had boiled over, and for the first time, a slight hate lingered to his brain for Jade. He still was not sure because he thought that if she had never loved him, then she would never have kept him.

"Thank you very much, Gloria, and see you," Jade said.

Gloria started to look frightened herself, but that was quickly replaced with anger.

"Why does she do it?" Gloria asked. "What am I saying? This should never have happened."

"She always calls me bastard, what does bastard mean, Mama?" Anthony asked. Gloria became speechless because she clocked what it was all about, and she had no doubt in her mind that what Anthony was saying was all true.

"Come here, my love, come here." She called Anthony and then she gave him a cuddle, not even a loving bear would have given so much to its cub.

"Bastard is just a swear word that some adults use when they cannot find any other word to express themselves," Gloria said. She hoped that Anthony bought it because she realized how sensitive and intelligent a boy he was.

"But, why me?" he asked. And, that was the question that made her understand why Marie could not wait to see Jade, sometimes crying her heart out to see her mother return, which was fine, but the opposite was true for Anthony. She cuddled him even more, and at that moment, Anthony seemed to have found peace and security at last. There were other children, about two others, but they had not fixated their lives on Gloria as much as Anthony and Marie. Perhaps, because of the peculiar needs, but Gloria always spoke of another boy and his name was Wayne. Wayne lived upstate New York with the rest of Mama's family.

"I wish you could meet Wayne because then you would see someone who feels your pain," Mama said.

"What?" Anthony asked.

"Not to worry," Gloria said as she got them all dressed for school.

Nine a.m. and they were all at Allan's kindergarten. It was the usual motions of schooling, listening to the teacher, making notes of the alphabet for Marie, Gabriel, and Anthony, simple arithmetic and basic skills of logic and mental ability. It was at recess when Anthony was looking for his brother when another boy of his own class grabbed his lunch box. "Give it back, now!" Anthony shouted.

"Let's see if your mother makes better sandwiches than mine," his horrible classmate teased as he took his first bite. Before he could take another bite, he got one kick to his feet, and before he knew what had hit him, he was punched in the face.

"Are you going to watch me or help?" Gabriel said to Anthony. Of course, Anthony mustered the courage and grabbed the fallen lunch box on the floor, and then he wacked it on the shoulder of the boy. "Is that all?" Gabriel asked before walking off with his brother.

Weeks like that followed, and Gabriel became not just a brother, but a protector, also. Gabriel had the personality of a giant, and through that, he was popular and respected. Everyone knew of Anthony's link to Gabriel, and for that reason alone, no one messed with Anthony. "You know, Gabriel, you are the best brother in the whole wide world," Anthony said.

"We should call ourselves all for one, one for all," Gabriel suggested.

"That is call, you truly are the best brother I have ever had," reiterated Anthony as they walked together with Marie in the middle, holding her brothers' hands from both sides.

One weekend after the other had passed and Mama had her way. Jade thought nothing of allowing Anthony to stay with Gloria, in fact, there was no challenge in that decision, and when he stayed with Jade, all went well. He could remember the most memorable Saturday when she had Anthony on her lap and she kissed him. To Anthony, it was the kiss of life. He so wanted to please her and he felt that he was doing something right. He was not sure what it was, but he believed he was, until that dreadful day in July, 1976. He was eight years old then and he remembered that it was the last day of school, a Thursday, when every school had broken up for the 4th of July two days later. It was a time when everyone was in a festive mood, and it would be a time to change everything, at least for that day. Jade had picked up Anthony and Marie from school the Wednesday and she had a whale of a time with both of them. On the Thursday, she gave Anthony the bunch of keys since there would have been no other way for Anthony or Marie to enter the house when they left school. Mama insisted that she bonded with the children more, and so she insisted on Jade keeping the children for at least a week. Anthony felt proud to have been given the responsibility by his mother to keep the bunch of keys. Eleven o'clock and Anthony checked his pocket, but there were no keys. He checked his bags, and still no keys. He then found Marie. "Have you seen the keys Mommy gave me?" he asked her.

"No. What have you done with those keys?" Marie asked.

"I do not know," a worried Anthony answered. Anthony then started to cry as the day wore on. He knew that he had lost the keys. He searched the entire school, but still no signs of the keys. It was at one o'clock when everyone had left the school that Anthony gave up and took his sister home. Fifteen minutes later they reached home, but could not enter.

He thought carefully on what to do. For the first time, he realized that he had to approach his neighbors, the Tomlinsons. He knocked at their door.

"Coming!" a female voice uttered. It was Mrs. Tomlinson, she and her family were devoted Christians and like Gloria, they tried to live what they preached. "My, my, what is it, kids?" she asked with Anthony at the front door and Marie behind.

"Well, ma'am, I live next door and my Mom gave me the keys to keep, but I lost them," Anthony explained.

"That happens to the best of us, you come in. In fact, you both came at the right time. I just finished the family loved fishcake, all homemade with two jugs of cool lemonade!" Her chirpy persona showed as she talked to the children. No one else was at the home, it was her alone. Her son, Richard, was away for the day and her husband was due home within the next five hours.

"Thank you, ma'am," Anthony and Marie said simultaneously as they were led to the kitchen. They ate a scrumptious fish cake washed down with the lemonade, just as it was promised by Mrs. Tomlinson. Mrs. Tomlinson had made her new acquaintances very comfortable, so comfortable that Anthony had forgotten that he had lost those keys.

"Go out and play, have fun," Mrs. Tomlinson suggested to the children, and so they did. They played everything there was to play; skipping, quizzed each other, and even played hide and seek until Anthony looked on the floor of the veranda. There, he saw the sun reaching the twentieth tile of the veranda's floor, and he knew that his mother would have only been five minutes away. The game was over, and like old times, his old personality had kicked in very well. He became withdrawn, worried, and confused. He did not know what to do. He was right. Five minutes to be exact and his mother in her thick, red buttoned uniform matched by her black stiletto heeled shoes entered the gates.

"What are you doing outside and still in your uniform?" an upset Jade asked.

"I lost the key, Mommy," Anthony answered with the tears trickling down his cheeks.

"Lost what?" she shouted. "I knew I was taking a risk when I gave you those keys, you stupid boy!"

"Hi, I am Mrs. Tomlinson, it has been three weeks and we never met, but these kids broke the ice," Mrs. Tomlinson interjected.

"Oh, hi, I am Jade."

"Yes, I have been keeping them, so it is alright," Mrs. Tomlinson said.

"Thank you, but I will need to get in still," a calm Jade said.

"I've got an idea, go back to school and see the caretaker. Maybe he has it. Don't you worry, I will continue to look after them. After all, is that not what neighbors are about?" Mrs. Tomlinson asked.

"Oh, you are so kind. Also, can you keep my bags here with you?" Jade asked.

"Of course, why not?" she replied. Jade did just as Mrs. Tomlinson suggested. She went to the school and there was the caretaker, walking around the school.

"Hi, sir, my name is Jade and my children attend this school," Jade explained.

"Yeah," he said, waiting for more.

"Well, I gave my son the keys to the house to keep, but he lost them, and I was wondering..." she started, but he butted in.

"Yes, I think these might be yours," he interjected as he quickly took his middle aged body as fast as he could to his quarters. Within two minutes, he returned with the bunch of keys. "Are these yours?" he asked.

"Oh yes, I am so grateful," Jade gleefully answered.

"As long as I made someone happy, then I am happy," the caretaker said. They then parted.

As she walked alone, she kept muttering to herself.

"You watch me and that bastard," she was muttering. Then, on her arrival, she knocked on the door of Mrs. Tomlinson. "Thank you very much, you have been so kind!" Jade said to Mrs. Tomlinson as the children stood outside.

"I see you got those keys. If my husband wasn't in such a rush, I would have invited you in for a meal, but we are going to my in-laws, so you could return the favor by watching our home, please?" Mrs. Tomlinson said.

"That will not be a problem. It was thanks to you that I can get into my home, so I will guard yours, of course." They chuckled together. "Come along now, kiddies," she then said to Marie and Anthony. She never changed her clothes when she entered. Instead, she got Marie in the bath and washed her. The usual powdering was being done when she saw the green Ford reversing from the car park to the road. She knew that the coast was clear and no one was around. She went to the wardrobe where she saw a thick belt, the one she had brought for Anthony. He wore it around his trousers, now he was to wear it around his skin. "Anthony!" she called him to the bedroom.

"Yes, Mommy?" he answered, following the direction of her voice.

"If you run off this time, expect it to be ten times worse because if I do not catch you now, I have the next eleven years to catch you. Now, stretch that hand out," she instructed. Trembling, Anthony stretched his hand out, and with all her might, she used the leather belt to whack him within the palms of his hands. She did that five times, but still was not satisfied and without warning him, she began to mercilessly beat Anthony anywhere the leather strap caught him. Anthony curled into himself like a hedgehog, shielding his face with his hands, but still she whacked him, sometimes catching his face. Still, she was not satisfied. She wanted blood, and so she held the strap, exposing the ends of the metal buckle, and there she started to hit him, mercilessly still.

"Stop, Mommy, stop!" Marie shouted. It was the first time that his sister had ever intervened and it helped. Jade stopped, but the damage had already been done. The bruises, cuts, and pain were all there to be seen. Anthony still could not find it in his heart to hate his mother, especially one day later when the same woman who would have killed him called him nicely. It was as if she were a different person.

"You know what you did was wrong. Losing those keys and putting me through such embarrassment was wrong," she said to Anthony, but he remained silent. "When I was a child, I was beaten and it did me no wrong, in fact, it made me a better person," she continued, but still Anthony just listened. He was fearful that he might say the wrong thing and again be assaulted. "The bible says spare the rod and spoil the child," she finished, and then dismissed him. He was not so sure what the quote meant, but he was pretty sure that she did not understand it herself. He wanted to believe that his mother had beaten him because of her love for him. He wanted to believe that because he still was not sure why; why she kept assaulting him.

It was needless to say how happy Anthony was when the time had come for him to return to Gloria, his only savior whom he saw as more than a mother, but close to divine. However, it was to be his last week, he just never knew it. "Hi, Gloria, it is so great to see you again," Jade greeted with the two children close to her.

"Jade, I must tell you so that you are not surprised when you return," Gloria said

"I am fine with it, tell me," Jade said.

"I am immigrating to Canada in two months," Gloria revealed.

"I see," was all that Jade said. It must have hit her like a ton of bricks because she went into loop to say the next word.

"But, that is in eight weeks time," Jade said.

"Yes, but I would like to be able to detach the emotions of these children from myself and vice versa," Gloria explained.

"I see," Jade said again, this being a clear blow to her plans. Again, Anthony could not wait for her to leave because it was the only way for him to release the tension, pain, and emotions that he had built up.

"Jade, before you leave, I need to say something else to you," Gloria said.

"Yes?" an innocent, naïve, and softly spoken Jade said.

"When are you going to stop beating Anthony like this?" she blurted.

"Gloria, do you know the bad things he has done?" Jade said, trying to justify herself.

"Jade, when will you stop? When you have killed him?" Gloria blurted again. All was being said in earshot of Anthony. Anthony was not sure whether it was good or bad, but it was subconsciously the signature of approval that he needed to stand up for himself. Finally, he had an ally who faced up and tackled his number one enemy.

"OK, Gloria, I won't hit him again," Jade said. Nobody was certain how sincere Jade was, but Anthony knew her all too well. It was all a show as far as he was concerned. She left looking flustered and defeated, but that was not Jade, for to Anthony, she was truly the devil's incarnation.

"Mama, she was really bad this time," Anthony said.

"I know," Gloria replied. She could see the signs of abuse, so she allowed Anthony to spit it out, and he spat it all out.

"You know, Anthony, Gabriel is now a member of the boys brigade. I think you should join, too," Gloria suggested.

"No, she would never let me," Anthony predicted.

"Gabriel will beg her because after I am gone, you will need an outlet. My husband and Gabriel will be here, but you will need something else to get your mind away from everything," Gloria advised.

Marie was around, but in her own little world, still daddy's little girl. Anthony never heard a conversation between them, but he saw them together, sometimes leaving for a dentist appointment, a visit to the mall, a visit to a funfair, and on his good days, a long stay at his home. Anthony could not say unless Jade boasted and compared Nate to Joseph, which she so often did. More and more, Anthony had a need to know his father and it bothered him so much. In bed, on the toilet, walking, and even in his dreams. What had bothered him more was the inevitability of Gloria's immigration. His worries increased more, though, when the clock struck five thirty p.m. that evening. His heart skipped a beat when the gates opened and he recognized the rhythm of her footsteps.

"Hi, Gloria, how were the children today?" Jade asked.

"They were fine," Gloria answered sharply. She became cold toward Jade and the feeling was becoming mutual.

"OK, thank you very much, anyway," Jade replied as she again took her children with her. Throughout the walk, she said not a word, one of her regular tactics to instill fear. Anthony knew that something was up, he just was not sure what it was. As soon as she reached home, she indulged herself in some work. That was not abnormal, so Anthony was not so worried yet. She got all the dirty linen and clothes together. Anthony was glad, it seemed as if she had intended to live up to her promise, and that was comforting to know. She hand-washed the clothes vigorously at the back of the yard, so much so that she began perspiring profusely. "Anthony!" she yelled. Anthony beckoned to her call immediately. "Please, get me a glass of water to drink," she asked.

"Yes, Mommy," Anthony said, going into the house to fetch the glass of water for her. However, what he was to observe next frightened him more than anything else could. As Jade held the glass to her lips, her hands trembled uncontrollably. Her lips also trembled, it was as though she had Parkinson's disease, but he thought not. It could only have been her nerves, he thought. That triggered a thirst of knowledge and he wanted to know more. He walked away scared, numb, but quietly as he hid his emotions. In one hour, she had finished washing and the house was to be cleaned. It was madness as she moved the chairs away, and anything else in her way. With the wet mop, she wiped the floor, and then polished the floor carefully, not missing a crevice.

"Anthony, it is time for you to shine the floor!" she commanded. Anthony did everything, even went on the round of borrowing money from her friends.

Anthony did whatever she demanded with a sense of pride, even when he passed on the note to her debtor begging for more. He dared not read the note, but he always knew as her debtor would sometimes chastise him. Anthony continued to shine the floor with the dry cloth attached to the mop of which he made the floor shine like a crystal, not even missing a single spot. He was proud of himself, so much so that he felt brave enough to talk.

"Mommy," he affectionately called to Jade.

"What is it now?" she asked.

"I want to join the Boy's Brigade and I will need uniform and fee for joining. The others I saw in it look so smart and great," Anthony said. He must have forgotten himself because it was the first time that he was so opened up with his mother. Jade looked at him carefully, as if he were mad.

"Anthony," she said before pausing. Anthony listened as he stood still with the mop in his hands. "Where the hell do you expect me to get the money?" she barked. "What do you want me to do, you want me to whore out my body?" she demanded angrily. Anthony mustered all the courage he possibly could and for the first time at eight years old, he challenged his mother.

"You should tell me where my father is, you find everything for Marie, but not me. Marie can never be wrong," Anthony protested. Jade was dumbstruck.

"Where the hell are you getting this from? It is that woman Gloria, you will never speak to me like that again!" she promised Anthony with an evil look in her eyes like Anthony had never seen before. Anthony saw what was coming and so he ventured to run as he dropped the mop. She picked up the mop and with the stick, she connected it to his arms.

"You promised to stop, Mommy, don't do it, please, please, don't," he begged. His plea was, however, too late, and with the stick, she aimlessly hit Anthony across his back, his feet, hands, and his face. Anthony ran to the veranda, hoping to get someone's attention, and at least hoping for her Jekyll and Hyde moment, but that never worked. It was as if she was possessed. "Help! Help! Help!" Anthony screamed as she continued beating him mercilessly. The mop stick cracked, then broke in two, but that still never stopped her. It was the intervention of John Tomlinson that stopped her as she puffed and hissed like a raging mad woman.

"Jade, what are you doing? Are you going to kill him?" John asked. John had just come from another state, Massachusetts, from the rest of his family. Anthony, still lying on the floor in a fetus position, recognized John's voice as the one he had eavesdropped on when he had first arrived at the cursed house, as he described it.

"If you only know what he did." Jade held her breath as she tried to justify her actions.

By that time, the entire Tomlinson family came out, John and Norma, they must have been in their mid twenties and were evidently brother and sister, and Mr. and Mrs. Tomlinson. They all had something to say to condemn Jade and she seemed repentant.

Anthony realized how dangerous things had become as he ran to see himself in the mirror. The marks across his back, across his shoulder, and feet were not his worry, it was his face. The puffed up eye with a gash underneath it scared him to death. He got closer to the mirror as he examined and nursed it at the same time. Then, he thought of several ways to hiding it from his school friends, but that, he realized, was impossible. The only way he thought to hide it was to lie. So, he concocted a story right there before the mirror. It was a fight, a fight with a stranger on the street, and he was the winner. The story, he thought, sounded plausible enough to make him feel good. He never had a dad. Other children asked him about his dad and now he could not say he had a mother who hated him so much to have done this to him. He just had to stick to the concocted story.

Chapter 10

It was true that Anthony had built up a courage like he had never done before, but it was because of a need for his survival. But, more so the idea that he had an ally, someone he knew held him dearest to their heart, and that was Gloria. She was, however, less on the scene and since the next day he had to go to school alone, he started to feel alone. Anthony sat during recess with other children, Gabriel seemed not to have been at school that day. He was just as mischievous as the other boys.

The mischief of that year was to have mirrors and aim them up the skirts of the girls. Anthony found that intriguing and as he covered his right eye for most of the day, he helped the rest of the boys aiming the mirror under their skirts. That never caught on well when pupils were being suspended, and the last thing Anthony wanted was a letter of suspension from school, so he shifted the purpose of the mirror to the magnifying glass where the reflection of the sun would burn papers. That became the craze, even burning unsuspecting victims on their legs, arms, or anywhere else. He then saw Jerry and Dorothy. He was crazy for Jerry, and finally the two girls were coming toward him.

"Hi, Anthony," Jerry said. Anthony felt as if he was in heaven. Jerry had spoken to him for the first time.

"Hi, Jerry," he blurted.

"We were just wondering. Your eyes seemed very swollen, what happened?" Dorothy asked.

"Oh, nothing serious, just a fight with this strange coward on the street. You should have seen how I decked him to the floor. That coward ran," Anthony said.

"That is strange, because rumor has it that your mother is responsible," Jerry said. Anthony said not a word for a while, he remembered that it all happened in the open and opposite to him was a family whose child attended the same school.

"That's what it is, rumors, all rumors," he said, looking grim. It was a double blow for him because the love of his life did not approach him out of genuine interest, but out of simple gossip, and worse, his secret life of torment was now out. Matters only got worse when he saw Mrs. Tomlinson approaching him at around noon.

"Anthony, I just spoke to your head teacher and I got her permission to take you home. I can't believe your mother allowed you to come to school," Mrs. Tomlinson said as she took Anthony home, that was, to her home.

There at her home, there was a basin of warm water with a nice, clean sponge. Like a true mother, Mrs. Tomlinson applied to sponge to Anthony's almost closed eyes. As she tended to Anthony, he had flashes of his mother's poisonous words, the series of physical assaults, and in contrast, he saw how playful and kind she was to Marie. He started to think that she never liked him at all until the penny dropped. It was his father that she never liked and every time she saw him, she saw his father. She hated his father for leaving her the way he did, and the only revenge she could take was acting it out on Anthony himself. He was sure of his theory and so the tables started to turn. He pledged to himself right there as Mrs. Tomlinson tended to his bruises, *That woman is not my mother, I hate her, she will pay for this*, he said to himself. But, first he had to understand more about her if he were to put the pieces all together. Anthony, however, had an even more daring quest. He was going to leave her house and no one could stop him. He had to, he thought, as he reflected on her trembling hands and lips. *A dangerous woman indeed*, he thought. "Thank you very much, Mrs. Tomlinson, but why?" Anthony asked.

"I could not have lived with my conscience or answer to my God knowing that I could have done something and did nothing," she explained. Anthony was moved by what she said and wondered how many were suffering like him, but most importantly, how many sat back and watched as a promising life was destroyed, thinking that it was none of their business. Anthony was ahead of his time because he believed those very ones who ignored could very well be the victims of the very ones they chose to ignore in time of their needs.

"Thank you again," Anthony said humbly.

"Where are you going now?" a panicked Mrs. Tomlinson asked Anthony as he stood up, but he said not one word. "My living God, what have I called onto myself?" a distressed Mrs. Tomlinson said as she held her head to the heavens. Anthony, however, proceeded through the gate and walked calmly away. "Come back here, come back," she pleaded.

Anthony knew where he was going and when he reached Gloria's home, there he saw David as well. "I can't go back, Mama, I can't, I just can't," Anthony cried.

"Oh my God!" Gloria exclaimed. Everyone looked in awe as they saw the state of Anthony, but Anthony wanted to show all and so he stripped his shirt and revealed his back, chest, shoulder, and arms. "Oh no!" Gloria screamed as she rushed to the toilet where she regurgitated almost everything she had eaten that day. "How could any mother do that to her own child?" Gloria asked herself out loud.

"A sick woman, she ain't a woman," David said in disgust. Anthony, in that moment, saw not only a true mother, but also a true father, and he was determined more than ever never to leave their protective sides. However, Jade soon arrived at Gloria's house to plead with Anthony to get him to return home.

"Anthony, I'm sorry, I didn't mean to hurt you," Jade pleaded.

"Doesn't seem that way to me," David interjected, wondering how a girl like Jade could cause anyone so much pain.

Whatever was the cause, the once petite, innocent, and quiet girl had changed into a monster, angry at what her own family had done to her, but worse, angered by her first love. "OK, Anthony, I was wrong, I will never do you any harm," she said with the most sincere face, a face that anyone would believe.

"You said that before!" Gloria barked.

"You promise, Mommy?" Anthony asked.

"I promise," she said as she held Anthony's hand and they both walked away as Gloria watched them leave, the last time she would see them, at least for a while.

Jade kept her promise. Weeks had passed and she never touched him in any way other than a loving, maternal way. It gave him enough time to do just what he wanted, and that was to get to the root of the problem. Anthony had so many opportunities to visit the Queens library, and he did. His main subject of study was mental disorder, learning the difference between being psychotic or simply just mad. It was during his studies that he became scared, because his worst fears were realized. He had read up about bipolar disorder, and what he read terrified him. He then decided on a course of action. He went over to the librarian and spoke. "Where can I find books on finding loved ones?" Anthony asked.

"Are you looking for any book on the topic, or is there a specific title?" the librarian asked.

"Any will do," Anthony replied.

"Then, you are best looking in call number 153.9695 Garrisons. He is good, should I help?" she asked.

"I'll be fine," a less modest reply came from Anthony. He was focused. He knew what he wanted and so he skimmed and scanned through as he gathered ideas for seeking his father. He spent a great deal of time there, and the more he scanned and read the books, the more he learned, but the answers he was searching for seemed to escape him.

Weeks turned into months, and months turned into years. Soon, without realizing it, Anthony had become a very mature twelve year old boy, intelligent, and yet calculating. Due to his harsh life, he was forced to grow up quickly, and that had both a positive and negative effect on him. For Anthony, the world was a jungle, and it was one in which only the fittest would survive. Over the years, Anthony had continued what seemed to be an impossible task, but thanks to his determination, he was finally given an answer. He had been at the library for six hours, and Anthony still scavenged through the leaves, writing all he could and finally, he saw something on a page that, for him, was more precious than gold. There, he saw that his surname, Redford, was one of the least popular surnames. That, to him, was a good start and when he was given a suggestion of tracking someone with the use of a directory, he was overjoyed.

"Young man, you must be tired now, besides, we are ready to close now." The librarian ushered Anthony out of the library.

"That's all right, ma'am, you are open at the same time tomorrow, nine a.m.?" Anthony asked.

"Yes, I will expect you then," she said, looking at

Anthony as she held her pen to her chin as she twirled it, wondering who the kid was. She had pure sympathy for him, knowing full well that he must either be fatherless or motherless, or rather, she assumed that to be the case.

Jade had calmed down for a long time now, and she just about tolerated him. Perhaps, because she was conscious of his awareness of her true feelings toward him. Sometimes, she could not help it and said something distasteful, but that became seldom. "Mommy, I will be at the library again tomorrow. I need to complete my science research for Ms. Crawford and I am enjoying it," he said.

"OK then," she said.

Saturday could not have come fast enough, and at six a.m., Anthony got up, put his books together, and his most important object, his notepad from the day before. He made certain to complete the chores he knew Jade expected of him. Cleaning their part of the yard, sweeping and polishing the floor, and making it glisten were just some of his chores. That day, he tried to impress so by seven thirty a.m., everything was spic and span.

"Wow, you sure worked hard today," Jade said, looking relaxed. She had prepared cornmeal porridge that morning. It was not to Anthony's highest expectation with the lumps in it, but he bypassed them, gulping down the spicy fluid parts. Eight a.m. came and he clutched his knapsack and rushed to the bus station where he got the 001 bus at eight ten a.m. In ten minutes he had arrived at Park Lane, leaving him with a five minute walk. He seemed a loner, in his tight jeans and checkered yellow and blue short sleeved shirt, but he never cared. He had an objective and as far as he was concerned, that objective was to be met. Two hundred yards away, and Anthony could clearly see the Queens public library. There was only one problem, he had forty minutes left, and that, for him, was a long time, but he was a very innovative young man. In the interim, Anthony took his notepad out and on it, he made his plans; the money, the time, the information all had to be spot on, otherwise, he would have wasted all of his efforts. The forty minutes were well spent as the doors to the library were now opened for public use. Directory and Redford were the only words on his mind as he dashed to the second floor to see the same librarian he saw before.

"Hi, it's me again as I promised," he said cheerfully.

"I can see, you are a man of your word. So, what can I do for you today?" the zealous librarian asked.

"I need to use a very detailed yellow book directory," he answered.

"Tell you what, I will get one for you." She smiled as she moved with grace. After a few moments, she returned. "Here you are, young man," she said as she placed the directory on the table where Anthony sat.

He carefully scrolled through the names, addresses, and phone numbers. He carefully scribed the information to his notepad and before he knew it, he had fifty three names with their particulars. Anthony was becoming the most charming male there and when he wanted something, he knew how to use those charms.

"You know how good I was, and today, you have been so nice. Could you be just a bit nicer and allow me to make a few calls?" Anthony craftily begged Jane, the librarian. Her badge had her name in black and bold.

"It is our policy not to do such things, but it is not busy here at the moment. In fact, it is just you and I, so I can't see the harm," Jane conceded. She led him to the phone where she guided him to make outside calls.

"Not being rude, but they are personal calls," a shrewd Anthony said.

"OK, whatever you say," Jane replied as she deliberately empowered the boy she so wanted to help. Anthony took full advantage of an opportunity he needed more than ever before. He dialed the first number and spoke.

"Hello, is this Eleanor Redford?" Anthony asked.

"Yes, it is," came the reply.

"Do you know a Joseph Redford?" he asked, holding his breath.

"I'm sorry, but I've never heard of a Joseph," the voice crackled before the receiver was down. It was the first disappointment, but Anthony never felt defeated. He moved on to the second, third, and fourth numbers.

"Is this Alfonso Redford?" Anthony asked.

"Yes, I'm Alfonso Redford, what can I do for you?" a shaken voice asked.

"Sir, my name is Anthony, and I am trying to locate my father, his name is Joseph Redford," Anthony explained.

"Joseph?" the voice asked with a renewed tone.

Anthony's hopes started to build up with his nerves well high.

"Yes, Joseph Redford," Anthony replied.

"I am his uncle, but let us see if we have the right man," the voice continued. "His father, my brother, died in 1967, he was murdered." The voice became even more crackling. His emotions got the better of both of them, but Anthony began to cry first because now he knew he was near to finding his father.

"Yes, you are right." Anthony sniffed.

"You will need to see me, son. How old are you, though?" Alfonso asked.

"I am twelve," Anthony answered.

"I am your grand uncle, but I need to see you in person to explain everything to you. Put your mother on the line," Alfonso instructed.

"I am not at home, my mother already approved, but for some reason, she does not want to talk," Anthony lied.

"Well, you will need my address," Alfonso said. "Have you got your pen and paper?" he asked.

"Yes, I have," Anthony replied.

"009 Green River Road, Hillsdale, NY 12563. That's in New Jersey, son," he informed.

"Got that," Anthony replied.

"Son, we are looking at about thirty five miles, put your mother on the line and let me tell her how to get there," Alfonso instructed.

"I don't know why, but she just doesn't want to speak to you," Anthony lied again.

"She has changed, I must say. OK then, you need to

know how to get there," Alfonso said before explaining how to get there. Anthony already had his intentions and plans in order, so he knew exactly what the next stage was.

"OK, thank you very much, ma'am. I am so happy, I am so close to finding my dad," he gleefully exclaimed. Jane said not a single word, only to smile and to show her glassy, watery eyes.

Anthony ran as fast as he possibly could as he ventured outside. Anthony was so elated, he made such a loud scream of delight that a stranger had to stop and ask him what the matter was. He just smiled. "I am the happiest boy in the world today," Anthony said. His smile became infectious to that stranger. He then looked to see if he had everything in his knapsack, but most importantly, he looked to the side of the bag and checked for the fifty dollars he had stolen from Jade. He knew very well that should his plan come alive, then he would have needed at least fifty dollars, so that very morning while everyone was asleep as he did the chores he called slave labor, he helped himself to the fifty dollars safely put away in the cabinet drawer well positioned in the living room. He gave the cabinet a special clean, making sure that the mahogany shone through the house.

Chapter 11

"Anthony! Anthony, where the hell are you?" a very upset Jade shouted. She thought he had returned home. It was natural to think so since it was two thirty p.m. and the library was closed at noon on Saturdays. Besides, she had been waiting two hours before when she discovered that her fifty dollars was missing. Anthony, however, had other plans as he boarded Coach USA, fully occupied. He had his ticket. He could have gotten away with being on his own as he had a well developed body, he could have been mistaken for a young adult. The coach had a destination for Hillside. It was one of those coaches used for random tours and sightseeing and the average traveler. There were children, grandparents, uncles, aunts, just about every type of family member going. Some sat with excitement, and the adults were not excluded. Anthony sat in the back at the rear window where he got a full view of the goings on. The coach left promptly at two p.m, which was shown on his $20 ticket. He worked it all out in his head; he calculated a two and a half hour journey for the thirty five miles, the latest, he thought, would be three hours. What he never planned for was a police alert for him as a missing person. At about three thirty p.m. while he comfortably viewed Merrick Boulevard and eventually 237th Street, police cars with uniformed officers, about three of them, were all at Jade's house investigating a missing person. "He was meant to be at the library," she said to a Detective Stone.

"What was he wearing?" Detective Stone asked.

"I think it was a pair of blue jeans, and his favorite checkered yellow and blue short sleeved shirt," she said, looking on with worry.

"Yellow and blue checkered short sleeved shirt, blue jeans, roger that?" Detective Stone spoke into his radio. He was speaking to a Sergeant Henry, who was feeding the information to other sources; sources that could develop to good leads. "Do you have a picture of the boy?" Stone asked.

"Oh yes," she said, quickly providing him with the requested picture.

"So, what does he look like? His height, color of his eyes, hair, and does he have any distinctive features?" Detective Stone quizzed as he received the picture.

"He's about 5'2", slim, about 48kg, and pronounced brown eyes," Jade said. At that point, she broke down and started to sob her eyes out.

"Oh, ma'am, don't you worry. We will find him, we will," Detective Stone assured her. The problem was that Jade broke down not because of her missing son, but the words pronounced brown eyes, words that reminded her so much of Joseph, the man she had loved but now loathed, to death. The detective gathered all the information and there was a lead, Jane was their crucial lead.

Anthony, by that time, oblivious to the special interest in him, had reached Barren Island where, for the first time, the world was his oyster. He now realized just how much he had been cheated by his mother and father. As he looked across Rockaway Peninsula, South East of Brooklyn, and saw a spacious land with little to no development, he wished that he had a parent who could have shown him the world, one who would have had a deep interest in him. However, when the coach reached Coney Island and the children got from their seats with sheer excitement, their parents endorsing their anxiety with love and devotion, his blood boiled with vengeance. The sight of Deno's amusement and kiddie park and the wonder wheel was just too much for Anthony to bear, and then he slumped in his seat looking defeated and rejected. Everyone seemed too absorbed with the glitter, excitement, and wonder to have noticed the twelve year old boy drenched in self pity boarded by revenge. "Hi, little one, are you not going to Coney Island with the rest?" an old gentleman asked Anthony. He must have been the only one to have taken an interest and might have noticed a void in Anthony's life.

"No, sir, I am for Hillsdale," Anthony answered.

"OK then," the gentleman answered, and walked away. Anthony looked at the mature gentleman and a thought entered his mind. *That man could have been my great uncle*, he pondered to himself. He then saw the positive of better late than never, but he wondered with a mission explanation given to him by Alfonso as to why Joseph left him before he was even born. The view of Veragano Bridge in its most majestic splendor shifted his focus for that moment in time. He looked at its architecture in awe, but the Hudson Bay River captured his imagination with the boats, ferries, and the river itself. It was refreshing for him to be able to forget the wretched world he knew and to be taken in by the wonders of the scenes around him, and all that lasted for more than two miles, the length of the journey of the Narrow Bridge, a wonder he would never forget.

"So, he asked you to use the library phone and you allowed him? Did he tell you who he was speaking to?" Detective Stone asked.

"No, but I remember him being so ecstatic about finding a trace to his father," Jane answered. Stone looked at the phone, and then at the other officers.

"Find out what number he called and find where it leads to. See if the mother will give the father's name," Stone said to the other officers with him.

Anthony's coach had long crossed Slater Island, littered with fields and linear settlements, then went north west past Bloomfield, further north to Trenton, and finally left to Hillside Avenue where, like a pro, he connected himself to a yellow cab. "Please, take me to 009 Green River Road," Anthony said. The driver responded and in less than five minutes, Anthony turned up in the leafy suburbs of the 1.9 acres land fronted by the detached Potter Heritage house in all its glory. It had Anthony wondering if he had the right address, but it was too late as the cab had already left. Anthony timidly walked up the driveway fifty yards from the door entrance and pressed the buzzer, feeling very nervous. A mature looking man, at least sixty to seventy years old, opened the door. He must have seen Anthony from a distance.

"Are you lost, my son?" he asked.

"I hope not, are you Alfonso Redford?" Anthony asked with a whimper.

"Yes, I am, oh my God. You can't be Anthony?" Alfonso said.

"I am, yes, I am," Anthony said, still with a whimper in his voice.

"Where is your mother?" a concerned Alfonso asked.

"She just would not come," Anthony said.

"You should be with your mother," Alfonso reiterated.

"I am fine, I just wanted to know about my father," Anthony insisted.

"My son, what I have to say is very sensitive, you need to be older," Alfonso said. However, the look in his eyes showed that he wanted to say it. It was a look that Anthony never liked, but he had to take the risk, it was a matter of life and death for him.

"Put it this way, you not telling me now will have done me greater harm than good. I can live with the truth, but I can't live with the lie or not knowing. And, I just am not sure what I am capable of doing, it could even be suicide." Anthony masterly manipulated Alfonso, not that Alfonso wished otherwise.

"Sit down, son, and let's have a chat," his granduncle said. "I'll get you something to eat first," he added. Anthony was too besotted by his granduncle, to say the least. After all, it was the closest he had gotten to his dad and the ticket to finally contacting his father; his long lost father. He sat on the antique settee where he reflected while Mr. Redford prepared some sandwiches and drink. Anthony wondered what he needed to ask; how much would his great granduncle be able to help him in contacting his father. The image of what his dad would look like had so many faces flashing in front of him. There, without any warning, he blurted out one word.

"Why?" he asked himself with drops of tears falling from his cheeks. He wondered if he was the problem, but then the real Anthony stood up. "No, it was never my fault. No man of good would treat his son like this," he muttered to himself. "A father should be there to protect and defend his children, and his woman," Anthony insisted. "I would like for him to suffer for all the pain he caused me," Anthony continued to mutter as he wiped the stains from his cheeks just in time to compose himself for his newly found great granduncle.

"You like my home?" Mr. Redford asked.

"Yes, it is beautiful, sir," Anthony said sheepishly.

"My home is your home. In any case, you will soon have your own home, you are an intelligent and courageous young man," Mr. Redford hailed Anthony.

"Oh, thank you," Anthony replied.

"You really came here on your own. I still can't believe it. Joseph did not have a clue what he was missing. My nephew had been a stupid man," Mr. Redford mourned with a touch of anger. It was just the road that Anthony wanted him on, and he thought that it was the time to spare no punches.

"So, will you be able to help me contact my father?" Anthony asked. He could not afford to beat around the bush.

"No, son, I can never help you with that," Mr. Redford answered as sharply as the question was thrown at him. Anthony became numb with shock and disappointment.

"So, why did you not tell me on the phone?" he asked, pausing for a moment and counting to ten just in case he said the wrong thing.

"Well, I never expected you to be here so soon, and besides, the conversation on the phone did not develop to that stage," he explained. Anthony sat sullen, looking rejected and defeated.

"I am sorry, but, please, tell me why you cannot help me contact my own dad?" Anthony asked. He felt his emotions threatening to overcome him, and his grandaunt, who had been standing in the room, went to him and held him in an embrace.

"You see, son, you father is dead. How he died, I cannot say now, but never let it be told that he neglected," she whispered in his ears. At that moment, Anthony shook like a tree, and she could feel that tree shedding all its leaves. She then held his arms firmly and stooped to his eye level. "Your dad never met you, but I can see him in you, and in time, I will tell you the entire story, but not now," she said before letting him go.

"Gran, I promise, I am strong. I can take it all in, but I will die, too, if you do not say it now," an equally fearless and bold Anthony uttered.

"Oh my God, you surely are the reincarnation of your father. He was just as stubborn, determined, and courageous like you, but I still...cannot say," she said with a whimper, holding her handkerchief to her nose. She sat him down, and Anthony was all prepared to hear everything when the commotion outside halted his world. The siren was the first thing they heard, and a couple of moments later, they saw the flashing lights. It was like the entire district unit covered the premises. Augustine Redford almost had a panic attack. "This is not good for my heart," she shouted. "I suppose no one knew of you coming here," she surmised. "Look, son, I am a sick woman, dying of cancer, I am not strong enough for all these theatrics." She moaned as she approached the door. She opened the door to two policemen, both holding their waits, while three other cars with more police officered waited, infringing on her wide, open, beautiful green lawn.

"Hello, ma'am, I am PC Jones, and we have good intelligence that you may have a vulnerable lost child," PC Jones politely addressed Augustine.

"As a matter of fact, I do have a child here, but he came to see me, his grand aunt, without me expecting him on his own," she informed them.

"We are well aware of that, ma'am, but we will need to see Anthony Redford, and for formalities, we will need to ask you some questions," Jones said.

"Please, come in," she said.

Anthony, looking stone faced, sat on the same antique settee trying to absorb all of the misfortune of the day. A social worker entered after the police, and she went directly to Anthony. He was still stony faced, as if he had not a care in the world, but who could have blamed him? In the space of three hours from a long and tiring journey, he had learned of his father's death without any background story, he had no hopes of ever meeting his father, he learned of his only grand aunt, whom he had only just met, was soon to die from cancer, and now the police and, worse yet, the social worker were all there to take him home.

"Anthony, are you hurt in any way, have you been harmed in any way?" Lauren Apple, as her badge indicated, asked.

"What do you think? She is my grand aunt," a feisty Anthony replied.

"We checked it out, and, yes, she is your grand aunt, but she could have been anybody, Anthony," Lauren said.

"Yeah, OK," he replied. In the interim, Augustine calmly answered PC Jones' questions.

"Are you aware that his mother does not want you to have any contact with her son?" PC Jones asked.

"No, but I won't be living for long and whatever is mine will be Anthony's, and that she can never stop," she replied. Anthony could lip read her very well and in his mind, he was now more determined to fight whatever Jade represented.

"I am sorry to hear that. I hope I am not being impertinent here by asking what the matter with you is, ma'am?" he asked with sincere concern.

"Oh, that is OK, it is lung cancer. It is in its infancy stage and I have been given two to three years. Some survive it, I doubt I will," she said.

"You will beat this," he said as he got up. "Thank you, ma'am, I have gotten the information I needed and all is well," he said.

"So, what will happen with Anthony now?" she asked.

"We will take care of him, drive him home, and leave him with his doting, loving, and caring mother," he said.

"He will be fine then." She smiled.

"His mother will be more relieved. My supervisor told me how she was close to a break down, worried stiff about her son," he said. The social worker was satisfied that all was well, although Anthony's distance and now gaunt appearance worried her. She knew of the terrible news he had only just received, but her inkling told her that there was a deeper, underlying issue, one that was out of her jurisdiction.

Anthony entered the back of the Honda police car, where he began the journey home. For him, it was nothing now but a mundane journey, and yet, a time to reflect on his next move, a move that he believed would be his only gateway to freedom. Freedom of his mind and deliverance from his own mother. Anthony would have been tired, but he could not stop thinking about the information his grand aunt was withholding from him. He believed her, though, when she said in due course he would get the information. The suspense, he thought, would kill him, but for that time alone would tell.

"Are you OK?" a concerned Lauren asked.

"Yes, but, please, I am tired and just want to be left alone," Anthony answered with a slow slur followed by a smile, a superficial smile. She understood, they all understood, and so they left him to it.

He leaned his head horizontally toward the door of the car with his eyes closed as if he were about to sleep. As the car paused, Anthony was deep in his subconscious, some psychologists would say his superego, as he mapped the changes that were to follow in his life. That change, he decided, was a commitment to fight any and every child abuser. His fantasies grew when he realized how sinister his mother was toward him because of the absence of his dad, a dad he now believed had no choice of being an absentee. He was focused on revenge on culprits like his mother. That was a mammoth of a task for a twelve year old, he thought, but thought he could think through a plan and make it work. First, he thought of Gloria, whom he knew very well would fight in his cause, but he knew how unrealistic that was. Gloria was in a far, distant land, Canada to be exact, and for him, he needed someone he would have been in constant contact with. The librarian was his only option. She showed deep empathy toward him and for him. She was all for the cause since she went beyond her calling to break the rules and allowed Anthony to make that all important call. As he continued his mundane journey, his deep thoughts turned into plans. He began mapping his thoughts. The first attack, he believed, was to secure a convenient and strategic location. The library was crossed out of his mind. His mother's rented home crazily came to mind, and he just laughed at the thought. Then, the school flashed into his mind. "Yes!" Anthony blurted triumphantly to the air. They all looked at him. He knew what the cops and the social worker were thinking. "A mad boy," he whispered. The school was, after all, the best place. It was territorial for children, many who needed a voice of their own. Many, like himself, who needed the support in order to be stronger in making the right decision, and to be at peace with themselves, knowing at least that it was never their fault. A tear fell from his eyes, but it was a tear of joy. Finally, he felt as if there was some hope for himself and others. A small voice whispered in his ear.

"What is the main aim of your group and where will you get the money from, little boy?" It was his own thoughts in reflection. The main aim was to empower helpless, abused children, and to empower them as confident and worthwhile human beings, he thought to himself. "As for the abusers, I will make sure that they are held accountable and be made an example of," he pledged to himself. "I will get lawyers, mayors, the state, radio personalities, and all those who are powerful on my side, that's how the money will flow," he continued to dream.

The plan was in his head, but as he approached his own town, he anticipated what his mother would do. He knew Jade very well. The crocodile tears, the scornful hugs, the unimaginable thanks to the social worker and police unit, and once they were gone, he was certain that the Hyde would come out of her. After all, she was unknowingly suffering from bipolar disorder and her circumstances with her made him the target, so he believed. However, he was convinced she had a genuine hatred for him and for that reason alone, he refused to be understanding. Anthony had made up his mind that should his mother touch so much as a strand of his hair, he would use it as a catalyst to stop her from ever doing it again, and from there, many others would follow suit, he promised himself. Ten minutes later, the convoy of police cars, about four of them, drove up to the gate of Jade's rented home. Just as Anthony had predicted, Jade was at the gate. She must have seen the flashing lights and cars earlier from a distance.

"My baby, oh my God!" she screamed, running to meet the opening door of the car as Anthony's feet emerged first, followed by his head. Jade held him tight with tears covering her cheeks. Anthony was confused. For that moment, he really believed Jade to be genuinely concerned. He actually felt good to be getting the tender, loving care from his mother. "Thank you very much, officer, thank you!" she continued. Anthony looked at her and his suspicions aroused him to fear. She was so to the script that he had to remind himself of the plan. Of course, Jade never disappointed. Her predictability had become boring. Anthony could not be surprised for too long.

The police, social services, and the wind were gone. It was Jade, Anthony, and Marie behind a now closed door. Marie was a strange one to Anthony. She was almost never there, he had forgotten that she was living there because she was so untouchable. It was as if her silence made her nonexistent. "If I had known that you and your father would have turned out like this, I would have taken a knife and pushed it straight through my womb before you were born," Jade said to Anthony. Anthony felt it really hard. He had just learned of his father's death and he already knew of her hatred toward him, but he never know how much worse words could have been compared to a sledgehammer hitting him in his head. He truly would have preferred her hitting him than saying those words. And, so he became true to his words.

"I wonder what makes you Jade? Does it make you worthless, because it sure does not make me worthless, as I am not the one with two children for two different men. Sorry, my mistake, three different children for three different men. One is on the way, I hear," Anthony fired back. Jade was speechless for a moment. She was in shock, after all, she was used to a passive, helpless Anthony, but the tide had turned and unfortunately for him, she had now passed the doldrum.

"You ungrateful good for nothing, I bore you in my womb for nine months and this is how you repay me?" she screamed.

"Anyone can do that. Keeping a fetus in the womb for nine months does not give you the license to abuse, misuse, and refuse another human being a fair life," Anthony retorted. She suddenly made sense of his silence, and deep observations and concentrations. She realized that he was no ordinary child and that he had calculated her actions all along to the 'T'. It was too much for her to handle, and so she charged at Anthony, that time with the hot iron she had left on since she realized the convoy of cars and Anthony's arrival. Anthony was a step ahead of her when he saw the direction of her eye toward the iron a few seconds before she had taken it up. He ran as fast as he could, but she chased him, determined to have her way, but unknowingly allowing Anthony to have his way. Anthony ran in the street, while behind him, Jade had the hot iron in her hands.

"Help! Help! Help! She wants to kill me, she wants to burn me with the iron!" Anthony screamed, knowing very well that he was calling out for witnesses. Jade's Jekyll and Hyde was there for all and sundry to see. There was no escaping that one. It was ironical that Marie was the one who called the police, and since they were there only a few moments ago, it was in seconds that they returned to see a few people from the neighborhood surrounding Jade.

"He caused this, what a wicked boy. I never had any luck with men!" she rambled away.

"He is not a man, he is your son!" a loud voice from the crowd uttered. Anthony realized what could have happened, and he knew that he had to think fast, very fast. Jade's mind was falling apart, but if she was to be sectioned, then the shame would be greater than he could imagine, but worse yet, he and Marie would be carted off to anyone, possibly putting him in a less controlling and more dangerous position. He realized how much it could have backfired on him, and so he started.

"I want my daddy! I should have killed you with the iron, you whoring bitch. I would do anything to stay away from you, and Uncle Raymond is the one I would rather be with!" he shouted. Everyone, including Marie, was confused. By that time, Jade had calmed down, but Anthony had seemingly had a break down. He was kicking at the police, spitting and shouting incoherently. He had proven to the police and social worker what they already suspected. Jade was seen as the victim, and indeed the mother with too much burden on her shoulder. What was supposed to have been an act for Anthony had become a reality. The emotions were manifesting itself, interestingly enough, against Anthony's will, and so it took five of the policemen to hold him down as the ambulance drew nearer.

"Hold his hands down!" was the next thing Anthony heard from the thin figured nurse dressed in white. He could see her as she had the needle of the syringe to the two ounce bottle. He couldn't see the words on the bottle, but he could tell that it was a sedative, enough to make him weak and lose that melancholy he had before. It was a feeling of peace and calm like he had never experienced before.

"Oh, my baby, my baby," Jade cried as he was driven away from the quiet neighborhood, well sedated.

It was extreme, but that was what it took for Anthony's escape; but what he could never have envisaged was the impact that this could have had on everyone. Soon, the word had spread that Anthony had gone mad and could be sectioned. It was shame on the family, and no one could afford that, least of all, the Jackson family. For the first time, for weeks Jade's family head emerged once again. The first week, at around six p.m. in the evening, the dogs were first to start barking, clearly disturbed by the knocking on the gate. Jade shifted the white curtain by the side as she peeped to see what all the commotion was all about.

"Oh my God!" she gasped when she realized who it was. It was Crystal, a bit overweight, but the structured face with the outstanding eyelashes stood out just the same. Jade quickly got her pair of slippers on and any old overalls would have done as she hastily rushed to the gate. "Oh my God, do my eyes deceive me?" a blissful Jade shouted to the echo of Crystal. They hugged each other as if they would never have let go of each other. "My, my, I never saw these kids, are they yours?" Jade asked.

"Yes, this is Kamila, and this is Andre. Kids, say hi to your aunt," Crystal coerced.

"Hi," they said in a chorus.

"Hello, little ones, you are both as beautiful as your mother, my, my," Jade said. "So, what breeze blew you here? Come in, come in, how dare me," Jade apologetically invited them in.

"Ah, so this is where you have been hiding," Crystal said.

"Not quite, you found me, so you must have known before."

"Well, let us make a correction first, you have kept yourself from the family, second, news of your missing son was on the news, radio, and the television. My God, your life is in a mess, Jade," Crystal chided her sister.

"Cup of tea, coffee, or hot chocolate?" Jade asked as if brushing the subject away. Crystal sat herself to the edge of the bed and continued.

"Your bedroom located to the door entrance, one bed. Is that for three of you? And, you seem pregnant, is that for a different man?" Crystal dug in.

"Enough, enough!" Jade screamed.

"No, it is not enough, not when your actions have called shame onto the family," Crystal retorted. It must have been the most silent argument since they could have hardly been heard. "You know, Jade, when I realized from the media, good God, the media, the area where you lived, I came here one week ago and it was a neighbor who told me everything, everything about the abuse and the melodramatics of Anthony being whizzed away by the psychiatrics. Neighbors told me, sis, damn strangers!"

Her tone cracked at that point as she covered her face in tears. Jade became speechless, it was not the Crystal she was used to. Crystal wiped her eyes and then held her head up, it was time for business. "Jade, I hate to say this, Mama was right about you, you are selfish, insensitive, and cruel, but worst of all, incapable of running your own life," Crystal said. Jade still said nothing. "The family has decided that Anthony will not stay with you when he is out of hospital. He will stay with Ma's brother, Stanford, it was his decision."

"You come to my house speaking on your terms as if you all care about my son, daughter, or myself, and as for Doreen!" An abrupt pause came from Jade with one smack in the face by Crystal.

"Doreen? Mommy, Mother, or Mrs. to you and the rest of us, the least she deserves is our respect. No wonder she wishes never to see you again. You will do as we say, the entire family will be on you should you decide otherwise!" commanded Crystal as she let herself out, meeting Kamila and Andre playing on the lawn.

Jade, left on her own, reflected on how it could have reached to this and slowly started to accept her responsibilities, but still chose to blame everyone except herself. She would not, however, be given any respite as two days later, she had another visitor. It was not Crystal that time.

Anthony had already been discharged from hospital. Jade was careful not to upset him, well, common sense had told her that he could easily have another breakdown. She took care to give him his daily anxiolytics medication at the right time. The doctor told her how he had suffered a mild nervous breakdown, and that the anxiolytic tablet was a form of tranquilizer and that he would be calm and quiet beyond what was normal. He was meant to be on it for three weeks as the psychiatrist believed his condition not to be serious.

"Jade! Jade!" A shout came from the gate. Jade looked through the window and her heart skipped a beat or two. It was Nadine and Doreen. Jade was not sure what to do. She wanted to pretend as if she was not at home, but they had seen the shifted curtain.

"Jade, we saw you!" Nadine cornered Jade. She had no choice as she got her slippers on and her long, chiffon, flowering dress. "Are you not glad to see us?" Nadine asked as Doreen watched in silence.

"Well, I never expected anyone to visit, so I had to get myself properly dressed," Jade explained.

"Come on, my dear, all is behind us now. Come and give your mother a big hug." Doreen finally broke her silence. Jade obliged, but the hug was short and very insincere. They both knew, but they both understood that the feeling was mutual. Nadine was, as usual, less subtle with her feelings and views.

"Let us cut to the chase, Mom, this is about preventing more disgrace on the family," she said as they entered Jade's humble dwelling. "So, this is the guy causing such a stir?" Nadine said as the door opened, exposing Anthony on the bed. Anthony pretended as if he was asleep, but he was awake with all his faculties in the right place.

"Such a beautiful grandson and you reduced him to this, Jade," Doreen said.

"He needs to go today, we can't risk with another day," Nadine said. Anthony smiled malevolently, as he knew his strategy was on spot to destroy his own mother and the taste of blood only just got sweeter; he wanted more.

"I do not mind him going to Uncle, but what about Anthony and what he wants?" Jade asked.

"OK, let us wake him and ask him. If he says yes, then he comes with us, and if he says no, he stays with you," Nadine said.

"OK then," Jade said, shrugging. "Anthony, darling, Anthony," Jade calmly whispered in his ears as she cowered over his shoulders.

"Mmm, yes, Mommy?" he asked, pretending as if he only just awoke.

"Meet your grandmother and aunt," Jade said. Anthony gave the widest smile with his brown eyes wide opened. He was the most handsome teenager on the block and they both fell in love with him instantly.

"What took you so long, Grandma and Aunt?" His bravery revealed as usual in a crowd, that time to Jade's pleasure. "I so wanted you to be here long ago to save me," he went on, wiping the smirk from Jade's face. Jade knew how calculating Anthony was, but that one threw her off guard.

"You bastard, take him, it is obviously what he wants," she hissed. The first time Doreen and Nadine had seen the Jekyll and Hyde Jade, even Doreen was taken aback. They also realized how desperate Anthony was to get away when he dashed to the bathroom and emerged in his jeans, and checkered green and blue long sleeve shirt. Quick thinking Nadine now understood that Anthony might very well be a risk to his great uncle, who was seventy two. She didn't liked the manipulative side of him and in her mind, he was capable of doing just about anything.

"Mother, I believe we need to discuss more with Jade," Nadine said.

"What for?" Doreen asked. She pulled Doreen aside.

"Look at how Anthony manipulated the situation. For all I care, he might have been pretending about this illness, we could be biting off more than we can chew," Nadine warned her.

"You have always been the sensible one, so what do we do?" she whispered.

"Reverse psychology, we will get in both of their mad heads," she revealed.

"God, I can't believe I produced such offspring," Doreen moaned.

"Are you ready, Anthony?" Nadine asked.

"Yes, Aunt," he gleefully answered. Nadine summoned everyone around the table, including Marie.

"Anthony, I did not like what I saw of you. It makes me confused about the plight of your mother and I do believe your concerns are genuine, but because I believe they're a dangerous element to you, Jade will see you at least every two weeks and the minute you are too much of a burden to Uncle, you will be with Jade faster than you can call her name, understood?" Nadine explained. Anthony summed up Nadine. He knew that she was no bullshitter, but he was determined in his head to achieve his aims and not even a bull with its raging horn was going to stop him. He had decided.

"Yes, ma'am," he humbly answered as he took his packed suitcase. He looked back at his sister and he could see the connection in her eyes. He now believed that Marie was actually on his side and that meant a lot for him because he always believed she was conveniently unaware of his sensitive issues with their mother. He believed she was silently feeling the same pain, only that she was as powerless as he was. Anthony entered the Ascot car as Nadine drove away to a new suburb called Mandela Estates, only four miles away, just outside of the inner city, a further four miles from the central business district of New York. Very ideal, ideal for as many dysfunctional families you could ever imagine. Piece of cake for Anthony, even though he had to travel further to get into school, but the prospect of realizing his dream with the convenience of meeting the right victims was convenient enough for him. Not much was said during the journey, it was as if they were surmising each other. Anthony, on the other hand, made sure to capture and interpret the socio-economic conditions of the houses as he moved from the Central Business District through the factories, inner cities, and working class to his new suburb environment. It was not as extravagant and vulgarly rich as grand aunt Redford's house, but it was just fine. Soon, the escort approached the driveway.

"There he is, my has he grown," Stanford said. A slim, mature man looking younger than seventy two, his true age, more like fifty or even younger, came out to meet and greet Anthony.

"Yes, Uncle, there he is looking so saintly, but I doubt it," Nadine proclaimed. Anthony just stood looking around at the grilled house. He could have easily mistaken his location to be Alcatraz, located just off of San Francisco. Anthony immediately psychoanalyzed Stanford as either an insecure freak or a man who had the most horrific experience.

"So, what's your name?" Stanford asked an obvious question, which would give him the obvious answer. The reason was also obvious.

"Anthony Redford," he answered, saying nothing else.

"New surroundings, he won't open up to us as yet," his wife, Margaret, interjected. She was a short, stout, but lean lady who took total pride in her appearance. Her hair looked like she was trapped in the sixties, but Anthony saw in her what many did not see. He saw a lady trapped in a relationship and his strength was their weakness. He believed that once you were on the side of anyone through their weaknesses, then they would always be on your side. But, how did you know and get them on your side? Ah! He knew how to make his problems parallel to theirs by just talking. "Let me show the young gentleman around, after all, this is his new home," she said. In the meantime, Nadine briefed Stanford on Anthony.

"Watch him, he seems like a crafty bugger, just like his mother," she said.

"A handsome young man, though, can't believe she treated him this way," Doreen said. Doreen had lost her sting. She, herself, was getting on, although in all fitness she never got back her sting since the death of Douglas. Douglas was everything to her, they were school sweethearts, that said it all.

"What made you say that about him?" Stanford asked, putting on the features of scholar in his face.

Since he won the trifecta and guinella in the seventies giving him more than $80,000, he suddenly became one of the Bourgeoisie. No one dared to remind him that he was nothing but a bell boy at the Claremont Hotel in Chicago, sometimes having a great day from a tipper.

"Well, you already know about his breakdown and running away from home for hundreds of miles, well, we saw something most sinister of him today," Nadine said.

"And, what was that?" A curious Stanford drew nearer to learn of his new resident.

"It was as if he wanted everything bad to happen to his mother, it was as if he was manipulating or plotting the sequence of events. It's hard to explain, but I would watch him carefully if I were you," she warned.

"Not to worry, I had spotted his personality from a mile. The boy is a lion, someone of my heart, my own heart," he said. Nadine gave a wry smile, biting her lips with worry. She saw how they were clearly attached to him already, but she still believed their hearts could not take it all. "You think I am too old for this, was I not the one who suggested this? If things got to the worse, then we would just return him to Jade," Stanford said.

"Everything will be fine, he only needed a change of environment, he'll be fine," Doreen said. Coming from Doreen, then all was well.

"Nice grandfather clock," Anthony said to Margaret.

"Oh yes, we had that clock since Whoppy killed Fella," Margaret said.

"What?" Anthony giggled away.

"Just an expression to say we had it for so long we cannot remember. Passed down through the generations," she explained.

"I see, as long as you and Uncle Stan has been together?" Anthony started making his web of control.

"Mmm, yeah," she said lukewarmly.

"I understand. I always got away from my mother, even though it was in the same house. Even seeing her, I built my own escape world in my mind," Anthony answered.

"Oh my God," Margaret said, cupping her mouth with one hand. "Come on, let me show you your room," she said, quickly walking in front. They understood the mind reading occasion, and so he followed. Somehow, Anthony felt at home. From Margaret's reaction, he was certain they would be more than new found relatives, but friends as well.

"You take care and you know my number should you have any reasons to call," Nadine said as she rattled the keys, holding the car key cocked as some of them usually do, an air supreme. Anthony, on the other hand, retired to bed, but before he went to sleep, he did the most unusual thing.

"You've cracked it, Anthony. This is the perfect breeding ground for me to empower myself and all those suffering like myself." He was speaking to himself. He then knelt down and prayed, thanking God for his deliverance. To him, it was true luxury. His own king sized bed with quilted sheets covering layers of smooth sheets. He was in heaven, it was the quickest time he drifted in his sleep.

Chapter 12

March 1981

The crack of dawn was like he had never seen it before. "Did you have a good rest?" Stanford asked. It was six a.m. and everyone was up, at least Stanford and Margaret were. He was not sure if they were the only ones living there. It was clear how Stanford doted on Anthony. He went back to the adjoining bedroom. Soon, Margaret came out.

"Come on, Anthony, let's go out," Margaret said. Anthony eagerly got from beneath the silk quilted sheet and accompanied his grand aunt he now finally called Aunt. They walked to the backyard where there was at least an acre of land, and he could not believe how self sufficient they were.

Oranges, apples, cherries, tangerines, and as many more were thriving. Anthony picked on the directions of Margaret. He loved it. She then took him inside where he manually juiced the freshly picked oranges. He was not sure if it was all for real. He had pricked his hands to see if it were all a dream. It was for real.

Day in, day out, he got used to the routine, getting

up early in the morning – six a.m., chairs on the veranda turned back on its feet. It was some superstitious routine to ensure the ghost of whoever never got a chance to sit on the chairs, even the moon futon was turned upside down. Stanford would then take his slender body to the moon futon sitting upright, tapping the cigarette box, and then one smoke leading to another. That was perhaps the only thing Anthony detested. He hated the smell of the cigarettes and he was very concerned about Stanford's health. After a few puffs, he would lay on that comfortable moon futon. Margaret was always in the kitchen preparing breakfast, lunch, and dinner. When not doing that, the furniture was being dusted and the floor being left to sparkle. Stanford came from the era of the chauvinistic age, so you would never have caught him doing any of the work, and he warned Anthony not to.

Anthony, however, soon joined Margaret more often than not and to appease Stanford, sit with him chatting pure gibberish, but soon Stanford would seek wisdom from Anthony. Sometimes, pretending as if he was testing him, but Anthony knew very well it was for Stanford's own knowledge, like when he asked him how many zeroes were in a million. Anthony answered five and Stanford agreed, then Anthony later told him it was six zeroes. Stanford said he never wanted to embarrass anyone, then cautioned him to listen more to his math teacher. Anthony chuckled, he always chuckled with Stanford. Days turned into weeks, weeks turned into months, and the relationship got stronger, so much so, Anthony was close to forgetting the pledge he had made to himself.

The spring of 1981 seemed to be the perfect, ripe time. Six months had passed and Anthony seemed to have forgotten the pain he endured or the plans he envisioned. He had been at the same high school for three years. Puberty had kicked in, and he was popular. Gabriel had immigrated to Canada to join Gloria and he desperately wanted to contact them again, wondering why they had abandoned him. Devon had become his new comrade, they had so much in common. Devon was, however, the boy who never grew. He was short, about 4' 4", but his voice and strong personality made up for it.

"Have you studied for the physics exam?" Devon asked.

"No, I hate the teacher and the subject. I have no chance with that subject," Anthony answered.

"I will help you to pass," Devon suggested. Devon was that type of guy, a selfless individual who thought of others before himself.

"Should I come to yours or you to mine?" Anthony asked.

"Up to you," Devon replied.

"Come to mine," Anthony suggested. Devon seemed relieved. Anthony was good at reading expressions. That day, they both arrived at Stanford's house. "Hi, Uncle, this is Devon, he will be revising with me," Anthony informed them.

"Are you a good boy?" Margaret asked.

"Yes, ma'am," Devon answered. Anthony excitedly

went to the back with Devon and understandably so. The football game began. Anthony had no one to play with, so the least chance he got, he took advantage of it. Thirty minutes in the game and Devon shouted.

"Stop, let's stop," he called.

"Why?" Anthony inquired.

"Remember, we came to revise physics," Devon reminded him.

"OK, Mr. Boring, if you say so," Anthony said.

"Let us look at calculating the velocity of the car, and then on how the circuit works." Devon took the lead. Devon was good at work. Nothing else mattered to him as he worked out the five questions on velocity and the other five on electrical circuits.

"Is this your escapism?" Anthony abruptly asked.

"Excuse me?" Devon looked puzzled.

"I have noticed how much you would buy time out of your own home, how intense you are in whatever you do. Sounds like my life, so again, what are you running from?" Anthony asked. Devon gritted his teeth and gave Anthony the stare of death.

"What are you, some shrink?" Devon asked. "I got no problems, man, and even if I did, what is it to you?" Devon demanded.

It was so weird that at that same time Devon's mother had made a discovery that was enough to give her an instant heart attack, instead, it gave her a minor stroke. Her name was Blossom, and she, like many women of the time, doted on her family. Cooking, washing, and cleaning the house was just a part of women's chores of which many were proud of; unless you were a feminist or a feminist sympathizer. That day, the same time Anthony quizzed Devon relentlessly, about three forty five, she got the washing together. There were two baskets, one for her and the other for Brian Diamond, her recently wed husband, making him Devon's recent step dad. One year marriage was good, but they had moved in together two years before. Brian was a muscular, tall man who was so vain, no one took notice of that at the time. In fact, it was one of the features which drew Blossom to the heartthrob forty three year old man looking like he was still twenty five. Anyway, they all said that marriage was an eye opener and it was with Brian.

It was only after her marriage to Brian that she realized how domineering and possessive he was. Now, the dirty clothing opened a nasty can of worms, but on whom, she herself was not sure. As she got Brian's clothing, shorts, shirts, trousers, briefs, it was all good until she got Devon's shirt, shorts, trousers, and a big pause at his briefs. The backside of his white briefs was colored red, stained red. It was blood and like all caring mothers, millions of things crossed her mind, but what if it was sexual abuse?

"Pull yourself together, Blossom," she spoke to herself. "It could be just piles or bowel cancer," she continued speaking to herself. "Brian!" she screamed. "Brian!" she screamed again. The emotions were too much to bear. She could not rule anything out.

"What is it, dear?" Brian came running in, frightened.

"Look at this, look at this! What do you think?" she

screamed, still an emotional wreck as she had the briefs in the air exposing the bloodied part, shaking as she supported her body to the washing machine. Her trembling body was about to fall when Brian held her frail body. She slumped in his muscular, caring arms. "He should be home already, we must take him to the hospital the moment he arrives," she muttered. What she did noticed, even in her confused state, was that Brian himself was trembling. She put it down to him being in shock equally as her.

"Don't worry, we will get to the bottom of this, no pun intended," Brian said.

"Yes, we shall," she agreed as she sipped the sugary drink given by Brian. In the interim, Anthony and Devon were still at logger heads, but Anthony would have no joy.

"I think I am best going home now. You are some paranoid guy who thinks everyone is having the same issues like you and you want to be their hero. I won't be your guinea pig," Devon said before walking off.

"Sorry, man, let's forget this all happened," Anthony said.

"No hard feelings, but I just need to get home. We are still friends," Devon answered from a distance. Anthony got the key to the grilled gate, allowing Devon to leave. He had a distance to travel, about an hour's journey.

"What was that all about?" Margaret asked. She was evidently eavesdropping.

"I overstepped by boundary with Devon," Anthony answered.

"From what I heard, I do not think so. It sounds as if he is running away from his own demons," she surmised.

"I think there is more than meets the eye, Aunt. He is in some kind of problem at home, I just can't put my finger on it," Anthony said.

"But, how could you, you are recent friends, are you not?" she asked. Margaret admired and respected Anthony because she saw in him a whole man, more intelligent and braver than she ever anticipated. "You will get far, I tell you, no experience is bad. Look at your own and it makes you so conscious of others feelings with such great adept," she said. Anthony quickly glanced at her with a glimpse of shock. "Ah, you never saw me in that light, did you? I will have you know that I was a nurse, young man," she debriefed him. He ran and hugged her, tighter than someone could imagine.

"You are the only one apart from Gloria who knows me inside out," he said.

"And, who is Gloria?" she asked.

"It is a long story," he said.

"I have time," she answered.

"She now lives in Canada, but she took care of us during the absence of Jade. She was like an angel, so protective and helpful," he explained. "In my deepest distress, she was there for me, she gave me all this confidence and courage I now have. She loved children so much, I just know that God sent her to protect me just as I think He wants me to do for those weaker than myself," Anthony elaborated.

"Wow, she sounds like a great human being. Where is she now?" Margaret asked.

"We lost contact and I must find her. What if she has been writing me letters and I have not been getting them?" he wondered.

"Don't worry. If that is the case, you will find out in due course," she said.

An hour had passed and on time, Devon arrived at the door of his home. "Devon, come here now!" a loud whisper came from Brian. Devon knew that with Brian, you complied, and then you complain.

"What now, dad?" a passive Devon asked.

"You listen to me now, son. Your mother saw blood on your briefs, how could you be so careless?" he asked, staring Devon in the eyes.

"I did not know, tell her it's piles," Devon said.

"She is getting dressed. She is taking you to the doctor, there is no way out of this now," Brian said.

"So, what do you want me to do?" Devon asked, looking scared.

"You tell your momma that it was the caretaker at the school that done it. You ain't putting no shit on me," he said in a threatening voice.

"But, you know the caretaker is innocent, you know it was you," Devon said with some courage.

"You are forgetting what I can do. You listen, if I go down, my boys will bring you and your mother down. You know what that means?" Brian continued with the rhetorics.

"I'm dead, my mom is dead," Devon muttered. He had heard the threat for so long, so often, that Brian never needed to repeat those sentences.

"Damn right, now get your shit together," he said, but he could not resist slapping Devon on his ass before he timidly left the room.

"Oh my gosh, you are here. Come on, we must see Dr. Asprio now," she said, looking fidgety.

"Mom, I need to change my clothes," Devon replied.

"No, dear, we have no time. We don't want to be late for Dr. Asprio," she said. Devon complied and immediately they left, entering the car of Brian. Brian was quietly waiting in the driver's seat. He turned once to look at Devon in the backseat. In ten minutes, Devon was in the doctor's office.

"OK, young man, sit on the chair," he said.

"Yes, sir," Devon replied, complying.

"So, your mother tells me she found some blood stains on your briefs. Is there anything you wish to tell me before the tests I am about to perform?" Asprio asked.

"No."

"Did you notice any blood from your stool or on your briefs before?"

"No."

"OK, what about pain when you go to the toilet, in your stomach?"

"No."

"Hmm, I see. Please, get your trousers and underwear off, I will need to examine you," the doctor said. Devon did as he was told while Blossom sat in the waiting room holding Brian's hand. Anxiety was about to kill her. The doctor, in the meantime, got his gloves out and using his fingers, he inserted it into Devon's rectum, examining him for hemorrhoids or any unusual suspect. Other tests were done, including taking blood samples, only to rule out bowel cancer. It was all routine because Doctor Asprio had already determined the diagnosis the second Devon opened his legs, exposing his rectum. "OK, Devon, I have done all the necessary tests. I am going to ask you one last question. There is evidence that shows penetration to your back passage, is there anything you wish to say?" Asprio asked. At that moment, Devon began to cry. It was just as the doctor had suspected. "OK, I will be calling in your mother and father in where you will need to explain."

"Only Mom, please," Devon begged.

"Is there a reason for this?" a quick thinking Aspiro asked.

"No, just embarrassed," Devon said with fear in his eyes. Dr. Asprio calmly went to the waiting room.

"Mrs. Blossom Brown, please, enter the doctor's office," the receptionist commanded. Blossom and Brian got up, and hand in hand they walked to the door. "Sorry, Mr. Brown, only Mrs. Brown," the receptionist clarified.

"There must be some misunderstanding, he is my husband. I need his support," Blossom explained.

"Sorry, but those were the doctor's instructions," the receptionist said. Brian seemed agitated.

"It's OK, darling, I'll be fine," Brian said before returning to his warm seat. There, he fiddled his thumb, anxious to know the real deal.

"Please, sit down, Mrs. Brown," Dr. Asprio instructed.

"What's the problem, Doc, please tell me it is not too serious," she said. He allowed her time to compose herself, even offering her water.

"I'll be fine when I am told what is really going on," she said.

"Well, Devon, would you like to tell us? Because I am in the dark just as your mom."

"No, you, please, tell first," Devon said.

"Well, I have done all the tests and I can tell you that I have ruled out hemorrhoids, or piles as it is commonly known, other possibilities such as bowel cancer. I have sent off the blood samples amongst other samples."

"Please, get to the point. So, what is the concern?" Blossom asked.

"Well, the laceration to his rectum suggests forcible penetration."

"You are only fourteen, Devon, are you gay then?" Blossom asked. It was her only rationale to avoid hearing what she feared from the start.

"No, Mrs. Brown, your son has been repeatedly sexually abused by an adult," Dr. Asprio clarified.

"I figured as much," she calmly muttered, wiping her face. She glanced at Devon, who had his head hung in shame. "Look at me, Devon, you did nothing wrong, but who was it, son?" she asked. Devon looked at her and as his lips moved slowly, he barely could have said the words.

"The caretaker at school," he answered.

"Who?" she asked.

"The caretaker at school," he repeated. That time, it was as if he believed it.

"Thank you, Doctor Asprio, the police must be called," she said. "Come on, Devon, let's go," she said as they walked out, only to have Brian meeting them halfway.

"What's wrong, dear, how serious was it?" an overly concerned Brian asked.

"Sexual abuse, I want to kill that caretaker," she barked. He smiled, looking back at Devon as if to say job well done.

Chapter 13

Thursday, March 5th 1981 came. It was one of those memorable days every teacher, student, dinner lady, and anything that breathed on Kingsmill Secondary campus would never forget. In fact, to forget that day, even when you got old and senile, would mean a crime had been committed by that person against the campus. It was early in the morning, approximately eight thirty a.m. School did not officially start until the tannoy sounded at eight fifty five a.m. Most pupils and teachers were about, though, some gossiping, some being the usual early bird and some like Mr. Steward, who had no choice.

He was thirty two, a pleasant man and everyone knew him. He was affectionately called Stewy. He was the caretaker, so it was fair to say that everyone's lives were in his hands. The job was his life. He had it for five years and coming from a poor background, he was grateful for the job. He even had his own residence on site. The accommodation went with the job so he could not afford to lose it. Stewy recently had a little baby boy with his fiancée of one year and they all lived in the one bedroom house, but it was alright. If no one knew Stewy well, Anthony did. Anthony was an inquisitive boy and in jest, his jokes always led to Stewy sharing his private life with Anthony. So, when Anthony arrived at school Thursday morning at eight forty, he knew something was wrong when he went to the quad block and there was no sign of Devon. If no one knew where Devon was, Stewy would, or should, he thought.

"Hey, Stewy, you're looking rough this morning, what's up?" Anthony asked.

"The sky, the moon, the sun, the stars, the clouds..." Stewart got in first with the jest.

"OK, you got me, but on a serious note, have you seen Devon?" Anthony asked.

"Devon who?" Stewart asked, looking puzzled.

"You do not know Devon, eh?" Anthony said.

"Everyone assumes I know everyone when everyone knows me, but I do not and cannot know the names of a population of eighteen hundred kids," Steward blabbed away.

Sirens could have been heard from a distance, but in no time it was clear where they were heading. Anthony was mindful of sirens and was somewhat eager to get away. So, he started walking. He only got twenty feet before the cars pulled up in front of Mr. Stewart. With them, emerged Devon and his mother. His mother had her purse clutched under her armpit walking behind the police in quick and sharp steps.

"Is this the caretaker you have accused of molesting you?" the police in uniform inquired. Anthony looked on, bemused by everything. The word molestation and

Stewy just did not match. For him, it was all a folly, but the words molestation sang abuse in his head, and it was like a kettle boiling with the steam now clearly visible.

"Yes, this is he," Devon answered. By that time, the crowd of pupils and teachers had gathered around the scene.

"Mr. Stewart, we are arresting you for sexual abuse on a minor. You have the right to remain silent. You have the right to an attorney. If you cannot afford an attorney, one will be provided to you by the court." The police officer read him his rights. Mr. Stewart looked flabbergasted, to say the least.

"Just when was I supposed to have done such a crime?" Stewart asked in protest.

"Mr. Stewart would never have done that!" Anthony shouted. The children agreed.

"Free Stewy, he would never have hurt any of us!" they all shouted.

"You animal, you pedophile!" Blossom shouted. She was not allowed to get too near. In the midst of chaos, Anthony's eyes connected with Devon. Anthony saw the guilt in his eyes.

"What are you afraid of? Is it the truth? How could you? You can talk to me, you know that." Anthony tried to get in as much as it could hit home to Devon. It was all too late, though, because Stewy was driven away. His fate was ironically left in Devon's hands. If he never knew Devon before, he sure did then.

That was, however, the real catalyst that set Anthony ablaze once again. He was determined to get to the bottom of it all, and there was no better time.

The children, the school would have been well placed to back him on his dream campaign, a campaign against the real offenders of abuse. Those who abused children physically, sexually, or even verbally. It was time, he believed, to visit an old acquaintance, but before that, he now had a mandate to put his plan together. For him, it was a real war, a war that had to be won and Devon was at the heart of his first case. Devon, he decided, would be his accomplice and associate. With no time to waste, Anthony rushed to Mr. Baidoo. Mr. Baidoo was the physics teacher. "Hello, sir, how are you?" Anthony went to his form room. Mr. Baidoo was sure enough sitting at his desk waiting for the students to arrive. They had five minutes remaining.

"So, what can I do for you, Anthony? I do not have you for physics today," he said.

"No, sir, but I need your help more than anything else in the world," Anthony said in a begging mode.

"I am listening," Mr. Baidoo said.

"Well, sir, I really do not believe that Mr. Stewart committed such a hideous crime and I want to see him vindicated of such accusations."

"What makes you so sure he did not do it?" Mr. Baidoo asked.

"Well, sir, I was physically abused by my mother and I know when someone is lying, and Devon is lying. The thing is that I want to help Devon because I believe that he really was abused, but not by Stewy," Anthony explained. He surely got Mr. Baidoo's attention.

"Again, what makes you so sure he, Mr. Stewart, didn't do it, and how do I come into this equation, anyway?" asked Mr. Baidoo.

"Well, sir, you see, Devon was at my home yesterday and we had an argument because I sensed something being wrong, and he would not open to me. The fact is that most sexual assault is perpetuated by someone closest to you, such as your family and..." he started to explain, but was cut off.

"You still have not said how I come into the equation, though," Mr. Baidoo said.

"I was just on that. Devon loves physics and he was at my home to revise physics. I want your help to convince him that I believe him that Mr. Stewart did it."

"I thought you said you did not think Mr. Stewart did it?" a confused Mr. Baidoo said, scratching his head.

"You are right, sir, but I need to get closer to Devon because I earlier chastised him for accusing Mr. Stewart, but if you help me to get closer to him, then I will be able to get closer to the truth and at the same time, help both of them," a conniving Anthony revealed. He was always a strategic individual, but more so dramatic as the tears dropped from his eyes.

"If this is any consolation for you, I am fully on your side and am in total defense of Mr. Stewart and his family. If I would trust any gifted intelligent student, it would be you, but for the last time, what is my role in this?" Mr. Baidoo asked.

"Tell him that he needs someone to talk to, and that you are certain that I am the best candidate. Let him know that we will work together, any crap like that," Anthony said.

"Well, not very convincing, but I will do my best to get you closer and the test results will do the trick." A sly Mr. Baidoo surprised Anthony. Anthony knew exactly what he meant. The tannoy had gone ten minutes before, but Mr. Baidoo had taken Anthony in his office to complete the plan while the assistant tutor took charge. "You do not want to be late for your first lesson, here is a note of excuse for being late." Mr. Baidoo handed Anthony the note from his notepad.

"I never thought you would have been so helpful, but you turned out to be more than a confidante," Anthony said.

"Call me a confidante when I have changed my sex." Mr. Baidoo growled in laughter.

"You know what I mean," Anthony replied.

"You go on," Mr. Baidoo said.

Anthony hurriedly got to his English lesson where his body was there, but surely not his mind, nor his intentions. Instead, he took his small book out where he trotted on with his plan. On the first page, he scribbled the name Mrs. Merchel. Mrs. Merchel was the deputy head, she was also the head of year nine and she was very influential. He never wrote her note, but he did write very important person. Next on his list, he wrote YPAA, and beside it he wrote the meaning of the acronym – Young People Against Abuse. Pretending that he was doing the class work, he quickly scribbled, *need own office and must link it with the media – this will be big*. He had it all figured out but it was an advice he knew he would need and there was no better person but the 6'3" lady standing in front of him. He remembered her saying, or rather boasting, about her law degree. He smiled at her. She returned the smile, thinking how much an impact she was having on her favorite student, only she had no clue of his true intentions.

Twenty minutes later and the lesson had ended. "What was that smile about, Anthony?" Ms. Jones asked him.

"Just how helpful you would be to my cause on child abuse," he said.

"That's so honorable of you, Anthony, but I am busy as it is already," she politely declined.

"Miss, do you have a child?" Anthony asked.

"Yes, I have a beautiful daughter, she is two," she dotingly replied.

"What if I told you that between your daughter's current age to at least the age of sixteen, there is a ninety percent chance of her being abused?" he gesticulated with his fingers.

"If you were not a child, I would eat you now," snarled Ms. Jones. Anthony was, however, unrepentant, staring her in the eyes. She looked at him, but in her heart she knew he had touched a nerve. She knew his statistics were flawed, but even a one percent chance was enough to drive total fear. "OK, Anthony, you got my attention, what do you want me to do?" she asked.

"Let's leave it for lunch break, Miss, and then I will return to discuss the details with you," Anthony dictated. He knew that he had her emotionally in his pocket. That was what he was best at. She could not believe a thirteen year old could be so successful at using reverse psychology on her.

At the same time Anthony had been to the lessons in between lunch, Devon was under careful examination by so many different organizations. The social services, police, psychologist, prosecuting attorneys, they were all there. By that time, he did not need the intimidation of Brian. He had lied so much he started to believe his lie.

"So, tell me, Devon, when was the last time that Mr. Stewart sexually assaulted you?" asked the prosecuting officer. She looked like a no nonsense woman dressed in her military style suit.

"I can't remember, my mind is just too messed up at this time," Devon replied.

"The underwear found by your mother indicated a recent assault. You will be questioned with shit like this, so you are doing neither yourself or the prosecution any favors by holding back any information," the prosecuting officer advised him.

"I just can't answer any more questions now. I prepared for a test tomorrow, and I need to rest to get my mind prepared for this." Devon requested his exit.

"Sure," she said, looking at him suspiciously. She asked implicating questions and she noticed how he always dodged those same questions. She left, but she made sure to leave him with one message.

"The truth always prevails, so never try to play the smart ass guy. I have been in this job long enough to tell you that the body always talks and the mind tells the truth," she said. She left without saying another word.

Anthony was right, Devon would need someone to talk to, but he had a problem, though. His problem was that Anthony was the only person he had to talk to. Mr. Stewart had the same experience of cross examinations, except that it was done from a less pleasant atmosphere. "OK, Mr. Stewart, you claim not to know Devon, but the evidence here from the principal's table showed that the 12th of February of this year, you were instructed to see to his safety as he was one of the last people to leave from the lawn tennis training," the same prosecuting officer questioned him.

"I have hundreds of directives from the principal because I am the chief caretaker, but it does not mean that I will oversee these jobs," Mr. Stewart explained.

"Are you saying that the other caretakers are responsible?" she asked.

"Well, he pointed me out three times, so I am not suggesting that at all. I was just answering your question," he answered.

"So, you are playing the smart ass, too?" she asked. "Why did you do it, Mr. Stewart? Where did you assault him?" she demanded. She took a breath. "Mr. Stewart, I will be honest with you, we cannot even use an alibi to nail you, so we need your help. If you just admit to what you did, I promise you that your sentence will be cut from fifteen years to seven," she continued. It was the years that did it. Mr. Stewart thought of the years of his newborn child passing by. He could not handle it any longer. He cracked and started to cry. "It's OK to cry, Mr. Stewart, just make your admission when you are finished," she said.

"You just don't get it, do you? I have a kid, how could I do such a disgusting thing know that I have a child myself? Even if I never had a child, I would rather slit my throat first before doing such things." He let it all loose. The prosecuting officer did not see any pretence. She was actually moved, but she could not give away her own emotions.

"Well done, great performance. You should get an Oscar!" She shouted out her barrage of sarcasm. "When we meet again, I want a better performance. Just come with the answers I need to hear," she said, having her briefcase packaged with all the paperwork of the day. Her mind was, however, shaded with doubts on Devon, and it was eating her out because she could not crack him. The problem was that she could not question any other without sufficient evidence. She needed an ally desperately and fast. That ally, unknown to her, was Anthony, but chances of their paths crossing was very slim.

Lunchtime had come and Anthony had found his way to Ms. Jones. She was at her desk waiting for him, looking intrigued to say the least. "So, what is this all about, Anthony? Spill the beans," Ms. Jones said.

"Well, you heard what happened to Mr. Stewart?"

"Yes," she replied.

"Well, I have been abused and so I do not take it lightly when I say I believe he is innocent, and so I want to help and other children in this school and everywhere," he explained.

"How gallant of you, so how can I help?" she asked.

"Well, with your law expertise and your command of the English language, I need you to support and establish my new club – Young People Against Abuse," he explained.

"Hmm, sure I can help. When do we start?" she asked.

"We can start now. How about you preparing the visionary statements and investigate all the legal apparatus that will be useful to this club, by that I mean all the loopholes these assholes have been using to evade justice," he calmly advised. Ms. Jones gave Anthony the most stupendous look, showing just how intrigued she was.

"At your command, I will get back to you next week with all your requests," she said.

"Thank you, Miss, well appreciated," he replied.

Anthony was indeed a unique individual, but then again, his intelligence combined with his ruthlessness may have been developed from his own battle of injustice against himself from a very tender age. Next on his list was Mrs. Merchel, he knew exactly where to find her. Her office was adjacent to the Head Master's office to the second floor, just after entering the admission entrance of the school. Luckily for him, the door was left ajar, exposing the very lady he so wanted to see sitting at her desk, busily at work. He knocked at the door nervously, nervous because he was prepared for a fight; a fight to have his plan accepted and put in place as soon as possible if not immediately.

"Please, come in," she answered.

"Hi, Mrs. Merchel."

"Hello, Anthony," she answered. She knew his name and that broke the ice.

"Miss, you know my name!" Anthony gasped.

"There are three types of pupils who will always be known," she said.

"And, what are they?" he asked.

"The very bad and dull, the very good and intelligent, and the very indifferent students," she answered.

"And, what category do I fall under?" Anthony asked.

"The very good and intelligent," she answered. It was indeed a great start for Anthony.

"I see, very is the operative word then?"

"How intelligent of you, so what is it?" the short, middle aged, and immaculately groomed woman said. At that moment, Anthony slapped a document half an inch thick onto her desk. She cautiously opened it, and there on the front page she saw a lovely presented introduction explaining his aims and cause. She turned and seemed more curious as she read his needs. At that point, she closed the small manual and faced up to see Anthony examining her expressions. "Interesting stuff here, Anthony," she said.

"And, I wish for the club to start as soon as possible, but you know I have come to you for its implications and, most important, funding."

"An adult..."

"Ms. Jones and Mr. Baidoo have committed themselves already, and you can be on board by supporting us now," Anthony cut short her question.

"I am actually proud of your initiative here, Anthony, but we are dealing with sensitive matters here, so sensitive, a child could commit suicide by a small mistake made by yourself. We, as a school, cannot take such a risk. We already have an experienced, qualified student counselor in the school who has been doing a great job," she explained to him.

"But, Mrs. Merchel, how many students haven't gone to Mr. Bennett because he is not like them? He is an adult and for many, a male who represents an abusive father or simply an out of touch individual?" Anthony backed up his corner.

"Point taken. Tell you what, the best I can do is speak to Mr. Bennett. His office is only next to mine."

"I will get him now," Anthony said before rushing to Mr. Bennett's office. She hung her head, shaking it. It was a few short moments before Anthony re-entered the office with Mr. Bennett.

"This young man just pulled me in your office, what's all the fuss about?" a bemused Mr. Bennett inquired. She handed him the YPAA manual of which Mr. Bennett scanned quickly. "I think this is a brilliant idea. I for sure recognized this glitch a long time ago and am prepared to work with this fine young man," Mr. Bennett said, much to Anthony's delight.

"I knew you would understand. Thank you, sir."

"OK then, have it your way. We will set things in motion. You will get your office and most of your demands," a defeated Mrs. Merchel replied. Anthony was delighted, to say the least. Then again, he usually made things happen his way. It was the shortest day ever for Anthony, like he had never seen it before, but he was glad because it was the most productive day of his life with many more of the same where it all came from.

"You look well haggard, Anthony," his auntie said. He had finally reached home that day. "Look in the stove where you will see your meal," she directed him. He went to the kitchen and opened the stove where he saw the Chinese plate covered by another. With his bare hands, he took the plate out. It was not too hot, it was bearable. The food was his favorite – steamed fish with fried chips. The grape drink was on its way to wash down such savory. "Here is your drink," Margaret said as she poured the grape juice from the glass jug while Anthony chewed on the fish and chips.

"Thanks, Auntie."

"You're welcome. I got something else for you," she said with a mischievous smile. She disappeared for a few seconds, and then reappeared with a bundle of letters. Anthony continued to enjoy his well prepared meal, still unaware of the magnitude of Margaret's find. "These are for you," she said with a smile. She finally got his attention as he slowly and cautiously peeled away the elastic bands from the covered two dozen letters. When he saw the return names and address, he first dropped the fork, and then his mouth literally dropped as he saw the first name was Gloria Williams, then on the other letters he saw Gabriel Williams. He was blown away.

"How did you do this? Are you saying they have been writing me all along?" he inquired.

"Oh yes, thank your Great Uncle. He only made one call to your mother and before you knew it, we got these letters from her in the flesh," Margaret explained.

"Can you now see what I have been through?" Anthony asked.

"I must admit that she comes across as one of the most misunderstood women I have ever set my eyes on. Do not judge her too harshly, she is due a child soon. Anyway, I will not take up any more of your time, I see you got a lot of catching up to do," Margaret said to a quiet, still stanced young boy. He could not have eaten another bite, and Margaret understood as she took up the remains of his food and placed it in the dog's mix.

Anthony could not read enough, many of them desperately trying to find out about his well being and some wondering if he has died or changed address. The one that was most poignant was the sixth letter he read. It was from Gabriel, saying how much he missed his brother and what he would have done to trade places, but he left a number. The letter was more than a year late, but all the same, nothing beat a trial but a failure, he thought. Anthony ran to the phone and dialed the number he saw in the letter. The phone rang, but no one answered. He hung up the receiver, but his spirit could not rest until fifteen minutes later he rang again.

"Hello?" someone from the other end answered.

"Hello? Is this Gabriel?" Anthony asked.

"Yeah, it is. Anthony, is that you?" Gabriel asked.

"Yes, it's me!" Anthony confirmed.

"You are kidding me,   Mama, Daddy!" Gabriel shouted. "Anthony is on the phone!"

"Thank You, Jesus, thank You, Jesus." The voices came from the background. "Anthony!"

"Yes, Mama?" Anthony answered.

"I have been trying to get in touch with you for so long."

"I know, I only just got the letters that were being hidden away from me," he answered.

"My God, is she still trying to kill you?" Gloria asked.

"I am no longer with her. I managed to be taken away by the rest of the family," he explained.

"We have worried about you for so long. We have prayed for you and there is a God who watches over us," she said. The gaps were being filled. "Your dad and I have gotten a good job here in Canada, we will send you something when we can," she pledged to Anthony.

He felt better, his prayers were answered and now he felt as if was renewed with a different type of confidence to move on. It then dawned on why people were made and not an individual. His philosophy of life was that people were made to help each other and if they were unable to do so, then they were less of a human being. He was tired, so he went to bed earlier than usual, at seven p.m. that evening. The phone, however, rang again. It was Margaret that answered the phone

"Hello?" she said.

"Good evening, ma'am, may I speak to Anthony?" the voice requested. She recognized his voice.

"Hi, Devon, how are you?" she asked.

"I am fine, ma'am," he replied. She knew the score, but she knew better to mind her own business. She went to Anthony's room where he was well asleep, but she knew how important the call would have been to him.

"Anthony, wake up, someone is on the phone for you."

"Hmm?" he moaned, rubbing his eyes.

"The phone, go and answer it," she insisted. Anthony thought it was Gloria or Gabriel on the phone once more.

"Hello?"

"Anthony, glad you answered the phone, I needed someone to talk to," Devon said. He got Anthony's attention completely. Now, Anthony thought, was a strategic chance to build on something.

"Before you say anything else, I want you to understand that I am here for you, and I believe you when you said Stewy did it. How could he?" Anthony said.

"It's nice of you, I am just scared at the moment."

"You have done nothing wrong, so don't be scared," Anthony answered.

"Well, I will be back at school tomorrow and..." He stopped there.

"And, what?" Anthony asked.

"I can't say over the phone. When I see you, I will show you instead, it's not good for me," a worried Devon continued.

"Please, tell me!" Anthony practically screamed.

"I have noticed some things in the palm of my hands. Some rash of the sort and, please, don't let me say it now. I don't even know if I can make it at school."

"Sounds like you got..." Anthony paused. "Come to school tomorrow, I will have your back, no matter what," Anthony promised him.

"OK," he said, concluding the conversation.

As Anthony put the receiver down, he thought with a smile, *This really is my lucky day.* He realized Devon had something that would give him enough ammunition to lead him ten levels above his original target. He felt like a conduit that nothing could block, leading him to stardom if he pleased. He knew he bagged it now and so, his plan needed another two hours and if it meant that the day would go faster, he was prepared to let it go faster.

He built up on paper strategies that would lead to the empowerment of the abused, ways to get them to talk without fear. He wrote that the Young People Against Abuse (YPAA) must not just be a fancy school's club, but a national, if not international, organization. Early detection, he thought, was necessary, so he wrote friends, family members, and even strangers must make it their business to be involved in every facet of a child's life.

He wrote that because he remembered how, if it were not for the vigilance of Gloria or other family members, he would have been as good as dead. Lastly, he wrote that the guilty culprits must be known and pay a dear price for their sins and for him, that was possibly the most crucial aspect of the manifesto for his organization. He then scribbled the media before falling asleep.

Chapter 14

Six a.m. and the sun beamed through the curtains onto Anthony as he sprawled his legs and arms out, causing him to rub his eyes, waking up to the realism of another day when he had to get out of bed. The usual mundane job of brushing his teeth, having a bath, and getting dressed in his uniform was done in a rush that day. He could not wait to see Devon. After all, the suspense was killing him. Eight thirty a.m. arrived quickly, and he had arrived at school passing the gate unmanned by security. Five minutes later, from a distance he saw the image of Devon as he approached the school's gate.

"Devon!" Anthony shouted.

"Said I would be back today, so here I am," Devon said.

"Go on then, let me see those hands," Anthony said.

"Gosh, you could not wait," Devon said.

"You bet," Anthony replied. Devon took him by the side where there was no one around and showed him the palm of his hands. It was that confirmation he waited for. He stared at Devon as if he had seen a ghost.

"What's the matter?" Devon asked, looking embarrassed.

"Nothing, I just never expected it to look this badly," Anthony said. "At least you can cover it, no one will notice. So, what do you think caused this then?" Anthony asked.

"To tell you the truth, I am not sure, but I have my suspicions," he said.

"Suspicions, what do you mean?" Anthony asked as he cleverly became the buffoon.

"It is not important, do not listen to me," he said.

"You know you got to see the doctor?" Anthony suggested.

"I am too embarrassed, to say the least," Devon revealed.

"Too embarrassed? Too embarrassed?" Anthony shouted. "Boy, you've got syphilis, syphilis kills," Anthony whispered in the ears of Devon.

"Is that what you think it is?" Devon asked.

"Devon, not think, it's what I know. You were absent the day we studied this in science," Anthony said. Devon was now too upset and embarrassed, he walked away. "Come back to me and do not run away from the problem, face it with me," Anthony ordered. At that moment in time, Devon fell to his knees and clasped his hands between his eyebrows and started to cry.

"Why me, Lord, why me?" he screamed. Anthony felt bad for his friend and stared in space, searching for one million and one answers to give Devon. The solution, at least part solution, he thought he had, and he was about to reach out to Devon.

"Are you ready to expose that bastard?" Anthony asked. He held his lips when he realized his thoughts of words were seriously an imitation of Jade's.

"Please, let no one know of this," he pleaded to Anthony.

"So, that is all you are concerned about? What about getting some medical attention?" Anthony asked. Devon knew of the domino effects to follow and was walking on eggshells.

"It goes away sometimes, just disappears. It heals itself," Devon said.

"That's what syphilis does, you are playing Russian roulette with your life, Devon," Anthony whispered loudly into his hears.

"Not another word of this, as a matter of fact, leave me alone!" Devon shouted before walking in the opposite direction to Anthony.

"No, I will not leave you alone!" Anthony whispered to himself as he walked northwards to the science block. His destiny, Mr. Baidoo. "Mr. Baidoo, you need to forget all that I have said to you."

"About what?"

"Trying to convince Devon that I believe Stewy committed such horrible crimes against him."

"Hmm, I see. Why the change of plan?" Mr. Baidoo asked.

"Devon has just made it easier for me to prove Stewy's innocence," Anthony replied.

"My Lord, I really would love to get into that brain of yours just for a day," Mr. Baidoo said.

"I really don't think so, Mr. Baidoo," he replied.

"There is one thing I will need, though, and that is your attendance to the YPAA's first meeting this Wednesday, starting time fifteen thirty hours sharp."

"You did not need to say the time, the notice has been on display board of all the faculties of this school," Mr. Baidoo said.

"Very funny," Anthony said.

"Of course, I will be there, but am I useless otherwise?" Mr. Baidoo said.

"Thank you, your support makes you more useful than you could ever imagine," Anthony said. The next stop was Mrs. Jones, and, of course, for him, her usefulness would have to be a call beyond her duty as a teacher. She had no time to have a discussion with Anthony. She went to her desk and from it she picked up a parcel, a fat parcel.

"Here, Anthony, it is the fourteenth amendment. I would suggest you read it for when we meet at the opening of your organization. I have highlighted the important bits for discussion," she explained.

"I wanted to..." Anthony tried to speak, but was cut off.

"No, Anthony, not now. I am very busy," she interrupted him.

"Miss, Devon has syphilis and he is afraid to get treatment," he blurted. His statement hit a nerve.

"Really? Oh my God, this is serious!" she exclaimed, now finding the time to talk.

"We need to find a way of getting this information to the police and allowing them to match the evidence to his stepfather or Stewart," he said.

"You are right because whichever of them have it would have been implicated to be the culprit," she agreed.

"Exactly," Anthony said.

"I am not going to the police, though, I will not get that deep into it," she warned.

"That is fine. I will go, I just need your advice."

"The school has an obligation to report this, so I will have to call social services, I advise that you leave it to the authorities," she told him.

"OK, ma'am," Anthony conceded. He said it, of course, but he had other plans. He left with the packed parcel, determined to carry out his plan.

Nothing happened out of the ordinary for Anthony that day, except that he crossed paths with Devon in physics class and they kept their distance from one another. During his breaks, he went to his office where he prepared a manifesto for his organization as if it were a proper political party. He had other things to do, but he chose to open the parcel where he noticed highlights with scribbled guidelines. He noticed the emphasis put on the interpretation of the statement. *'State level child protection laws that allow parental assault upon children as long as the motive is retaliation for displeasure with the child.'* He understood the full impact of that, especially when he had placed it in retrospect of his own experience with Jade. He thought it horrible, and agreed with Mrs. Jones suggestion that his organization had to align itself with social work organizations, reputable ones that understood that most states had no restrictions in the laws and were helpless. He got the phone directory and searched for a social work company, but his eyes were set upon the most popular radio company. He could not resist the temptation of calling Radio for the People. Unbeknown to Anthony, they had a talk show called *Let Us Sort Out This Mess*.

"Hello," a timid voice said.

"Hello, young man, you are on the air, that's how we do it. What is it that you want to share with us?" Barry Johnson, the ever so popular DJ said.

"Hi, my name is Anthony, and I really think that the 14th amendment needs to change to protect children like me who have been abused by my own mother and millions of others out there. We are talking about children!" Anthony voiced his opinion.

"That is very honorable and brave of you, but for change to come about, we need so many more as brave as you not just talking, but doing something," Barry said.

"I agree, and that is why at my school, I have organized a club to help those abused to come and speak out, and my organization will help them in every way, but most of all, help them to nail those cowards, those pedophiles."

"That is so admirable," Barry said. "But, what has given you such motivation, your mother abusing you I would imagine?" Barry asked.

"Yes, but I have a friend who has been sexually abused and I know they got the wrong person, and tonight with my evidence, I will get the right man behind the bars. This pedophile has destroyed a boy's life forever and to know that this man was supposed to be protecting him makes me sick. The amendment can't even protect us, so there you go," Anthony spoke out.

"How old are you?" Barry asked.

"I am fourteen years old," Anthony answered.

"You know what; this boy has just put us all to shame. If we do not respond for anyone else, we must respond for this courageous boy," Barry said. Barry then thanked Anthony for calling before ending the discussions, but the number of people trying to get on the radio program after crashed the line twice. Unfortunately for Anthony, one person was listening who he would rather not had listened. His name was Brian Diamond. He ground his teeth as he continued to drive, but decided to make a quick detour. Anthony felt good about his call and it was a treat worth ending the day on.

Four thirty and he was ready to make a move. The police station visit would have been the icing on the cake. The local police station was only a mile away and for him, that walk was a piece of cake. Anthony walked briskly along the road, keeping a pace twice his usual. The road was a lovely one with no one except himself. He liked it that way since it gave him space and a chance to reflect on anything he desired. Anthony started to reflect on his accomplishment, and although it was not much, he was thankful for the start. He truly wanted to make a difference and he believed he could do more. He saw a vision of a successful organization fighting in the corner of children like himself; helpless and unrepresented. As he turned onto the next street, completing about a quarter of his journey, he heard the engine of a car. He looked behind him to notice a VW. The car looked familiar to him, but it was not near enough for him to identify the driver. He noticed the car had slowed down. It was nearer to him, so he turned full on and looked closer. He had been to Devon's home twice before and on those two occasions he knew the face of Brian. Once he realized it was Brian, his survival instinct had kicked in. Anthony started to run as Brian accelerated, directing the car at Anthony. Destiny had its place and it was Anthony's destiny to survive. Luckily for him, a man who could not have been older than forty five was jogging that same time and chose to turn toward the road where he saw the VW teasingly chasing the fourteen year old. The sight of someone caused Brian to make a U-turn where he sped away.

"Oh, thank you, sir, that man wanted to kill me!" Anthony screamed as he panted, trying to catch up on his breathing.

"He was probably trying to scare you, he would have killed you already if he really wanted to run that car over you," the mature stranger suggested to Anthony. Anthony realized that he was really trying to scare him and keep him silent; but he was determined now more than ever before to fulfill his mission, and so he completed his journey to the police station.

Brian was hysterical and his mind became more and more irrational. He knew that everything was about to close in on him and he had one last chance, he had to destroy the evidence, and, like Anthony, he was just as determined. He knew very well that Blossom would have been at work and his view of her was that of a naive, stupid woman. He parked the car to the curb of the gate and calmly entered the house. There, he saw the tall, but timid Devon sitting in front of the television screen watching his favorite show, a new show called *McGuyver*. It was that show that got him so keen on science, particularly Physics, and the episode in question had him glued to the TV. The television was, however, switched off, with Brian standing in front of his usual target.

Anthony, in the meantime, ran into the police station. "Help, help me!" he frantically shouted.

"Calm down, have a glass of water and speak to me," the senior police officer calmly said. He went and fetched a glass of water, and gave it to Anthony. "OK, I'm Detective Armstrong, you look as if you had just seen a ghost. Tell me, what's the matter?" Armstrong asked. Anthony gulped the water down as he tried to calm down. He spoke so fast, it was as if he felt that he was running out of time.

"A man, I think his name is Brian Diamond, just tried to run me over. He knew I was on my way to you guys," Anthony revealed, still trying to compose himself.

"How could he have known this?" Detective Armstrong asked.

"I was on the radio about protecting children and I know that he sexually assaulted my friend, Devon, and framed it on Mr. Stewart, the caretaker of the school," Anthony answered.

"Yes, you are the young man on the air only forty minutes ago, and I do remember the case of Devon," Armstrong said. "But, what evidence do you have to say that it was Mr. Diamond and not Mr. Stewart?" Detective Armstrong asked a valid question as he, too, started to show some emotions. He believed every word that Anthony said.

"Devon has Syphilis. I believe he got it from his abuser and, therefore, his abuser would have that disease. He might have realized that I had something well incriminating," Anthony replied.

"Easy, tiger, you are trying to take my job from me, I can see," Detective Armstrong said. It was Armstrong's style as he tried to take some of the anxiety away from Anthony and himself.

At the same time, the manipulating Brian got on his knees in front of Devon. "I really am sorry for what I have done to you. I mean it from the bottom of my heart," Brian pleaded with watery eyes. Devon was bewildered, to say the least, and the sincerity of Brian was too much to bear.

"I can forgive you, but you know how Mommy will feel. We must tell her and save Mr. Stewart, if you are really sorry," Devon said.

"I agree, and that is why I will take my own life. I want to end it all so, please, write my suicide note for me," Brian calmly asked of Devon.

"I can't do that," Devon said.

"Well, I can't help Mr. Stewart or your mother

because I will not go to prison for life. I would rather take my own life and I do not have the courage or strength to write my own suicide note," he said with a slight oratory skill.

"OK then," Devon said. "Tell me what to write." Devon caved in. Brian had the note and the paper at hand.

"Only write what I say, nothing added, nothing subtracted, you hear me?" Brian demanded.

"OK," Devon answered.

"I am sorry for the hurt to my family of being gay and causing all these problems," Brian dictated. Devon wrote, and then he paused.

"But, how does this..."

"Just write, I will write two notes, one to admit who I am, and one to say what I did," Brian convinced Devon.

"Alright," Devon said.

"I cannot take it anymore, even with the sexual disease that I got from some random guy, and so I will take my life," he dictated. The words were all written down. Brian then grabbed the note from him with the most sinister laugh one could ever have imagined. "You idiot, you have just written your own suicide note and now I will be vindicated of all evidence, you fool," he mockingly teased Devon. He had the knife in one hand and the suicide note in the other.

"You will not get away with this, Brian!" Devon bravely said to him.

"Yes, I will, when you are in your grave," Brian said as he slashed at Devon. He rushed as Devon got the vase, throwing it in Brian's face and running, but Brian got the blade to Devon's wrist and there, blood spewed. Brian was pleased with the accuracy and his thirst for more blood became evident as Devon staggered to the bathroom, but the door was locked.

The living room faced the back of the garden; a lovely groomed garden with lily hibiscus plants and many exotic plants. Brian had Devon cornered and Brian was certain of his death as he became weak, staggering to the floor. His head becoming light and his social awareness became beyond his grasp. Brian held his inflicted hand. He wanted to make the wound deeper at the same spot, but before doing so, he carefully placed the suicide note by the neck of his victim. He then took up the knife to make that final slash, but one bullet to the very arm had him dropping the knife and running at the same time. His one mistake was having his back to the patio door, unaware of Detective Armstrong's strategic aim at him. It was panic as he shattered the glass and ran for Devon. They could not move him, CPR and first aid had to be administered.

"Emergency 911, can I help you?"

"Get an ambulance at 297 Springfield Road now!" one of the officers shouted. Then, two of the officers pinned Brian to the floor as he was handcuffed, but the more serious case of Devon had the well experienced Armstrong pouring peroxide onto the wide, open wound, a clear sign that his tendon was inflicted. Simultaneously, one of his first aiders frantically opened Devon's airway as he tilted his head, and soon he locked his mouth onto Devon with his nose being held and he would breathe into him, making his chest rise. He then compressed his chest with the heel of his hand in the middle of Devon's chest several times. Detective Armstrong watched his officer and seemed impressed.

"Officer Leung, I am well impressed. Look, he is breathing."

"Oh, thank you, sir, you have not done so badly yourself with the peroxide. That was quick thinking. Where did you get that from?" Leung asked.

"Any good woman in the house with children knows that must have one of these. I found it in the bathroom," he answered. He had to knock the door down, but it was worth it. The ambulance arrived, taking Devon, who was now partially conscious of his surroundings. Anthony watched from the outside as he witnessed his friend being taken away, but the commotion was just too much to bear.

"No! No! Not my son!" Blossom screamed, arriving home just in time to make her way to the back of the ambulance. The grief etched on her face said it all. She had already been briefed on the situation and the betrayal by her Brian made her wish he had slashed her wrist instead. "I will be strong for you, my son. I am so sorry, I should have known," she kept whispering in the ear of Devon.

"Mom, it is not your fault, I will be fine. Detective Armstrong was my hero," he said before drifting into sleep again. Within ten minutes, they arrived at the hospital and Devon was whisked to the emergency room.

"Anthony, where have you been?" a waiting Margaret asked.

"You would not believe what happened. My friend, Devon, was attacked by his stepfather and if I had not went to the police, Devon would have been dead now," Anthony told her.

"That is the reason for you to be here at nine fifty p.m.?" an unmoved Margaret asked.

"Yes, Auntie!" Anthony replied.

"Well, your granduncle won't buy that because he wants you to return to your mother," she said. Anthony felt gutted. He was not so sure as to what he should do and on impulse, he held onto Margaret's hands.

"Please, I beg you, do not let me go back. She hates me, she will kill me. Please, I do not want to go back," he beseeched to her. The genuine fear in his voice almost revealed the living soul of Anthony and Margaret saw. She felt the connection and for the first time, she realized the breadth and length of his situation, his abuse, and his fear. She walked off saying not one word.

"Stanford, we cannot send him back to his mother, he has developed with us. Let us not cause him to go ten steps backward," she pleaded to her husband.

"Fine then, but he must understand that he must keep to our laws and rules. I will speak to him tomorrow morning," Stanford said.

A confident Anthony was trembling with fear. He was not sure what to do. He thought to go to Stanford's room and beg him, but he feared he would make it worse. He chose not to go, and instead allowed things to run its course. Devon was the least of his problems as horrible flashbacks ran through his mind. The belt buckle hitting him across his face, the mop stick broken on his back as Jade wacked him across his face, sleeping on the floor, and stones hurled at him, some connecting his small body, kept unfolding in his memories. However, those were not the worse, it was statements like, "Go and find your father for the clothes." "What do you want me to do, whore out myself? I do not have it." "If I knew what you would have become, I would have taken a knife and pushed it in my womb with you in there."

And, those were only some of the statements of Jade that reminded him that her husband was all drown to the hate of his father. He believed that the hatred would never go away, that time not because of her, but because of his deep rooted hatred for her. He was clear on one thing, and that was he never wanted to see his own mother again. On those bitter reflections, Anthony fell sound asleep. There was one thing he realized more than anything else, and that was of all the people he knew, he feared his mother the most and it was not a fear out of respect, but a fear born out of hatred.

Four hours, Blossom waited patiently outside the medical emergency room before the doctor arrived. "Hi, you must be Mrs. Brown," the doctor said.

"Yes, I am," she answered.

"I am Doctor Baird, and I just wanted to update you on the progress of your son," he introduced himself.

"How is he, Doctor?" she asked with a nervous disposition.

"I can tell you that three tendons and one nerve was severed," he said. "The slash was to the bottom of his wrist horizontally to the center with one and a half inch long perpendicular cut," he explained. She looked confused, but with the sense she could make from what to her mind was non-sense, she knew that it was serious.

"So, he will be fine?" she asked again with worry in her eyes.

"The avulsion or nerve damage, I cannot say anything definitive yet, but I can say that he should be fine."

"Thank You, Jesus, thank you, Doctor," she said.

"Oh no, do not thank me. We injected some neprevesatucal dyes and this helped us to use the CT scan, which showed that there was no serious damage or any blockage. He is just lucky that the injury or cut was any deeper, otherwise, he would have been dead," Doctor Baird said.

"So, is there anything else that I need to know?" Blossom asked, still looking worried.

"Well, if after two weeks he should complain about a tingling sensation in the affected area, then consider that to be good news, this is one of the main proof of a near full recovery," Doctor Baird said.

"OK, thank you again," she said.

"Oh, before I forget, make sure that he does not lift any weights for months. This would only stretch the brachial plexus, causing greater damage to his nerves.

You will get some anti inflamatories as he will be in pain at some time, and we will be organizing some physical therapy sessions." Doctor Baird was as meticulous as they come. He wanted to make sure that he covered his back in everything. "Oh, and here is a tennis ball, I would suggest that in a week's time he squeezes this for at least thirty minutes in the day. This will help to repair his nervous system and develop his abilities to use his hands again." Doctor Baird would not finish, but Blossom was grateful, even though he was overzealous.

"OK, Doc, how is he now, though?"

"Come on, you can see him now, he is fine," Doctor Baird reassured her. Blossom followed him to intensive care ward and she finally felt relieved when she saw Devon sitting up with a smile across his face. His right hand was in bandage and a sling, but she could live with that. She ran and hugged him tightly as if she never wanted to let him go.

"Oh, Mom, my hand, you are hurting it now." He laughed as he told her.

"I am sorry, dear, I am sorry," she said, laughing as well. The problem, though, was that it was no laughing matter when Detective Armstrong returned to see Devon, and with luck, his mother was at hand. The visit was to find out about his progress.

"Hi, Devon, and how are you doing now?" Armstrong asked.

"A lot better now, thank you very much for saving my life," Devon said as his mother looked on.

"Don't thank me, thank Anthony. If it were not for

him, we would not have known that you could have been in danger," he said. Devon looked surprised, but still grateful. "While Doctor Baird looked after you, a blood sample was taken and the results has come back positive for syphilis. Can you tell us how you contracted this disease?" Asked Detective Armstrong. Devon knew it was pointless to lie. He was sure Anthony told them all and now that Brian was caught, he realized the need to spill the beans.

"I was sexually assaulted by my stepdad, Brian," he said, hanging his head in shame.

"You need not hang your head in shame, you did no wrong. How long has he been assaulting you?" Detective Armstrong asked.

"Two years. Since my dad moved out of the house and his presence replaced my dad," Devon answered. Blossom could not say a word, but she was shaking like a leaf and soon she was in revulsion. She slumped to the floor, her eyes rolling back and she started to choke on her tongue.

"Help! Help!" The scream came from Detective Armstrong. Nurses and doctors were immediately on site.

"Let us get her in, this is an epileptic attack," one of the doctors said. The thing was that Blossom had never had an epileptic attack. The shock of what she heard must have brought on the fit.

"I am sorry, Devon, I think that we have had enough for the day," Detective Armstrong said with his hat placed back on his head as he ventured through the door. For Devon, he believed it had only just begun because he was certain that he being the center of it all would demand greater pain, possibly greater than the slashed wrist he had sustained.

Chapter 15

April 2nd 1981 was a morning to remember. For Anthony, it was bittersweet. Bitter since he was unsure of his own destiny with his accommodation. Sweet because he had made a giant step that made him an ambassador for children. The usual happened that morning. Margaret having the chairs upright, and Stanford sitting outside with the cigarette to his mouth as he listened to the eight o'clock news. For him, it was not news if it did not come from the ABC. The news was done. "Anthony!" he bellowed. He only needed to call once.

"Yes, Uncle," Anthony answered as he ran to the veranda. He then sat adjacent to Stanford.

"What is it with you, Anthony?" Stanford asked.

"Nothing, Uncle," he answered.

"Do you want to continue to stay here?" Stanford asked.

"Yes, Uncle," Anthony answered humbly.

"Well, you must abide by my rules, and you know that you must get back here by four p.m. the latest," he commanded.

"Uncle, I truly want to stay here, but I started this club and I was on the radio, and soon I will be helping so many more like myself who were abused," Anthony explained.

"Four p.m. and no later," Stanford said.

"This club is my world, and I cannot promise you that I will be back by four p.m. Sometimes, I will get back by six thirty p.m." Anthony built up the courage to fight in his corner.

"So, you made up your mind then?"

"Yes, and I will not go back to that woman, but if I must, I will. Can I leave now?" Anthony asked.

"Yes, you can," Stanford answered. Anthony left to his room and there, he started to get his clothes from the drawers. In less than a moment, Stanford followed him to his room. "Anthony, for the first time, you stood up to me, you are becoming a man and I like that," Stanford said as he got closer to Anthony.

"Sorry for speaking to you like that, but this club means the world to me," Anthony explained.

"Put the clothes back, you ain't going nowhere," Stanford said.

"But, you said I must be here by four p.m. and that will not happen every day."

"OK, I understand, but do me one favor, let me know when this will happen," Stanford said before hugging his grandnephew. Anthony felt relieved, to say the least, because on that Wednesday, it was the launch day of his club and after what happened, he wanted to make it a blast. He was prepared to give it his all. He then rushed to the shower, pondered himself, and at no other time was he so quickly attired looking like a real gentleman in uniform.

"Who is this fine young man I am looking at?" teased Margaret.

"You are looking at the President of the Young People Against Abuse," Anthony proudly replied.

"Well, President or not, you should always look like that. If you ask me, you would already get a fine young lady to call your own," Margaret said.

"OK, Auntie, whatever you say," he said as he gulped down the egg sandwich and hot chocolate drink.

"Take your time, my boy, you are still pretty early," she said as she took his empty plate.

"You would not understand, I have so much fine tuning to do, it is just awesome," he said before grabbing his bag and running through the opened grills. The grilled gate was already opened because Margaret had been watering the front garden, one of her early chores. Later in the evening she would return to her beloved garden, watering every plant. It was as if each plant was her children. All her children were grown mature people and they lived in California, so for her, any substitute would do.

Seven forty a.m. and Anthony was present at school. As he walked to the unmanned gate, the thought of Stewy rushed through his mind. He was certain of Stewy's release and could not wait for his body at its right place, at the school gates where he belonged. "I will tackle this situation before anything else," he whispered to himself. On entrance to his office, he got rid of all of the unnecessary papers stock piled on his desk; they were important, some were claims as expenses he had to make, but the fourteenth amendment, he needed to complete and now saw how important that document was. It was easy for him to do so, including the official opening because it was a special day in school called achievement day where no traditional lessons were held, but organized, fun activities to ensure independent work. He had the entire day for himself. Eight fifteen came and he was still in his office making sure everything was to the 'T.' On the dot of eight fifteen, the phone in the office rang. It was the first time someone had called. "Hello?" he said.

"Hello, this is Barry Johnson, the radio DJ who spoke to you before."

"I know who you are, what are you calling about?" Anthony asked, sounding a bit arrogant. However, the trembling voice gave away his anxiety and reverence for Barry, the most listened to radio host.

"Well, I am calling you to say congratulations because your actions yesterday has now made you a household name."

"What do you mean?" Anthony asked.

"Well, I made sure to get you because I knew you would be in at this time, but you will soon learn that your call to my radio station and your action of being in the front line for a victim, I think his name was Devon," Barry said.

"You know about Devon?" Anthony gasped.

"Yes, and the eighty five thousand population of this Springfield town, and yes, the entire city of New York," an excited Barry J said.

"But, I have done nothing," Anthony replied.

"Don't be modest, you have started a revolution, young man, and so it will be at your school. The radio team will be at your school to collect you. You will be with us for part of the day, but for the most part you will be with LBC TV," he reeled with excitement. It was too early for Anthony to take in so much, but he felt like a star until he composed himself. He did not want to get his eyes off of the ball, it was one thing he had pledged to himself.

"Thank you, Barry, for this information, but you must know that I will be mainly focused on the protection of our children, and some people will not like what I have to say," Anthony revealed.

"The ball will be in your court, please, do it your way," Barry J said before bidding him goodbye. Anthony was a statue for at least a minute. The quick thinking activist called his home. "Hello, the Jackson's residence," Margaret answered. Anthony could never mistake her vivacious voice. It was as if speaking to another Barry J.

"Hi, Auntie, I will be on TV, I told you," the excited teenager revealed.

"So, you are a celebrity now, you go, my boy."

"I will be very late today and I want to tell Grand Uncle myself," he said. There was a brief pause before Stanford came onto the phone.

"Hi, son, I heard your name was in the radio," Stanford said.

"Auntie forgot to tell me that part," Anthony said. "Listen, I will be on TV today, so I will be late getting home."

"About what time, son?" Stanford asked.

"I don't know, please, understand."

"I understand, you just stay safe, and I love you. I am proud of you, very proud of you," an emotional Stanford said. Anthony knew when someone said something and meant it, and Stanford meant it all, every word that came out of his mouth.

The itinerary for that day was changed. The official opening of the club was masterly brought forward to ten a.m. Like wildfire, news got around the school of Barry J's presence and everyone wanted to see their celebrity; he was the town's celebrity. The block of the school was used; room 414, the second assembly hall of the school. Luckily for Anthony, the hall was tailor made to be opened extending to the outside of the playing field with the doors opening as the floor was leveled to the field. Another three hundred chairs had been added outside and although it was so inconvenient for a good view, the bright, sunny day complemented by the cool wind of the spring season. The headmaster, pupils, and even the caretakers quickly packed the hall, soon there were not enough seats outside, others had to stand to the back, forgetting the rule, not to trample on the well groomed grass of the playing field.

"The official opening of the club has begun," the headmaster said. He was not well liked, perhaps, because he was one of the most well liked, perhaps, because he was one of the most evasive headmasters. Some students did not even know who he was. "It is not the usual tradition for us to have such a formal opening or even gathering for the starting of any club at this prestigious school, but this is not an ordinary club, nor is the founder an ordinary student," Mr. Watson, the headmaster, explained, being the rightfully opening spokesperson. "I am sure many of you have heard what Anthony Redford has accomplished, which has validated his right to start this club and with him is Barry J, and you all know him," he said with a pause. The audience responded to the pause with chatter and whispers before a rapturous applause. It took a moment for the simmering of the applause, some standing to glimpse Barry sitting on the outside to the left of the platform. "Without any further ado, I wish to invite Anthony Redford to the audience of his choice," Mr. Watson said, finding his way to the center of the seating platform. Anthony, for some reason, looked less flustered. He had the calm, statesman appearance.

"Thank you, everyone, for making it to my, sorry, our opening of the club, Young People Against Abuse." His confidence and clear intonation had a well received and attentive audience. "It is amazing that today was meant to be an ordinary day until the achievement day kicking off from the offset, but if this is not an achievement, then my name is not Anthony Redford." The audience laughed and clapped at the same time. "Four years from now and I am an adult, for some countries it is sixteen, but no one wants an adult life if they never had a good childhood. I mean, what is the point when emotionally, psychologically, and even physically, you are under developed?" he said with every word coming from his soul. A pin could have fallen and it would have been heard.

"Our pledge is to empower every child beyond the gates of this school, to the boundaries of Springfield, to the boundaries of the fifty states of our beloved country, and to the boundaries of every sea and ocean of this world," he calmly, but valiantly spoke with a crisp undertone. It was as if he was speaking to every child around the world.

"To all those children that have beaten, raped, enslaved, and verbally abused, today I want you to know that you are not alone because we will all build a network that will crush the mothers, fathers, uncles, aunts, teachers, anyone who believes that at their disgusting whims and pleasure they can destroy a human life," he said loudly and strongly.

His words were both personal and sensitive, and many were wiping tears, holding their mouths, or just staring. They were all well captivated by the realism of his words. He continued, using himself as an example, showcasing his plans and the time of day to meet. If there was anything that one had to believe, it was that he came without fear or bias. He then handed the microphone over to Mrs. Jones. The problem was that she could not say a word for about a minute because of the standing ovation and the deafening applause for Anthony was almost unstoppable. The idea of a fourteen year old being committed was one thing, but the depth of his conviction stole the heart of every man, woman, and child. One was no longer sure who the celebrity was anymore, because Barry J was certainly upstaged. Anthony could not speak on amendment fourteen as this would show a more emotional, unstable boy. His feelings on the subject was so passionate, it would have certainly defeated the purpose on agenda. Mrs. Jones finally got a chance to show that the policy of the club would be to give guidance to the victims, protection, and support. She then showed how amendment fourteen would be used in two ways. One, as a tool to fight for the protection of children and two, a medium used to deliver change. As she showed off her legal prowess, she became monotonous and boring as the audience could not wrap their brains around the technicalities so early.

It was all good when Mr. Baidoo followed on for one minute to introduce himself and his role as the second in command to Mrs. Jones in supporting and guiding the children of the school. At least his stepdaughter, Gene Farrell, was present. Few knew of Gene's connection to Mr. Baidoo, in fact, only two teachers knew, but none of the children really knew of any connection. Gene sat in the audience, looking withdrawn as usual, but her silky, fluffy hair with the most flawless white skin made her the most popular within a paradox her social demise. Everyone was intimidated by her beauty and the brain of Albert Einstein. Her close attention to Anthony was, however, clear as she stared motionless with her slender body. She was fifteen, but a few months difference made little to no difference. Her eyes caught Anthony's as Barry J finally had his turn to address the audience. The well groomed twenty five year old Casanova with a flair for words, and the wit and maturity of a wise man had the girls screaming and the boys seated with aspirations or jealously. There was contact between Gene and Anthony, and they both understood the subliminal messages of attraction being passed on. However, Gene's messages were more intense and, yet, blended with too many mixtures, too hard to read, but with a certainty of interest. "Mrs. Jones, who is that girl with that yellow, flowery ribbon around her hair?" Anthony asked.

"Don't be silly, everyone knows that she is Gene Farrell. I have noticed the attraction." Mrs. Jones smiled.

"No, I am cool."

"Don't you worry, they will all want you so much. I fear they will be smothering you," she whispered to Anthony as the audience quieted down.

While Barry J had all in a frenzy, Blossom had gotten around, sitting up on the make shift single bed, still early in the morning for patients with the musty smell of sick people and the heart monitors bleeping away to their own rhythm. "Hi, Blossom, I am Doctor Kate, your personal therapist," Dr. Kate said. She was the psychologist assigned to Blossom, and it was all arranged by YPAA. In fact, she was the first guinea pig as the organization recognized that secondary victims can be affected worse than the primary victims.

"My God, look what I have come to, a shrink is seeing me now," Blossom moaned.

"Don't you worry, it is part of the hospital's support organized by Anthony Redford, the founder of YPAA."

"YPAA, what is that?"

"Young People Against Abuse," Dr. Kate answered. "Anyway, I want you to know that you should never blame yourself and for as long as I believe you can understand that, I will be your friend and your support," she promised.

"Anthony has been great, I heard how he has saved my son." Blossom bowed her head in deep thoughts.

"He has done a lot, I agree, but you have been just as good as Anthony. Think about it, it was your love for your son that also kept your son and yourself alive," Dr. Kate said.

"What do you mean?" Blossom asked.

"Were you not told that your son kept everything from you because your love was so great, he loved you in turn and decided not to tell anyone," she explained.

"Dr. Kate, you are still not making sense to me," Blossom said.

"Devon was threatened that if he ever told anyone that you would be killed and your love was so strong, he decided to protect you," Dr. Kate finished her explanation. Blossom had tear drops, a sign she fully understood what Dr. Kate was saying. It didn't put everything into perspective, but it was a good start. "Now listen, the first phase will be having you talk with Devon about everything, and hopefully you will at least direct the blame away from yourself and be the strength and pillar for your son. You know that he will need you now more than ever," Dr. Kate explained.

"OK," Blossom said.

"After that, you will need to be strong enough to

possibility go to court and face that son of a bitch," Dr. Kate said unapologetically.

"Yes," Blossom said again like an empty shell. She was a broken woman, but in her eyes, the determination was evidently there.

"Hopefully, his sentencing will give you some closure and even after that, I will still be by your side. Remember, I am your friend," Dr. Kate said cheerfully, holding Blossom's hands, and then comfortably hugging Blossom. Blossom looked peaceful at that moment, perhaps, a hint of security coming her way with Dr. Kate.

Interestingly, the same closure that Blossom needed was the same that Mr. Stewart required. The clattering sound from the bunch of cell keys had Stewy sitting upright. He was uncertain of which cell the guard approached because he had been hearing the same sound ever since he had arrived, and each time, he wondered to himself when he would be vindicated of the crime he had never committed. He wondered about his daughter, although, he saw her once a fortnight, but that was not enough. His trust in mankind had ended and his own passion kept ebbing away, but he thought of his God and for him, it did the whole works. Slowly, he saw himself as something else. It was as if he was not out of the box, but he was no longer a name, a person but an object that could be anything with freedom beyond his dreams and with that free soul. He was always with God and nothing else mattered, and nothing else would matter. He had no one, he was not a person, or so he thought. Yet, it was that imaginative way of thinking that kept him going for the days he had faced. The key fitted his cell gate, and Stewy looked bewildered, wondering where he was being taken to. He was hoping in his mind that they would not take him further from his hometown. Taking him further, or worse, to another state, meant that he would never see his daughter for much longer than he was used to, and that would surely kill him. He would need to be far more innovative than the current imagination he had held tightly and somehow learnt to appreciate.

"Mr. Jack Stewart, under the Federal law of the Government of the United States of America, you are hereby declared a free man," the guard announced. "You will need to fill out more forms and this you will need to follow me for," the guard said.

"Just like that? No explanation?" Mr. Stewart asked.

"Your lawyer is at the front, and I believe another lady is out there waiting for you," the guard said as Stewy walked behind. Another turn to the right, and at the front desk stood two professional women just as the guard promised.

"Mr. Stewart, I am Valerie Johnson, your attorney at law, and I am here to explain some developments and your position," Valerie said.

"And, I am Dr. Kate. I won't stay long as I have others to see, but here is my card and I will be seeing you with your wife," she said. Stewy took the card, trying to juggle both situations at the same time. "Please, make sure to call me any time," Dr. Kate emphasized before running off. Mr. Stewart signed his release papers, a paper showing the court ordered his release.

"I am sure that you want to get out of this God forsaken place. I have reservations at an upbeat and trendy restaurant only a few blocks from here, let's go." Valerie smiled as she walked. Her breasts bounced in the arrogant manner as her walk and her talk. Like a child, Mr. Stewart followed, still at his wits end as to what was going on. However, when he stepped outside and smelled the fresh air of freedom, he felt like a bird, waiting to fly away to any land far, far away. "Come on, there is the restaurant," Valerie said to Stewy, who stood still, looking around as if he were Alice standing in Wonderland for the first time. She then held onto his arm and pulled him to her direction of The Ritz Restaurant 24/7.

"Come this way, please." The waiter ushered them to their reserved seat. "Here is the menu, please, take your time," the waiter said. He walked off and left the two of them to decide what they wanted. He returned, and waited for them to order.

"I will have steamed fish and plain rice. What will you have?" Valerie asked.

"I will have the same," Stewy said. The waiter nodded and walked off to hand in the orders to the chef.

"OK, while we wait, let us get down to business," Valerie said. "You were wrongly placed in jail and so the state will compensate you. Wow, you are a lucky man hearing all this good news in the same day," Valerie said. Stewy, however, gave her a blank stare as he listened to her. "Well, you need to sign here, my friend, and then ninety thousand dollars is all yours. Here is the check," she said, still excited. Mr. Stewart had never seen so much money at any one time and he was in awe, but not flattered. Valerie could not understand his dead still face. "What's the matter?" she asked. "Is it not enough?" she asked when he never responded.

"Ninety thousand or ninety million, what's the difference? None to me. Not when I spent so long in jail for a crime I never committed. No money can give me back that freedom that was taken away from me," he broke his silence. Valerie calmed down, adopting a more sane persona. "Not when a boy's life was taken away by a man who only thought of his own evil gratification, not when a mother is left destroyed for the rest of her life. For me, yeah, the money will help, but it will give to one the illusion it only represents," chided Mr. Stewart. The message was somehow brought home to Valerie and she was out of her own bubble, even making excuses for not eating. Stewy was not hungry, either, he only wanted to go home to his wife and to his beloved daughter.

Jade had gotten wind of Anthony's celebrity status in Springfield, and his courageous struggle as she and Marie watched the controversial talk show *Say It As It Really Is*. It was a live show as always. "Mom, look at your son, you should be proud of him," Marie said.

"I am proud, of course, I am, but should he not be at school?" Jade asked.

"Well, I knew that this would happen because Lisa

told me that they had a sort of free day called 'creative curriculum day' and Anthony was supposed to have started this club. I suppose he is promoting of LBC television," Marie surmised. It was five o'clock and with an indifferent approach, she watched the program until she heard something.

"The way my parents treated me, I would die first before I have a child and not have the resources to protect him or her or worse, take my irresponsible, worthless self to abuse my own child out of my own failures, none being their fault." When she heard those words from Anthony, her blood boiled with anger, so much so, she got up from the settee and with the hump and stomped toward the kitchen.

"Self righteous, deluded, ungrateful boy," she said, and then snickered to herself. As she stomped into the kitchen, she shifted her direction to the toilet upstairs, and then her eyes glanced at the ajar door of Marie next to the toilet. It was a large parcel she glimpsed on the chest of drawers that caught her attention to Marie's room. Her curiosity got the better of her, and so she opened the door and went closer to the chest of drawers. She picked up the large parcel and through the transparent square of the envelope, she saw the address of a lawyer's company. She examined the envelope, and she then noticed that it was addressed to Anthony Redford. Thousands of ill-fated thoughts crashed into her mind, the most painful was of deception. She could not help but think that Marie was invading her private space, taking from her other personal items.

"Marie!" she barked.

"Yes, Mommy?" Marie innocently replied.

"Get up to your room now!" she barked again. Marie walked upstairs.

"What is all that tone for? Don't speak to me like that," Marie said as she continued the journey of the last two steps. She then saw Jade with the parcel and drawers opened with the clothes ruffled. "What have you done?" Marie shouted.

"Looking to see if you have been taking any other letters from me!" the wide eyed, stern faced Jade shouted.

"But, it was addressed to Anthony, and I had intended to give it to him," Marie said, looking at her mother, who still looking stony faced.

"You listen to me, Anthony is my son, and whatever belongs to him belongs to me. Don't you dare try getting between me and my son," Jade said, wagging a trembled finger in the face of Marie.

"Well, Anthony is my brother, and after all that you did to him, how can you even call him your son? Did you not just hear what he told the world of you?" jeered Marie. That was followed by a loud slap in the face of Marie, but unlike Anthony, Marie returned an equally pitched slap to Jade's face.

"Get out of my house! Get out!" Jade shouted.

"I can always go to my father. I may be only eleven, but he warned me about you, he warned me!" Marie screamed as she got her suitcase on the bed. As Jade walked out, she opened the parcel and in it she saw two letters, one from Alfonso Redford, and one from the lawyer himself. The letter, a personal letter from Alfonso, was not of any interest to her, but the lawyer's letter had her thinking strategy. She then realized that Marie couldn't leave. If Marie left then her strategic, sinister plan would be meaningless. She could not afford for Marie to have an easy ally such as Anthony Redford, not now, it would have been the worse timing she or anyone could have ever imagined. So, she humbly put her tail between her legs and slowly crept back to Marie's room.

"Marie," a softly spoken Jade said.

"What is it?" Marie snapped.

"You have all the reasons in the world to be angry, but I just want to say sorry." Jade tried to plant the seed.

"I don't want to hear it," Marie firmly said.

"I have lost a son, I don't want to lose my only daughter, please, forgive me," a crafty Jade begged.

"You have no right to slap me or anyone, you need help. I understand Anthony's cause so clearly now," Marie said.

"I agree with you and I have watched him today, and if anyone told me that my children would have been my leaders, I would have said hell no, but I submit to your guidance," Jade said. Like butter, she softened Marie's heart. Soon, her hands were off the clothes and instead, like sisters, they were talking, even laughing at some meaningless jokes.

Chapter 16

Fifteen minutes later, Jade left a settled Marie budging nowhere. She was satisfied at the outcome of her tricks and then the unfinished business was her next target, a target she was determined to meet. As if she was far behind time, she quickly dialed the number for Stanford, but she got Margaret instead. "Hi, Margaret, how are you?" Jade asked.

"I am fine, you are the last person I expected to hear on the phone," Margaret answered.

"Don't you mind me, let me speak to Stanford, please," requested Jade.

"Jade, you left us for a long time with Anthony. We are not young anymore and he needs you," Margaret said.

"I am sorry, in fact, this call was to let you know that I plan to see you tomorrow in the evening so that I can see Anthony as well," Jade explained. There was a moment of silence from the other end of the line. "Hello?" Jade said.

"How convenient. Did you by any chance see Anthony on the television Jade?" Margaret asked.

"Yes, I did," Jade answered.

"It is true that you'll never see smoke without fire," noted Margaret.

"And, what was that supposed to mean?" a slightly irritated Jade fumed.

"Never mind me," Margaret replied. Stanford was never a walkover, but he refused to entertain what he called idle talk.

"Hello, Gran Stan," Jade affectionately greeted Stanford with an innocent tease.

"Hello, Jade, how are you?" Stanford said.

"It has been a long time, but I will be there tomorrow at about six p.m.," she said.

"He is your son, so by all means, goodbye." Stanford became abrupt and yet courteous as he allowed Jade to say the last goodbye, pretty much after his goodbye. It was ironic that as the receivers were put down from both ends, Anthony turned up at his home.

"Hi, Auntie!" a gleeful Anthony greeted Margaret.

"Hi, love, your food is covered in the oven. It is your favorite, jacket potato with beans and I have done a special steamed fish with vegetables," she beamed at him.

"What have I done to deserve this royal treatment?" Anthony asked as he lovingly hugged her.

"Don't you be modest with me now, Mr. Bigshot," she teased.

"So, I suppose that you saw me on telly?" he said.

"Everyone saw and I am proud of you," she continued to beam.

"Thank you, Auntie, this really means the world to me," Anthony said.

"Hope you will tell your mother the same when she comes around tomorrow to congratulate you," Margaret said. Anthony's countenance changed instantaneously from bright to dull.

"I won't be here. She comes here only when it is convenient to her," Anthony said.

"I said the same thing," Margaret said.

"I won't be here to see her. What time will she be here?" Anthony asked.

"About six p.m., but your Granduncle wants you to be present," she said.

"I knew that I heard your voice," a more mature voice said.

"Hi, Granduncle," Anthony greeted.

"Come here, my son, give me a hug. You are an icon, you make me so proud," Stanford said, hugging Anthony.

Anthony was spoiled that day. It was a contented home with a contented family, and for the first time Anthony felt like he was invincible, he was like steel and that made him happy. The calm as darkness fell that Wednesday, however, made for a strange, unsettling moment. Stanford laid on his new Tennessee futon of simple mahogany wood, the fluffy mattress made him feel as if he were in heaven. Margaret sat by his side as they faced the front garden leading to their Avenue. Anthony sat with his administrative paperwork all comfortable in his mind when, without any warning, a fire bomb hit the veranda, missing Stanford and Margaret by a couple of inches.

"Fire! Help, fire!" Margaret screamed. The once frail Stanford got the energy from somewhere as he rushed for the key to open the lock of the grill, and as he rushed for the gate, another firebomb pelted through the ungrilled window leading to Anthony's bedroom.

Anthony, like a soldier, rallied Stanford and Margaret as they threw water on the bed, the sill of the doors and window, and even on the floor. The community never took long to rally around Stanford and Margaret as they helped prevent further damage. It was also no surprise when the two young men were apprehended only half a mile from the scene. The quick thinking community had several cars chasing the men as soon as they boldly made their second rounds of firebombs.

A citizen's arrest was made on the spot. The emergency services, the fire brigade, and the police had a presence, only a presence.

"What motivated you to attack these decent and honorable people?" one of the officers asked as he handcuffed the youngest culprit. He couldn't have been older than sixteen, but his unkempt appearance and psychotic glare showed there was more to what met the eyes. He would say not one word, except to say that he was no snitch.

"Are you alright?" asked the neighbor of Stanford.

"It could have been worse," Margaret said. Stanford sat on the partially burnt futon settee, deep in thought of his own world. Soon, everyone left them on their own to their private space.

"You know what caused this?" Stanford finally

broke his silence. Margaret nodded, that was all she could do.

"Maybe he is best going. He is a risk, his type of challenge will surely kill anyone," Stanford muttered. "Anthony!" Stanford shouted. "Anthony!" he shouted once more. He then got up, Margaret followed as they searched the entire house, but Anthony was nowhere to be found.

"Is it safe for us to spend the rest of the night here?" a shaken Margaret asked.

"They caught the men and after the quick reaction from the neighborhood watch, I am sure we are safe. But, where is Anthony?" Stanford asked.

Forty five minutes later, Anthony was outside knocking on the grill. "Wait!" Margaret shouted as she fetched the key to open the lock. "Where the hell were you? You had me and Stanford all worried," she said. She then went to her room, but Anthony followed to see both of them together.

"Uncle, Auntie, I went to the police station because I had to know who those men were. I don't know what the policemen did, but I now know that they were henchmen sent by Brian," said Anthony.

"How do you know this, son?" Stanford, still shaken, asked.

"The police told me, they must have forced it out of 'em," Anthony said. For some reason, Stanford said nothing to Anthony and neither did Margaret; perhaps, they had enough of the drama. They all retired to bed quietly. It was as if they used mental telepathy to express a distance between each other.

Anthony did not allow that to break his spirit because he believed the insurance would cover all the damage, and he believed that progress was more important than a slight hitch.

The drama, however, never ended at that. The following morning, there was total chaos. Dr. Kate ran, panting, out of breath, but still pushing herself as she ran to her 1980 Camaro Z28. She got in, started the engine, and revved it a few times before she sped away. She reached her destination in short order, about twenty minutes. She was at the hospital at close to eight am. She ran into the hospital and toward Blossom's room. As she reached Blossom's room, she saw Devon sitting beside her. He had been there for an hour, telling jokes and stories to his mother, having decided to be the pillar of strength that Blossom needed. It was the most awkward situation for Dr. Kate, but she had to hold herself together and do her job and painlessly as possible. "Now, this is what I like to see. How are you, Devon?" she asked.

"I am fine, Dr. Kate. What brings you here so early? You look like someone who has just seen a ghost," Devon replied.

"I feel as if I heard a ghost an hour ago. Look, guys, I have some news and I'm not sure if it's good or bad," Dr. Kate said. "I...I don't know how to tell you this."

"Don't you worry, just tell us," Devon said.

"There is nothing that we have not seen or heard, tell us," Blossom added.

"Blossom, Devon...Brian is dead," Dr. Kate said.

"That bastard! That coward!" Blossom shouted.

"I know, I know, they found him in his cell with the rope tangled around his neck in mid air. He took his own life," she said as she hugged Blossom. Devon firmly held his mother's hand as he brushed her hair.

"We will get through this together, Mom, we will," Devon reassured her.

"I wanted closure, but not like this," Blossom said. "I wanted that son of a bitch to look me straight in the eyes and tell me why, I wanted to see him admit it all to my face," she added, staring at Dr. Kate straight in the face.

"Don't you worry, he will burn in hell," Devon said. "Mommy, it was probably best that he went that way, at least we can now feel safe for sure," he added.

"Not totally true, as it stands now, you are probably both more unsafe now than ever before," Dr. Kate revealed.

"How so?" Devon asked.

"His goons actually firebombed Anthony's home yesterday," Dr. Kate revealed. "They don't know this yet, but you will all be given a secret location and some heavy protection," she explained.

"Are we still talking about Brian? He surely can't have been so vile, I had no clue," Blossom said.

"He was, I'm sorry to say, the leader of the second division of the poisonous reptile gang, linked to drugs and murder," Dr. Kate continued to explain.

"Urgh." Blossom sighed. Devon knew he was into something, but he never knew how sinister it was.

"How is Anthony? You said his home was firebombed?" Devon asked.

"They are fine now, the police should be at their home now," Dr. Kate said.

She was right. Anthony couldn't go to school that morning. At the same time that Dr. Kate was with Blossom and Devon, Inspector Armstrong was sitting on the veranda with Stanford, Margaret, and Anthony. "It was only by the mercy of God that we did not die last night," Margaret said.

"It is true, look at the window sill, the door is useless and my…I can't take it anymore," Stanford said as Anthony looked on.

"As a matter of fact, the main reason for me being here is to ensure your security. We have secured a secret location for you," Inspector Armstrong said.

"What are you on about?" Stanford asked, looking confused.

"Brian Diamond committed suicide last night, and we now have grave concerns for your safety," Armstrong said.

"Was that the reason his men came at us?" Anthony asked.

"No, they came at you because it was you who got him arrested. They also went after your friend, Devon, and his mother. We don't believe they knew he was dead. Had they known, it's possible that they would have tried harder to kill you," Armstrong said.

"Harder? You mean they weren't trying to kill us?" Margaret asked.

"Possibly not, it's hard to say," Armstrong said.

"For every problem, there is a solution," Anthony muttered.

"Don't you be silly and cause any problems," Stanford reprimanded Anthony.

"Oh no, Uncle, I guarantee that his goons will no longer be a problem," Anthony said. It was pointless trying to persuade Anthony as he was always an obstinate boy, even when it was dangerous for him to be so.

"Sir, with all due respect, thank you for trying to protect us, but we are going nowhere. This is our home and no one will chase us away," Stanford said firmly. Somehow, Inspector Armstrong saw his reply coming.

"I understand the attachment you have to this house, but your safety comes first and the new home will be very nice," Armstrong said, still trying to push his case.

"Will be?" Margaret asked.

"There is no will be, there is no point discussing this." Stanford stuck to his guns.

"Alright, but at least allow us to provide an armed guard for your house," Armstrong said.

"Very well," Stanford relented.

"Thank you. The state will also refurbish and repair your home, so at least you won't have to do that yourself," Armstrong told them. Stanford looked around for Anthony, but he was gone.

"Hello, this is Anthony Redford, I need to speak to Barry J, please." Anthony called the radio station to speak with his ally. After a few moments, Barry J came to the phone.

"Hey, buddy, I am so glad that you called, I meant to call you. Since you came to light, the ratings for t his station have shot through the roof," Barry stated with glee.

"I'm glad I could help, but I didn't call for that. I need you to do me a big favor," Anthony said.

"And, what is that, buddy?" Barry J asked.

"I need you to let the people know why Brian Diamond was in jail," Anthony said.

"That's the guy who tried killing your friend, Devon, after abusing him, isn't it?" Barry asked.

"Yes, that's the one. Can you do that for me?" Anthony asked.

"I'll have to clear it with my producer, but I don't see why not. Has something happened?" Barry asked.

"You could say that. He hung himself last night in his cell, taking the coward's way out. It's caused a few problems since he is a gangster, so I need everyone to know the full truth, and quickly," Anthony replied.

"Well, I'm on the air in ten minutes, so I'll broadcast it all since I'm due to talk a little about your club," Barry said.

"Now, that's what I wanted to hear," Anthony said, smiling.

"When this is done, maybe we can get you in the studio?" Barry asked. "The producer has been talking about giving you your own radio program."

"Well, we are on spring term break next week, so I can do it any time then," Anthony said. He then realized what Barry had just said. "Hold on a second, how will I have my own program when I'm at school?"

"Weekends, that's the timeslot we are thinking of. I

will get back to you on the specifics, but I've got to run," Barry said before hanging up the phone and departing. Anthony ran to Stanford, Margaret, and Inspector Armstrong.

"Listen to the radio, Barry J's show," Anthony said. Stanford turned on the radio, and everyone listened to what was being said. After a few minutes, Barry J reached the main part.

"Now, I've been asked to bring to light a matter of a sensitive issue. I've been speaking about YPAA, but I think it's time that everyone learned of their first successful case," Barry said. "Their first case was against Brian Diamond, a sick pervert who raped his stepson, banging him more than his own wife. I know that some of you have bad images of gangsters, but is this really a man that any group would want to associate themselves with?" Barry asked. "The coward, last night, took the easy way out and took his own life after realizing that all of his dirty little secrets were about to come out. Well, they need to be revealed, anyway," Barry said. Anthony smiled, as did Armstrong. They both knew that any sensible gangster would not kill in his name, and no one would want to be associated with him any longer. It seemed as though Anthony's quick thinking had saved the day once again.

However, at the radio station, Barry J was in trouble. His producer was fuming at what was being revealed, and especially the content of the words that Barry used. It didn't matter that he was helping people, he had crossed a line. Both Blossom and Devon heard the broadcast, and although they were pleased to hear the broadcast, they still had the emotional and psychological effects to live with for the rest of their lives, even with Dr. Kate's interventions.

Across town, another couple was listening to the show and smiling. Stewy was sitting with his wife enjoying breakfast. "You know, darling, we owe a lot to Anthony. If it were not for him, you would still be in prison for a crime you never committed," Marcia Stewart said. It was the announcement of Brian's suicide that triggered the conversation as they sat at the breakfast table with Marcia feeding their baby girl, Lisa.

"You are right, darling. I can't imagine where I would be now if Anthony had not intervened from the start." Stewy sniffed. "He rocks, I will ask him if I can volunteer to do anything. I would do anything to help that gifted boy," he finished, wiping away his tears.

"It's alright, dear, it's over now, so let's not speak of this again unless Dr. Kate is here. We need to move on," Marcia advised him.

"You are absolutely right. We have a beautiful baby girl and a lovely home, what more could we want?" Stewy asked, smiling at his beautiful wife.

That evening, Margaret made the best of what they had. Apart from the window sill and burnt door, which were currently being replaced, everything looked in order. Anthony knew that Jade was due, but he was still coerced to shower and told to look his best, although he secretly wondered why. As he had a shower, Margaret went to her room, making sure that there was an empty suitcase. They had already made up their minds that he had to go. He was just unaware of their plan.

"Come on, son, come and sit with us," Margaret said to Anthony when he was ready. It was natural that he would do anything they requested, considering what they had gone through and in the back of his head, he continued to consider the role he had played in the events. The tapping on the gate alerted them to visitors, Anthony was the only one who didn't know he was about to get an entourage of guests. He was a little shocked when he saw his whole family.

"My God, what have they done to your house?" Doreen Jackson asked. It was yet another family affair. Doreen, Nadine, and Crystal all entered the house.

"It could have been worse, we could all be dead," Stanford answered. Anthony was still oblivious of Stanford calling everyone to make an announcement. They were just waiting on Jade.

"Uncle is right, if it were not for our quick thinking actions, someone would surely have died," Anthony said.

"Yeah, right," Stanford said with a pinch of sarcasm.

"Look at you, even a celebrity I see," Crystal said with adulation. Doreen looked on begrudgingly at her grandson. With Anthony, the feeling seemed mutual as he totally ignored her except for when he gave her the superficial smile and greeting.

"Ah, here she comes," Stanford muttered. It was Jade, looking confident and determined with her devious plans. Anthony was about to be in the middle of a bidding war. He was starting to get suspicious, but the fire, the security threats, they still masked what was in store for him. Stanford and Margaret thought they were the only one in for the show until they were upstaged by Jade.

"Anthony must come home with me, he is obviously not safe here." She shrugged.

"Not safe? Anthony? What about us?" Stanford asked.

"And, what does that mean?" Jade asked. Stanford noticed the A3 parcel in her hands, it was then he realized the need to up his game. He thought to himself if he could know what was in the parcel before he could make any announcement.

"You wait a minute, can you support Anthony?" Doreen intercepted. "I thought the very reason you were quick to give him up was that you could not control or support him?" Doreen continued. Jade simply laughed.

"How dare you, you of all people, interfere! Wasn't it you who said that I was not your daughter? What right do you have?" Jade demanded.

"Well, he is my grandson, and let us cut to the chase, no one trusts you!" Doreen argued.

"Hey! We are all adults here, so can we not argue in front of Anthony?" Crystal asked, trying to calm down the situation.

"May I speak to my son alone?" Jade asked.

"Of course," Margaret replied.

"Anthony, I need to speak to you, please, come with

me?" she asked him, trying to sound more like a friend than a mother. Anthony had sized everything up and was keen on the developments. So far, things were...interesting. Stanford decided to watch and simply let things take their course. The truth, he believed, always prevailed. Anthony and Jade left the group, and ventured into the kitchen at the back of the house. Jade was prepared to play dirty, she always was, so she knew he had to be sly and strategic in the game. Jade then chose to open the parcel with Anthony's full attention. "Anthony, you know all that I did to you in the past. I am sorry, I truly am. I love you just as I love your sister, and I'm proud of you," Jade said.

"OK, sure," Anthony said, mentally shrugging his shoulders.

"I mean it, Anthony, so don't shrug me off with an OK," Jade told him.

"There you go, there's the real you coming out now," Anthony said, staring at her. He wondered what her game was, but he had already decided not to play it.

"Anthony, don't do this to me. I was in a bad situation, not of my choice, and you were in the middle of it." Her voice sounded teary as she spoke. She then opened the already broken envelope to reveal the most important document. She handed it to Anthony, but as he read it, he found himself falling back onto the chair, overwhelmed by the contents of his letter, putting his hand to his mouth. Jade was almost holding her breath. She wasn't sure if it was the dollars sign that stunned him or if he saw right through her.

"They have been out there for a long time, huh?" Nadine asked.

"Nadine, you've not said much today, you seem so tamed," Crystal joked with a sly smile.

"Oh, I have too much on my mind, the children, the job, and university at the same time. Dealing with such a load is enough to tame anyone," Nadine replied with a soft spoken voice. It was a complete switch from her former personality.

"Don't you worry, Stanford, Anthony is staying right here where he belongs," Doreen said in a solemn voice to a quiet Stanford Jackson.

"Alright, love, not to worry," Stanford said with a small smile. "Besides, Anthony is wise beyond his years. If Jade is trying some new game, he will see right through it."

Just as Stanford had predicted, Anthony was on fire, so to speak, standing up and glaring at Jade. He had indeed seen right through her. "So, this is what it is all about?" he shouted loud enough for those at the front to hear. "Is that what your love is worth? Two hundred and fifty thousand dollars, and I don't even get the estate until I am eighteen it says!" Anthony shouted. "You really don't have a heart, do you? Alfonso was my granduncle, he died and at both our expenses, you are trying to get what you want. That's the way you've always been, isn't it?" Anthony demanded.

"Not quite true, dear, but as it stands, you will be coming with me," Jade ordered with a smirk. "I am your mother, after all, and the law recognizes that I have the right to decide where you live."

"No! No way in hell!" Anthony retorted, storming through the house to the rest of the guests. Everyone stood when they saw Anthony.

"What's the matter, son?" Stanford asked, not happy at seeing Anthony upset.

"She hasn't changed, not one bit. She was not sincere about wanting me to return because I am her son," Anthony replied.

"What do you mean?" Stanford asked, confused.

"My granduncle on my father's side has died and left me with $250,000 and some of his estates for when I am eighteen," Anthony replied.

"What!" Doreen gasped.

"She only wants me in her care so that she can get the benefits from my fund," Anthony elaborated. Stanford looked both mortified and satisfied. He had now revoked his earlier decision and was very clear on his own stance, and faced Jade as she walked in.

"I want you gone now. Anthony is staying right here where he belongs, and you will never see one cent of his money!" Stanford told her firmly.

"Have it your way, Anthony! Have it your way!" Jade fumed before throwing the letter at Anthony and leaving. As she left, she hid a smile. She had stuck the dagger in, and now all she needed to do was twist it. As the group watched her leave, Anthony could almost hear Alfonso's words echoing in his head.

"My dearest grandnewphew, Anthony. By the time you get this letter, I will be long dead and gone. When you came to me, I promised you that I would tell you everything. I am sorry I cannot tell you in person, but I will tell you here, in this letter. First, let me tell you that your father loved you very much, but there is something you must know," Alfonso's voice sounded in his head. "This will be painful for you to hear, but you must know that your father died on the 19th June 1970. A part of me died that day; I never lived since that day. I found him in his room while in Canada. It was all the stress from how your grandfather died and your mother's, Jade, family knows all about it, ask them. I can't bear to write anymore." Anthony finished reading it, but Jade got up to leave. "You stay right there, you are going nowhere," Anthony barked. They all looked at Anthony, but his eyes said it all, the pain and bitterness was too much.

"What is it, son?" Stanford asked.

"You know what happened to my dad?" a rhetorical question followed.

"But, I do not understand, what are you talking about?" Stanford asked. Doreen, Nadine, and Crystal all looked numb, it was as if they had seen a ghost. Then, Doreen spoke.

"Let me see that letter there!" she demanded. She read the letter, and then she calmly responded.

"I know that this is painful for you, but both sides of the family have been to and from hell. Your mother never helped, she caused your grandfather, my husband's, death, and it all started from there," Doreen said.

"You just stop there!" Jade screamed. "Joseph's father's death started it all. If dad had not been a schemer, a gambler, and a loser, then none of this would have happened. It was because of him that I lost my man. I thought he had deserted me and our son, but it was my own family that had deserted me!" Jade screamed with tears rolling down her cheeks.

"You stop that!" Doreen shouted with a loud slap to Jade's face. Jade held her jaw and slowly turned her face to Doreen, and with her backhand, she fired back a shot on Doreen's face. Stanford was lost for words and he felt helpless in the family feud. Anthony listened more as he put the pieces together. He felt his mother's pain for the first time. He could never have forgiven her for all that she had done to him, especially when she confirmed his suspicions on why she treated him so differently, but it was a paradox that he understood.

"I forgive you, Mom," he blurted. Everyone turned to him and like a twist of faith, there was an eerie calm. Jade ran to Anthony, hugged him, and felt tears of joy roll down her cheeks.

"Oh, thank you, son, thank you. You know I love you," she said. Nothing else seemed to have mattered. "Come on, let us go home. There is so much to say, get your things," she said. Stanford and his wife looked on very disappointedly, but there was nothing they could do.

"I have forgiven you, Mom, but I can never forget. I can never trust you," Anthony said.

"What do you mean, Anthony?" Jade asked.

"I understand how this terrible family history caused you to be different, but I think it showed you up for who you really are, vindictive, spiteful, and dangerous. None of these incidents would have come to my attention if it were not for Uncle Alfonso's death, and I would remain hateful and resentful to my father who is dead. I would continue to think that it was all my fault and let us be honest, you treated me like trash because you also believed my father deserted you as well," Anthony explained.

"You know that it is more complicated than that, but it is all over now, let us go," Jade insisted.

"No, Mom, I am staying with Uncle Stanford, but my bitterness toward you is not the same, it is more love," Anthony replied. It was a pleasant surprise for Stanford as Nadine, Crystal, and Doreen, too, were mesmerized by Anthony's level of maturity, and great sense of reasoning and deduction.

"You made the right decision, son," Doreen said.

"Come off it now, none of you have been spotless," Anthony retorted. It was very discomforting for all present, and slowly they each made their excuses as they left feeling dejected, but satisfied that there was some closure. That closure was, however, not much for Anthony. He had a lot more sorting out to do and he knew exactly what he needed to do.

Chapter 17

Stanford and Margaret felt awkward, but happy and relieved with Anthony's decision. They realized that he needed the space. Anthony went to his room, the cream color of the walls did not help. He clutched the pillow to his chin, then changing his body in fetus mode, his mind went blank. He had not a care in the world. Then, his emotions got the better of him. He burst into tears, his breakdown was inevitable. "Why me, Lord?" he sobbed. Margaret heard his whimpering, but still she felt awkward not knowing what to do. It was too sensitive an issue that she believed her interference would do him or herself no good. His self pity had lent itself to glorious hallucinations and fantasies. He was someone saving all the children of the world, just a million dollars would be a good start. No child was in need of anything, everyone being happy and in his world, and no one could be abused in any way, shape, or form. At that point, he was talking aloud to himself.

"Is that Anthony talking to himself?" asked Stanford.

"As a matter of fact, it is," Margaret answered. She then left her adjoining room and ventured into Anthony's room. "We heard you talking, Anthony," Margaret said as she approached the boy.

"Yes, I was just thinking of saving the children of the world," Anthony revealed.

"How admirable, but unrealistic dear," Margaret said.

"No, it is not unrealistic, I could start my own charity and with my own radio program, children around the world would all be saved."

"Actually, you are right, but what would you call the charity?" Margaret asked.

"Young People Against Abuse," he answered. It was as if he had carefully thought that through.

"OK, love, I love you. I would be so glad to help you." Margaret said.

"I want to do it all on my own," Anthony replied. "Aunt Margaret?"

"Yes, dear?"

"Do you think I am normal?"

"Now, what makes you want to ask such a foolish question?"

"Well, everything seems so abnormal, everything has gone so horribly wrong," Anthony said.

"But, is that your fault? It is not your fault, it is just circumstances and you seem to have been coping so well. Look at you, even forming your own charity."

"Please, do not make light of the situation. In many ways, I am so much like my own mother, that was why I forgave her."

"I am lost, dear, what do you mean?"

"You have not been around her long, but her mood swings, sense of hopelessness, and all the other symptoms I read about at the library points to bipolar," he said. "What if I have bipolar disorder?" Anthony wondered.

"Don't be daft, mind you. I haven't got the foggiest idea about bipolar," she admitted.

"Can you please take me to a clinical psychologist, please?" Anthony pleaded.

"Now, the topic has done such a turn, I think you are right," Margaret said.

"Tell no one, though."

"I promise," she vowed. "Only Uncle Stanford," she then added.

"No, not even him," Anthony pleaded.

"I can't do that, I can't, he has to know," Margaret insisted.

"OK then, if you must," Anthony said sheepishly. At that moment, Anthony glanced toward the bed post where, in front of it, was the chest of drawers. Anthony turned his attention to the top of the chest of drawers to the opened letter Jade had given him from Alfonso. "Can you get me that letter, please, Aunt Margaret?" Anthony asked.

"No, not again, let it rest now," she said.

"I just want to read for the last time what happened to my dad," he said. She got up and held the letter, and then she handed it to Anthony. She had no choice, upsetting him at that time would be rather foolish. Anthony graciously took the envelope and began reading to himself, when he paused. Margaret noticed his pause. He stopped reading and then looked forward at the wall in front of him.

"What's the matter, love? You look as if you've just seen a ghost."

"I recognized the handwriting from somewhere," he revealed.

"Now you are making no sense. I will make sure you see that psychologist this week," she joked.

"Wait a minute, this is my mother's handwriting," he said with strong conviction. Margaret was not sure what to do. It was a good time for the Earth to open and take her in, she thought. It had gotten too much for her.

"Are you sure, love?" she asked.

"Yes, no one else makes their 'J' with a hook like this, and the I, even the Ts are unusual and only distinctive to her. It's as if they were her signatures," he said.

"It is getting late, dear, I am going to bed now." Margaret excused herself. She had already spent an hour by his bedside, and the situation had become too sensitive for her. Anthony was, however, too out of it to have realized her slipping away.

"She could not be so cruel, what is happening here?" he questioned himself.

"How is he now?" Stanford asked.

"Mad is an understatement. Now, he thinks Jade forged the letter from Alfonzo," Margaret answered.

"I would not put that past her," Stanford answered.

"Don't be daft, the guy is totally delusional. He

wants to see a psychiatrist and I could not agree with him more," she said. "Go and see for yourself," she invited Stanford.

"As a matter of fact, I shall do so now," Stanford said as he ventured toward the adjourning room.

"What is all this story I have been hearing?" a caring Stanford asked.

"Like what story?" Anthony asked.

"Like you thinking you need to see a shrink," Stanford answered.

"And, under the circumstances, would you not agree?" a clever Anthony asked. It was a different attitude to Stanford, though, he was less open with him.

"And, the letter?" Stanford asked.

"Perhaps, I was looking too much into that, I will let it rest," Anthony said. No one was sure if he was just appeasing the situation, but he was a sincere boy, so Stanford considered the problem solved.

"He is fine now, he had a hard day, that's all. Arrange for the psychologist to see him, do that first thing in the morning," Stanford instructed Margaret.

"OK, dear, first thing in the morning," Margaret said before turning the light off.

Anthony had the light turned off, too, but with his face toward the ceiling. He stared in space until his eyelids got weary, putting him to sleep.

"Good morning, Granduncle. Good morning, Grandaunt," Anthony said, kissing Margaret as she broke the egg in the frying pan. Stanford was already sitting at the table and looked up at Anthony.

"Calling me Granduncle makes me sound so old," Stanford said

"Being a Granduncle is a privilege, be proud and wear the title," Anthony said as he sat down beside Stanford.

"What's with you this morning? One minute you are below the ground, and the next you are on top of the world," Stanford said.

"Leave the boy alone, I called and made the appointment for this Wednesday," Margaret said.

"So, what about school?" Anthony asked.

"You will be late that day. Here is the letter for your teacher to tell her about that day."

"Thank you, I am already late, better rush out of here," Anthony said as he quickly took the last bite of the egg sandwich. He was rushing to school. It was the usual routine, catching the bus, and then from the bus stop walking less than two hundred yards to his school.

It was always a walk of meditation. That time, the letter that Jade had given him kept popping up in his head with suspicions lingering to the back of his. It was just the writing style, he kept seeing the letters Y, I, and F with Jade's name on all of them. He then reflected on how she turned out so well from the outcome of the family feud. It just did not feel right for Anthony. He reminded himself that he must figure out a solution. He would not rest until he worked it all out, that was a promise he had made to himself. His mood changed instantly when he saw Stewey at the gate. It was like the good old days.

"Hi, Mr. Stewart, how are you?" Anthony asked.

"I am all good, I am all good. Listen, Anthony, I just want you to know that to me, you are the King," Mr. Stewart said.

"No, Stewey, we are all kings. What happened to you could have happened to anyone. We are here to help each other, and we should never feel less than we are because of another man's help," Anthony explained.

"Wow, where did you come from, are you some sort of philosopher?" Mr. Stewart asked.

"No, a friend just like you told me that if someone helped you and reminds you more than once, he never helped you at all," Anthony replied. Mr. Stewart shook his head as he reflected on the thought provoking statement shared with him. It was enough for him to appreciate Anthony even more for the right reasons.

Anthony continued to walk toward his office. Contrary to his belief that he was late, Anthony was actually one hour early, just in time for meeting with Mrs. Jones, Mr. Baidoo, and the new member he had on his committee, Devon. His agenda was clear for that morning. It was all about the charity. He had it all planned in his head, and now it was all about putting the motions in place and he had the best people to put it together. Anthony was a product, and a valued product of the school. What he said was more or less gospel, especially when his actions filtered to the wider public audience. After all, it was because of him that the school had become oversubscribed.

"This is an exciting one, folks, we will make history with this one." He motioned his plan as he sat stately at the table. "You all know that my dream is clear and wide open," he started. "My dream is to see the reality of children like myself who have been abused to be empowered. I want to give all children all around the world a voice, a voice that will allow them to be heard when or if they are physically, mentally, or emotionally abused, and that is why I want us to concentrate on a charity for Young People Against Abuse," he explained.

"Actually, that is a very good idea," Mrs. Jones said. "I have worked with charities before, and it is not a difficult task to set up," she continued.

"And, what will I do?" Devon asked.

"You can be our Public Relations Officer, you know, spreading the word and making sure that we get as much support as possible," Anthony said.

"Sorry to be the dumb one here, but is this charity going to be all about you getting your name all over it?" Mr. Baidoo asked.

"Nothing I have done has ever been about me, listen, no one is being forced here," Anthony replied. It was clear that Mr. Baidoo was becoming the weak link, but Anthony stayed calm and refused to give him the ammunition. He was the teacher and he always believed that respect to the teachers was the ultimate expectations, besides, there was someone he needed and Mr. Baidoo was the man who could help.

"Please, guys, let us work in harmony. I have become committed to this cause and let us remember that no one is indispensable," Mrs. Jones interrupted.

"Sorry, guys, I don't know what came over me,"

Mr. Baidoo apologized. The meeting was adjourned and Mrs. Jones departed with the determination to fulfill her side.

Ten minutes was left before assembly began and soon, Anthony was amongst the crowd of students in the corridors when he bumped into Gene Farrell. "Hey, stranger," she said. "How can I believe Mr. Stranger when no one of my kind have had the privilege to exchange words with you?"

"Come to think of it, I believe it to be the first time we have exchanged words," Anthony cheekily added.

"OK, you have me beat on that one," she said.

"In that case, lunch is on me, being the gentleman I am," Anthony said.

"Well, I have no choice on the matter, being that I am the loser here," she replied. Anthony was a conqueror, an achievement he was most proud of. The chemistry was strong and so natural, both parties were relaxed with the other.

"So, what has kept us so far apart?" Anthony asked.

"Destiny, my mom always says that nothing happens before it's time," she replied. They never wanted to separate, but they had different lessons to attend and so they had to depart from each other. Lesson after lesson, one after the other followed, and five sessions later and the day was over, but his highlight of the day was one dream coming true. It was lunch time when he saw Gene approaching his table in the school main cafeteria. A spacious cafeteria, to be sure, but ten minutes into the lunch break and the cafeteria was almost empty. Most of the children were out on the playground for most of the time. "Here I am again, I have kept my promise," Gene said.

"So, I can see, I must be the luckiest boy in the school," Anthony said.

"And, I am the luckiest girl in the school," Gene replied. Eyes were everywhere, and it did not take a genius to work out that a relationship was developing. It was the envy for every boy in the school.

"Gene, I really would like you to be on my committee," Anthony asked.

"Oh no, that can't be," Gene blurted. It was as if she was waiting for the very question. Underneath the veneer, Anthony saw something else. It was as if she was running from something. Her countenance had changed dramatically.

"Look, Gene." At that point, he held her hands with their fingers interlocking with each other. "If it is your dad that is the problem, he will understand," Anthony said. However, it was that sentence that had put everything into perspective. It was as if Gene had locked down. Anthony knew right there and then that something was wrong and if anything, he had to turn it all around. He sucked his jaw in, his eyes popped out and holding his eyes, flopped it into a dogs shape. That had her in stitches. It was enough to sway her emotions from whatever it was that had been a sore point for her. All was forgotten and nothing else could have replaced that moment for Anthony. "So, will I see you again?" Anthony asked.

"Why not? A few lunch times together can't do any harm," she replied.

Tuesday had passed and another lunch meeting developed Anthony's confidence. It was, perhaps, the drug he needed, nothing but being in the company of Gene had made him most happy. The melancholy period had seemed over and done with, until Wednesday, when he had to go to his appointment with Dr. Semaj.

Chapter 18

"Come on, we have an appointment for nine thirty a.m.," Margaret said.

"I am ready. I need to look like a gentleman even though I am only in my school uniform."

"You really believe that I was born yesterday? I have noticed how much effort you have been putting in your appearance these days," Margaret said as they walked together.

"Her name is Gene," he whispered in her ears.

"I see, you should introduce her to me."

"I will, miss, seeing her this lunch time. I did not even remember to tell her that I may not make it for lunch with her today," Anthony shared with Margaret.

"Don't you worry, one day will not kill either of you," Margaret said. The bus, their usual mode of transport, led them to the leafy suburb of Red Hill, Springfields. The building was very modern, and when they entered the air conditioned building, they both felt a sense of peace and total calm. They both went forward to the receptionist.

"Anthony Redford?" the receptionist asked.

"Yes, madam?" Anthony replied.

"Please, sit in the lounge, I will call you," she said as she wrote in some details. They both sat in the lounge looking at the triangular boarded ceiling and the few art pieces etched beautifully on the wall. "Anthony, Dr. Semaj is ready for you," the receptionist said with a soft spoken voice.

Anthony left Margaret to the magazines she had been flickering through. Guided by the receptionist, Anthony opened the door where he saw three sofa chairs. They were so comfortable, the oval, modern leather types. Anthony felt as if he was at home, but when it automatically extended his feet out, he felt as if he was in heaven. Dr. Semaj seemed like the coolest man he had ever seen. His smile and soothing voice made Anthony feel at home, it was all well done to get him to open up.

"So, let's talk, Anthony, take me back to when you were five," he said. Anthony laid down comfortably on the sofa, his eyes closed as he slowly immersed himself under the spell of Dr. Semaj. "The world is your oyster, have no fear and tell me what you see," Dr. Semaj said in his soothing, calculating voice. It happened so soon, Anthony was hypnotized without his knowing it. He writhed his body as he moaned to his own discomfort. "Tell me what you are seeing, Anthony, tell me," Dr. Semaj insisted.

"He is there, who is he, Mom?" Anthony said. "Never you mind, you go out there and play with those kids," Anthony moaned to himself.

"Can you see who this man is?"

"No, it's a shadow, but I want to see him. Mom

231

wants me to go and play with the kids."

"Why do you think so?" Semaj asked.

"He is tall, am I seeing things, but Mom looks upset and, yet, she is pretending to be happy. I have seen that look before."

"Who do you think he is? Is he your dad, Anthony?"

"No, no, he could not be. My mother would have introduced us to each other," Anthony wailed.

"Take us to what happened after you have stopped playing with your friends," Semaj guided Anthony.

"Mommy, you look tired, what's wrong?" he said.

"Get to your room, you are both going to Ma tomorrow."

"But..."

"No buts, get to your room." All of it came from Anthony as if he was both himself and his mother.

"Go on, Anthony, tell me what happened," Semaj egged him on.

"Oh my God, what will I do? I have just cut Ma, I am dead now," Anthony said, looking very frustrated. "The ambulance is taking Ma, please, God, let her live, I never meant it." Anthony was crying now. It had gotten too much. Dr. Semaj snapped Anthony out of it. Anthony had had enough, he could not sustain more of his emotional baggage. Margaret was then invited into the room.

"How are you feeling, Anthony?" Dr. Semaj asked.

"I am doing fine," Anthony answered.

"Anthony, I need to speak to your grand aunt alone, do you mind?"

"Not at all," Anthony replied, leaving the room.

"Mrs. Jackson, it was an interesting session with Anthony."

"I am not surprised, but tell me what is happening with him," she said.

"I am afraid I can't say just yet, except that it is clear that he had a troubled childhood, and there in an underlying problem which will take several sessions to surface."

"Mmm, I see."

"Yes, I think the sessions will be very important, most of the problems surfaced around his mother, but my professional view is that it goes deeper than that."

"Tell me about it," Margaret said. "So, when shall the next session be?"

"The twentieth," he said.

"But, that's this Friday." Margaret replied.

"I know, but the quicker this is done, the better," Dr. Semaj reassured her.

"Very well," Margaret said. She then clutched her bag under her arms and left the building with Anthony. "He wants to see you again this Friday," she told him.

"Good, I found it very useful," Anthony answered.

Thursday could not come fast enough for Anthony. He had missed seeing Gene on the Wednesday, the usual lunch time, so when she never turned up for school on Thursday, he panicked. He later learned that Gene had gone on a French field trip with the school and would not be back until Monday. His stomach felt empty, his mind confused, not knowing how his future stood with Gene. Anthony was a shell of himself. He had lost a portion of his pride, courage, and his vivacious spirit of ruthlessness. At the age of fourteen, he was faced with too much, but the events unfolding in his life became more complicated with the latest information of his father. Anthony left school early that day and quickly, he changed from his uniform, putting on a pair of shorts and a t-shirt. He then went toward the oven where his dinner was covered. He began to eat it when Margaret entered. "You are home early today, and just do not look your usual self. What's wrong? Tell me," she said.

"Oh, nothing," he answered.

"I know you well enough, come on now," she begged.

"I just feel depressed, I don't know what's the matter, honest," he said. Margaret left him with a kiss on the forehead. She figured that something was wrong and in that moment, she thought how right it was for him to see the shrink.

Day two, and Anthony was at the psychiatrist's office on the Friday as was agreed upon. "Hi, Mrs. Jackson, Anthony, nice to see you again," the receptionist greeted them. "Please, sit in the lounge."

"Thank you very much," Margaret replied. Anthony said nothing. He still seemed withdrawn and depressed. It was the one time Margaret could not say a word to get his attention.

"Dr. Semaj is ready for you, Anthony, please, follow me." The receptionist led him to the office. Anthony entered the office where he sat at his usual place.

"You are looking on a downer, Anthony, now this is the place to drown your sorrows. Tell us what is making you so depressed," Dr. Semaj said.

"It's just everything, my mother, my daddy, responsibilities, and this girl, Gene," he answered.

"It is as if the world is on top of your head, right?" Dr. Semaj asked.

"Yes, I have just had enough, I can't take it anymore," he said.

"Anthony, you are fourteen and this is understandable, but of all of those problems, which of them bothers you the most?" Dr. Semaj asked.

"My dad, I wish I knew him, and I feel guilty thinking that he never cared for me, not knowing that he had died," Anthony divulged.

"And, which is the second biggest worry?"

"My mother, I wish I had a mother. I can't stop thinking about what she has done to me, and what she is capable of doing."

"And, what has she done?"

"Oh, the list is too long. Where should I start? Breaking the mop stick on my face, beating me mercilessly with her belt buckle, having me sleep on the floor at the age of seven, beating me with the stiletto of her shoes and...but, you know." Anthony paused.

"Go on, what should I know?" Dr. Semaj continued with his job.

"All of the physical harm was never as bad as the emotional pain. It was the things she said that hurt me the most. I would have forgiven her more readily for the beatings, the swollen face, and scars she left on me, but I can never forgive her for the things she said," Anthony lamented.

"And, what did she say?"

"Oh, like, 'If had known what you would have turned out to be, I would have pushed a knife into my womb, killing you.' She also told me regularly to go and find my dad, or, 'do you want me to whore my body out for you?' when I asked for a textbook or field trip money for school." Anthony stifled the tears and covered it all with a smile. "It was as if she rejected me. I sometimes wondered if she was my mother, even now I am not sure, but since lately, I have softened to her," he said.

"And, what has changed?" Dr. Semaj asked.

"Everything. That letter, I started to think that she, too, was a victim and have been feeling sorry for her, but with caution," Anthony said.

"You are so mature and intelligent, Anthony, you are like one of the seven wonders to me," Dr. Semaj said. "What makes you so suspicious of her then?" he asked.

"Oh, it is just the letter, nothing to really worry about." He cut the talk short. Dr. Semaj was convinced that his mother was the number one cause of worry for Anthony, and so he decided to tap in from that source.

"OK, Anthony, you have not a care in this world, not one care except for your mother, take us back to when you saw that tall, shadowy figure and your mother sent you to play with the children in the street," Dr. Semaj slowly and smoothly whispered in the ears of Anthony as he laid back in the same reclining sofa chair. Anthony went into a deep trance once again. It was weird how he went under Dr. Semaj's spell so quickly. "You are still five, Anthony," Dr. Semaj whispered.

"Mom, you look tired, what have you been doing?" Anthony mumbled to himself.

"Go to your room and get ready for Ma," he mumbled again. Dr. Semaj heard that before, but he had an awakening.

"It was as if she had seen a ghost or killed someone," Anthony mumbled. He then started to perspire, and from his mouth, froth came, and then his body started to quiver. Whatever he saw then was not the first time, but it prevented him from moving forward. Again, Dr. Semaj had to snap him out of it.

"Anthony, are you OK?" Dr. Semaj asked.

"Yeah," Anthony said as he tried to catch up on his breath.

"Anthony, can you remember the last thing you saw?" Semaj inquired. Anthony looked dazed, and then out of the blue, he spoke with a touch of anxiety.

"The letter, the letter, she wrote that letter. I must get to the bottom of it," he said to Dr. Semaj. The letter was just what had drained Anthony of everything he was made of. His resilience, ambition, and drive was stunted by that one letter and he felt as if the real Anthony was ready to re-emerge. It was as if he never needed Dr. Semaj anymore because whatever he saw, it was the piece of the missing link. Dr. Semaj wanted to learn more and he intended to, but he made sure to note a discovery he had made about Anthony. Bipolar disorder. It was not at the manic stage, but it was getting there and he feared Jade had suffered the same ill fate. He called Margaret in for another private chat.

"Mrs. Jackson, my diagnosis of Anthony is that he suffers from Bipolar Disorder," Dr. Semaj said.

"What is Bipolar Disorder?" Margaret asked.

"It is a medical illness where the patient has disproportionate mood swings, and I am afraid that his is pretty bad."

"Just how bad, Doctor?"

"Well, it can be hereditary and, as in his case, it is both hereditary and from the effects of social disorder," he explained. "I am afraid that his mother has destroyed his life and he may never have the normal social life of a grown man that many take for granted."

"So, what can be done?" Margaret asked.

"I will give him medication, but do not despair, he will possibly be exceptionally successful as he is so bright. He is beyond his years, his social life will be his main handicap, although, many like him have married with children."

"Lord, please, cover Anthony with your blood," Margaret said to herself as she looked to the heavens.

"There is just one thing, he has described some incidents which seemed disturbing," Dr. Semaj revealed.

"Like what, Doctor?"

"It is difficult to say, but the key to that disturbing event is in a letter that he was given by his mother."

"Oh, that letter," Margaret said.

"So, you know of the letter?"

"Yes, he mentioned something about it being in her handwriting," Margaret said.

"Well, to be honest, she is capable of anything, because I am certain that she also suffers from Bipolar Disorder," Dr. Semaj said.

"Say what?" Margaret exclaimed. She evidently did not understand the word hereditary.

Chapter 19

Margaret tried not to look discriminating, but she could not help staring at Anthony. It was a stare of wonder. *Perhaps, I wonder how he feels, or how mad or how dangerous he is*, she thought. They walked side by side returning to their home.

"No need to be staring at me like I am some freak, I always knew I had some disorder like that," Anthony said to Margaret, who had the guilt trip look, the type that a sorry puppy had.

"No, I was not thinking like that, shame on you."

"Right," a sarcastic reply came from Anthony.

"What's that supposed to mean? Look at the many strange things you did in the past and you think I needed a shrink to tell me you were mad as a hatter?" Margaret asked.

Anthony laughed at her statement, it was just what Margaret wanted, the old Anthony back. "Yeah, we heard how you ran away, and when you burst that clappers in the kitchen making me believe the gas had blown, you think I never knew you were mad." She just would not stop, but for Anthony, it was hilarious. It was just what was needed to break the ice.

"And, what will you tell Uncle Stanford?" Anthony asked.

"Just tell him that you have lost a few screws," Margaret said.

"It's just the euphemism that will get him scared," Anthony replied.

"Don't you worry, he is well mad himself," she said.

"He will not understand," Anthony insisted.

"No, seriously, he is mad as well, he will be glad for the company," Margaret said.

"No, be serious now."

"I am being serious."

"You don't say!" Anthony gasped.

"With stress and tension these days, you would be surprised how many are walking the streets just like you. Some in suits, some even doctors themselves. Have you never heard the saying 'there is a thin line between sanity and insanity' used before?" Margaret asked. It was food for thought for Anthony. It made him feel so much better. Margaret made it feel as if most people had some type of mental illness, some not knowing themselves, and after thinking about it some more, he spoke.

"You are so right, it is one of those unseen illnesses, and only the proud ones or some through embarrassment hide it," Anthony agreed.

"It is not as bad now, but in the past, you would be an outcast, no one in the family would want to know you. I think we have moved on as a people, we are getting better," Margaret said.

"Wow, in that respect you are right, but in many other respects, I think we have been getting worse as a people," Anthony told her.

"Sadly, I agree," Margaret said, sighing. They finally reached home and Margaret went straight to Stanford. "You have company, dear, the doctor says he is a mad one," Margaret said.

"Anthony?" Stanford asked.

"You heard me right."

"But, he doesn't..."

"Act mad?" Margaret helped him out with the words. "Like when you are not on your medications?" she said in front of Anthony. Stanford never batted an eyelid. Anthony was shocked because he felt it was something to be quite ashamed of.

"No, dear, his type is called Bipolar, and that explains his mood swings. But, the doctor says it could get worse, even deadly, that's why he, too, is now on medication."

"I see," Stanford said. It was all settled and Anthony was, yet again, in his comfort zone, but still one thing bugged him, and that was the letter. Being in his true form, a calculated plan came to his mind.

"If only I could get into my mother's home for just one day. A weekend would suffice," he mumbled to himself. On impulse and without wasting another minute, Anthony called his mother on the phone. "Hi, Mommy, how are you?"

"Anthony, it is so good hearing from you. How are you, son?" she asked, but Anthony wanted to rush the motion of events.

"I am fine, Mom, but I am missing you now."

"Anthony, hearing this is like sweet music to my ears. I miss you, too, and you know how much you are welcome back to your true home. You know that here is where you belong."

"I agree, Mom, but let us take it one step at a time. What if I stay over for the weekend, and then the following weekends, and let me see how we get on first?" Anthony suggested.

"That is a great idea. I think I already know, but what has really changed, Anthony?" she asked suspiciously.

"You know it was that letter and the fact that I now understood the pain you, too, were going through," Anthony explained himself.

"I know. I am just glad that the letter could have cleared up all those misunderstandings. So, when are you coming over?" she asked, sounding anxious.

"What about next weekend?" Anthony asked. He had a second thought, not wanting to seem too desperate.

"You can come over now, if you like," she excitedly replied.

"Not so fast, I must let Uncle know first. They need time, too," he said.

"OK, so tell me about school life."

"Oh, I must go now, Mommy, Uncle is coming." He cut the conversation short, he had already gotten what he wanted so nothing else mattered to him. Jade did not have the slightest inkling that her devious triumph's was Anthony's triumph, so her thoughts were blinkered with just one aim, and that was to win him over on the first day on his arrival. In her mind, pigs would fly and, therefore, he would not want to leave her home after that first day. "Aunt Margaret!" he shouted.

"Yes, Anthony?" she replied.

"I just had a word with Jade," he said.

"And?"

"Well, I will be staying at her house next weekend," he answered.

"Say what, now what is going on in that scheming mind of yours?" She caught on. Margaret had learned to understand Anthony well, and she always saw through him, even when he was the best for humanity. She realized that it as his survival traits instilled by his childhood experiences. She admired him and knew that he would most definitely make it in the world. She was, however, thankful that she understood him well enough. Perhaps, it was the fear of him seeing a need to use her to his advantage that was not so constructive for her.

"You know me too well, Aunt Margaret," Anthony said with the most mischievous smile to the corner of his mouth.

"I am listening." Margaret urged him to share the plan with her.

"Well, I need to get into her home because I believe that she did get a letter and it was not the letter she gave me."

"So, you think that she got the original letter in her house?" Margaret clarified.

"Well, duh," Anthony said.

"Don't be rude, let me give you a 'duh' then. What if she ripped or tore up the original letter?" Margaret asked.

"I know her well, she won't do that. She will want to keep it for as long as she can, just to prove that she won the battle. She will need to look at it from time to time," Anthony explained.

"She is your mother, you should know her well, but how will you find a letter like that in one day or a weekend?" Margaret inquired. She wanted to know everything. Then, she caught her breath. "Promise me one thing, do not get into her drawers," she animatedly warned Anthony. "A gentleman, and worse, the son of a mother, never does things like that," she justified her warnings.

"If she were a lady, I would agree, but considering that's where she keeps her prized secrets, I do not believe I can be that gentleman of yours," Anthony replied.

"No, you have been there before." Margaret gasped. Anthony refused to say a word; she realized the answer to that one.

It was good, though, that Anthony had spoken to Margaret first on the matter. Anthony knew very well that Margaret would have told Stanford everything, but more importantly, she would have done all the convincing. She always had. Margaret had not noticed the trend, but Anthony started it all, so he knew it all. He was already using her and she had not even realized it. He just could not help himself. As far as he was concerned, all's well that ends well, and so he just moved on to his next crusade, and that was his charity.

The peaceful, quiet, and lonely atmosphere was all he needed and he had it all. He really wanted the charity, Young People Against Abuse, to be set up, now more than ever before, and so he was determined to be on schedule with its complete set up. He hooked his index fingers into the dialing numbers, rotating the figures for Mrs. Jones call. "Hello?" her soft spoken voice answered the phone. Anthony must have been the only student to have known her number, and he seemed to be at liberty to call any time.

"Hello, Mrs. Jones."

"Oh, hi, Anthony, you are going to live so long. I just called your name," she said.

"And, may I ask what did I do to deserve such honor?"

"The charity, I was chatting to my friend, Paulette, a charity worker, about you. You owe her big time, Anthony, she has helped Devon and I get the application forms, putting together the declaration forms and with her expertise, the governing documents are all sorted," she briefed Anthony.

"All done and dusted then?" he asked.

"Sure is," she answered.

"So, what did Mr. Baidoo do?" he asked.

"Devon and he worked relentlessly in putting together the aims with some great statements, if I may add," she answered.

"Wow, so what has he said?"

"He looked on reasons for the charity, things like a

relief to abused children who are homeless, a tool to empower vulnerable children, and to educate the public on the need to protect abused children."

"I could not have said it any better," Anthony said.

"Stop being modest, many of the ideas came from your very speech when you launched Young People Against Abuse at the school," she answered.

"And now, I will be launching the charity on Tuesday, I just can't wait," Anthony said.

"I know. So, what is the next step?" she asked.

"Well, I have already arranged with LBC Radio Station and Barry J to host my own show for the day on Monday," he answered.

"That is wonderful," she said.

"Yeah, it will be awesome," Anthony said.

"Look, Anthony, I got to go now, but I will be listening to hear you. What time will it be?"

"Four o'clock, so I won't be at school, there will be training for the entire day," he explained. Anthony finished the talk to his total satisfaction. "All's well that ends well," he gleefully said to himself before putting the receiver down. His day had done, in fact, that was his weekend, knowing that he was content in his mind. Monday was all that was left to seal his fate and then nothing, absolutely nothing, would have mattered. He now believed Dr. Semaj's saying, 'Not a care in the world'.

Chapter 20

The defining moment had arrived for Anthony. It was THE DAY, the day that he had been waiting for so long. He was expected at LBC Radio Station at eighty thirty a.m. He had already gotten the itinerary for the day and in his head, it was as if the events of the day had already unfolded. He got up at four thirty a.m., and as he shuffled out of the bed, Stanford was awoken. "Margaret," he whispered.

"What is it now?" she asked.

"Anthony has gotten up, he is now in the shower, that's unusual," Stanford said.

"Oh yeah, the boy is excited about being on air at one of those big shot radio stations. Apparently, he will be having his own slot for the day," she explained.

"Why am I always the last to know what goes on in this house. He never tells me anything and I am his blood," Stanford moaned.

"Do not take it to heart, he loves you to bits, it's just that he thinks I am more open minded to accept things. He is one of those who believes that men are more difficult to convince and women are easier to understand," she explained.

"What station will he be on then?" Stanford asked, taking an invested interest.

"LBC, yes it is LBC, I think he said at four p.m., but it is a full day routine," she explained.

"Are you going to make him some breakfast?" Stanford asked with concern.

"I think you are right with that one," she said as she, too, shuffled out of bed and, with her nightgown on, she ventured toward the kitchen. The movements of the frying pan, and soon the egg frying and the whistling of the kettle made Anthony realize how lucky he was. He thought to himself that Margaret never had to do such things, but her caring attitude made him reflect on the hell hole that he had been in, and then the adrenaline with less anxiety, but a more fighting spirit, justified his cause for his charity. He promised himself there and then that he would hold back no punches. The emotions became even more unbearable when Stanford came in the room to do his part.

"I hope I am not imposing, but this is my favorite tie," he said as he handed it over to Anthony. It was just the tie Anthony needed, a silk grey and black striped tie. It went beautifully well with the silk striped dark grey suit Anthony had already put on. "Come on, let me put the tie on you," a proud Stanford said. Anthony obeyed, and Stanford gave him the gentleman tie and as he knotted it to his neck he looked proudly on. "You do not tell me much, but I want you to know that I will always be there for you, and I will be listening from the start to the end,"

Stanford promised. Anthony's eyes got watery, but he managed to hold back the tears.

"Thank you, Uncle, and I will always love you, too," an emotional Anthony said as he tightly hugged Stanford. It was astonishing to see how time had elapsed so quickly. Anthony's judgment of timing was spot on. It was six a.m. when he realized that time waited on no man. He dashed to the table, quickly gulped down the egg sandwich, but the hot tea he held slowed him down. He only managed half of the cup before giving up and then dashing from the dining room. Margaret ran to meet him.

"Arms up," she ordered. He quickly complied and she then sprayed the Brut cologne all over. "Here is the sandwich, come on, put it in the bag. You never know, you may also very well need this money," she said as she placed a twenty dollar note in his hand. He kissed her and then went through the gate, heading for the train station.

He walked briskly to the sub-station, and in less than an hour, he reached Manhattan. It was a different location, the branch of the big fish of LBS that he was going to. He pinched himself as he looked around and above to the high rise buildings. He turned down a street and it was not too difficult, the huge and bright sign of LBC was there for everyone to see. He had one problem, and that was he was well ahead of his schedule. He arrived at seven thirty a.m., but the security guard had let him in.

"Yeah, you are meant to be here, but you can only stay here in the foyer until Barry J arrives to take you under his wing," the security guard explained. The security guard did not know what he had taken onto himself.

The one hour wait went like nothing for Anthony, but for the security guard, a large strapping man, it was like one year. Anthony talked like crazy, and the closer it got to eight thirty, he talked even more. "Hey, Anthony, you made it," Barry J shouted to the relief of the security guard.

"I would not miss this for the world," Anthony exclaimed.

"Have you had breakfast yet?" Barry J asked.

"Oh yes, I have had enough fuel to take me half way through the day," Anthony said.

"Come on, let me show you around," Barry J said as he signed himself and Anthony in, and gave Anthony a visitor's badge, which he proudly wore. "Now remember, you will be filling my slot today, so you can't let me down. In fact, I expect the popularity to shoot through the roof." Barry laughed.

"You know me, I settle for nothing but the best," Anthony replied.

"Come on, the day has started, what I am about to show you will only take a minute," Barry J said. When Barry said just a minute, he must have meant hours because when Barry J started the routine, it was the entire radio station that he showed Anthony first, and then a health and safety drill had to be done. It was fine for Anthony, especially since he had gotten a certificate to prove that he had taken part in the drill.

His moment of glory arrived hours later. With

Barry J and an entourage of the director, program producer, technical support, and studio controllers, he had finally been shown his studio. Barry J sat beside him, but as far as everyone was concerned, Anthony was the man. Anthony looked around and as he did, he made a close examination of the two rooms separated by the glass window. There, the audio programs were produced, recorded, and broadcast. He felt so privileged, but he was mindful of his purpose, so he was totally prepared to forget himself and be selfless as he needed to do a fine job for his main cause. He remembered the children, the vulnerable, abused children, and within that space of time, he embodied a totally different, but strong and mature persona hungry to show his worth. Everything was set. Mike, the program's producer, sat at the producer's turret in the control unit with his body forward and mouth at the microphone.

"Are you all set, Anthony?" he asked.

"Oh, yes," Anthony shouted with confidence.

"Looks like this boy is set to take away your job, Barry," the producer joked.

"Tell me about it, I am watching him," Barry replied. According to the clock in front of them, they had five minutes left before the start of the show. Winston Turner, the director, sat in the control room facing Anthony and Barry. He was a middle aged bearded man who said little, but he chuckled away. He seemed relaxed as he got ready to monitor the on air program. He looked through the glass separating Anthony and himself, and pointed his finger at Anthony.

"You are the man, you are the man." Anthony lip read him. It was his way of boosting confidence. Anthony then noticed all eyes looking at the 'On Air' warning light. It was large enough to have been noticed, 150mm by 220mm, with purpose build aluminum. Then, the color red of ultra brightness and 12V LED illumination meant that Anthony was in the spotlight. Barry J had already used the announcer turret to turn the microphone on.

"Give it your best shot, son. Just be yourself," Barry whispered in his ear. And, the stopwatch was on. "And, here I am again, this is Anthony Redford, the boy who fights for the cause of vulnerable children," Anthony said. "Today, I will be sitting in for Barry J, although, he is right here, folks, he is right here."

"You know I would never leave y'all," Barry interjected. "So, what is your show all about, Anthony?" Barry asked, giving him that extra push.

"Well, I have lots in store for you all today. In five minutes, I will be taking calls from you, but for now, my crusade has begun," he said. "I have only just set up a new charity, Young People Against Abuse, and this was all thanks to Devon Brown, Mrs. Carole Jones, and Mr. Baidoo. Thank you, guys," he hailed them. It was four thirty one, and just as Mrs. Jones had promised, she was listening to the radio. Devon and Mr. Baidoo were all ears as well, as was Margaret and Stanford, along with a whole host of listeners in the big city.

"You go, my boy," a proud Stanford said.

"My Aunt Margaret and Uncle Stanford, you know you are my love and big up for setting me up this morning." Stanford had the widest smile then, just as Margaret tried to compose herself. "Serious business now, though. I don't know about you, but I am tired of seeing the rise in the abuse of children around the world. I am tired of reading in the papers that children have been neglected, beaten to death, and raped. It makes me sick, and worse, embarrassed to call myself a member of the human species," Anthony said with great conviction. "Give me a call, folks, and let me hear what you think," Anthony invited his listeners on his show.

"We've got a call," Barry said.

"Hello?" Anthony said.

"Glad to be the first caller, Anthony. I just wanted to say how I think you are doing a great job and as only fourteen, it makes me admire you even more," the caller, a woman, said.

"Thank you for calling in," Anthony said before another caller was put on the air.

"Anthony, I am just as livid as you. After listening to you for one minute, my conscience pricked me and I then had to call the police on my neighbor."

"Please, go on," Anthony said, before the irate caller continued.

"This man, every day he beats his son, he was like the caveman, clobbering his son with a stick, log, anything he found. I felt sorry for the boy, and besides, they are affecting my peace," the woman complained. Anthony felt it deep inside, but he had to hold it together, if for no one else, but the children. He clenched his fist, it was his only defense mechanism.

"Madam, I am so grateful for your call. It is people like you I truly admire, people like you who are not afraid to defend the helpless. You have allowed your neighbor's problem to be your own, no, let me get this right, it is not just your problem, but society's problem," Anthony lamented. He was only just getting started as he got in his stride. It was personal and he would pull no punches. Everyone was glued to the radio station LBC by then. Mrs. Jones could not stop herself from calling her friends, and Margaret did the same, demanding others to listen in. "We all need to do our part, we must let other's business be our own, because when you ignore their business thinking it is none of your business, think about what happens ten years down the line. In ten years, that child will make it your business when he starts to beat your daughter, when she begins to hate everyone for the wrong reasons, when their brains are so messed up they come into your home with a gun, when he or she commits suicide having smashed the community to pieces. It is all our business to get off of our bottoms and do something to get the abusers off of the street," Anthony lamented. The phone line was jammed up. For Barry J, it was the real deal, he could not believe it, his ratings must have soared, he thought, but for Anthony, it was all of genuine concerns.

"Oh my God!" exclaimed the caller on the line. "I am at the window now, and I can see the police cars pulling up. Gosh, it looks as if the social services are around as well," she revealed. "See you, and thank you again, Anthony." The line went dead.

"Whatever you guys do, be responsible, be careful not to bear false witness against your neighbor or anyone for that matter, not saying that's what my last caller did," Anthony warned. He knew the dangers and risks that could have come of it, you only needed the wrong over sentimental, irrational person with a grudge and an innocent man or woman would be in jail, he thought. That call was the highlight of the day, and it had set a precedent for the rest of the callers, but more so, contributions were pouring in like crazy. He could not believe it, his charity was in a great position to do its job, just as its aims had promised.

"You smashed it to pieces!" a jubilant Barry J screamed with delight. It was the end of the day at LBC for Anthony, but there was an element of surprise that he never expected. Barry took charge on the microphone and, live on air, he called Anthony over. "To all the good old folks listening, I just want to say thanks to Anthony here, the star of the day," Barry said. Anthony nodded, then said thank you. "Not so fast, we want to give you this as a token of our appreciation," Barry J said. Anthony reached his hand out and accepted a check, but he was gobsmacked the second he looked at it.

"Ten thousand dollars!" he exclaimed.

"That's right!" Barry J revealed. The check was paid out in order to Young People Against Abuse. That time, Anthony could not hide his emotions. He started crying all over again.

"I can deal with that, a young man crying," Mike teased on the other side of the control room.

"Thank you so much, I will make sure that this check is not given away in vain." Anthony was ready to leave.

"Oh no, you ain't going nowhere yet, that check was from LBC, but here is two more," Barry J said. The element of surprise was overwhelming. He looked at the other check and he saw seventy thousand dollars and fifteen cents. That check was from the public, all donated via credit card during his broadcast. He was also warned that more was coming in. What he never expected was the five thousand dollar check, a personal check written out to Anthony Redford.

"You didn't have to do this, guys," Anthony said.

He never knew what his highlight of the day was. There were too many highlights and so he left the LBC radio station on a natural high. He knew that whatever happened just then would have made him even more popular at school, and for him, it was just the perfect situation to help more of his own. Gene, he hoped, would be the icing on the cake. If ever he was to be selfish for the first time, it would be to use this to his advantage to get closer to Gene. Stanford and Margaret treated him like a king, but it was nothing unusual for Anthony. He took it with humility. Tuesday was the day he got jittery about, not knowing how Gene would respond.

Tuesday could not come fast enough, it would have been a busy day for him. The day when he was scheduled to launch Young People Against Abuse. The school had opened the presentation to the wider public. That was not the real challenge for Anthony, though. It was meeting up with Gene the usual lunch time. He got noticed and he was the center of attention, but still there was a sense of privacy for Anthony and he needed that, especially during the lunch hour. The usual happened, the cafeteria started off packed, and ten minutes later it was practically empty. Everyone had gone on the playing field or walking in pairs or groups around the school.

Anthony waiting in the cafeteria sitting on the silver metallic chair and around the matching silver metallic table all on his own. Five minutes had gone and still no sign of Gene. Twenty minutes passed, and now he could not understand. He wondered if he should have gone on the divided part of the school grounds where only the girls stayed. For some lessons, they shared the same classes as the boys. He was gutted until he saw from a distance, the bouncing walk and the hair moving in rhythm with her walk. His heart leaped for joy for it was her, the girl he so desperately wanted to see. "Be calm, Anthony," he whispered to himself as she got closer and his heart palpitated with total anxiety.

"Hi, Anthony, I listened to you on the radio yesterday," Gene said.

"Thanks for listening, I really missed you," he replied. He could not hold it back.

"Well, you were not here last Wednesday."

"That was my appointment," he quickly explained.

"What appointment?"

"Just a doctor's appointment," he said without elaborating.

"And, Thursday and Friday was the French Festival," she explained.

"Well, you are here now and that's all that matters," Anthony said. She then gave him a long lasting look in the eyes.

"Anthony, I am so proud of you, you just never would understand." She got emotional suddenly.

"I am so proud of you, too, darling." It was the first time he had gotten so personal. There was something extraordinary happening. She would not leave the topic. It got Anthony suspicious. "Is something wrong, Gene?" he asked.

"You know, I listened to your program and for the second time, I felt as if you were speaking to me alone," she said. With watery eyes, he looked at her intently. He wasn't sure if he should share his life with her, it was not supposed to be the time, but everything had gotten so spontaneous.

"Everything you hear was all because of my own experiences, my own pain. Gene, I, too, was abused, physically, verbally, and emotionally, that is why I feel the pain so much for others, it's all real," he explained.

"I figured that, and I suppose that is why I have become attached to you also," she revealed to Anthony. "I used to believe it was only girls who felt the pain of abuse, I never knew that boys went through those kinds of pains, too," she said.

"They do," Anthony said. "Devon and I are living proof," he continued, but kept track of her revelations.

"I never knew that some boys cried like girls for the same reasons. Like me, when my step dad had put his hands under my skirt for the first time, and then there was a second, and a third, and now look at me, you would think I am just that weird girl who has a normal life," she said with a straight face, but a body so tense you knew her body was in a prison. She was on lockdown. Anthony froze, he was as stiff as a rod, speechless. "I know, I am powerless and, yet, it is my schoolwork that gives me my freedom," she continued. Still, Anthony was speechless, it was as if he had become a mute. Finally, he spoke.

"Is this man in question Mr. Baidoo?" Anthony asked for clarification.

"Oh yes, no one else but the pure Anif Baidoo who sits on your committee, who teaches you and I," she answered.

"It all makes sense now. No wonder you looked as though you saw a ghost when I asked you to join the committee," Anthony reflected. "I could kill him now," he silently screamed. It was as if Anthony had hit the brakes so hard the veins stood in the length of his neck, the venom showing in his eyes. Then, he paused, the type of pause that meant the light bulb of destructive ideas was flashing. "You know what, you have no choice on the matter now," he said. "You will have something to do with this charity and you are a part of the committee," he coaxed Gene. "You will play an integral role and you will call the police for his arrest. He will sit amongst the committee at three forty five today during the opening of the charity."

"I am afraid, I can't," Gene said.

"Can't you see, Gene, if you really believed in what

I said to the world yesterday, then you will get that filth off of the street," he explained.

"But..."

"No buts, Gene. Can't you see how he has been laughing at us? He sits on the committee of Young People Against Abuse, he teaches other children, who's to tell that he isn't doing the same to others?" Anthony continued to urge Gene, and it was working. "You are not alone, Gene, you are not alone." It was those last words that swayed her full on. Without another word, she followed Anthony to his office. Anthony dialed 911 and asked for the police. When he was connected, he handed the phone to Gene.

"Hello, I am calling to report a pedophile," she said calmly with tears streaming down her cheeks.

"Another one, Johnny," the police officer said. "Ma'am, this is good of you. We have been getting thousands of calls since that fella Anthony was aired on LBC. Please, give us the details and we will also arrange for support, a counselor will come to see you," the officer explained. There, Gene went through a few of the painful details, but the details were so emotional that the officer himself felt tears streaming down his cheeks. "I believe you, you will need to come in and see us. How old are you? You sound quite young," the officer said.

"I am thirteen," Gene answered.

"Dear God, have mercy!" he exclaimed. Anthony wanted justice, but he could not bear it any longer. He took the receiver from Gene.

"Hello, officer, my name is Anthony," he said.

"You sound like that young lad on the radio station yesterday," the officer said.

"That's because I am he. Please, sir, you need to arrest this man today. At four he will be at the opening ceremony for the charity at Kingsmill Secondary campus, and he will be sitting on the pulpit as a member of the committee."

"Thanks for that information, I will personally pay him a visit," the officer said, the fire in his voice clear. He was a man who hated pedophiles with a passion. "Let me speak to Gene again," he said.

"Of course," Anthony said, returning the receiver to Gene.

"So, Gene, when will you come over to see us?"

"I can come now."

"Are you sure?" he asked.

"Yes, I am sure," she politely answered.

"We are proud of you, Gene, and thank you for putting your trust in us," the officer said. Gene hung up the receiver and left for the police station.

"I will follow you, it's only a few hundred yards away," Anthony offered his support. Gene was glad for it, and so they continued to the police station. Upon their arrival, a young policewoman took their details from behind the counter. Two minutes later, another female officer, at least forty five years old, took Gene away to a small room.

Gene never expected that half an hour later, she would be lying on a bed with the chief gynecologist thoroughly testing and recording all of the evidence found. It was intrusive, to say the least, but Gene felt fine, she knew it was for her own good and the good of the rest of the vulnerable children. Within an hour it was over, and they were set to leave the police station. As Anthony reached the exit, he stopped, turned back, reached for his back, and slid his hands in to take out the school's magazine. He yelled out for the attention of Officer Elaine Bell. "Look, page twenty two, I forgot to give Gene and the other officers this so you know what the creep looks like. This will save you time when collecting him," Anthony said with a scornful disposition.

"Thank you, that will be very useful. Gene is a lucky girl to have a young man like you around," Officer Bell said before walking away, leaving Anthony and Gene to head back to school.

Chapter 21

Anthony and Gene had returned at approximately three p.m., and Anthony was pleasantly surprised to see the entire set up replicating the original ceremony for the official opening of the Young People Against Abuse club. That time, however, it was to celebrate the beginning of the Young People Against Abuse charity. The same room, 414, the second assembly hall of the school, was used once again. The back doors were opened in the same way, extending to the outside of the playing field. The feeling was that of a great achievement and consistency. A mood of happiness covered Anthony until he saw Mr. Baidoo. He was very busy helping to get the chairs out. He took pride in the chairs being positioned in straight lines. Mr. Watson, the headmaster, was helping as well, and together, they approached Anthony. It was inevitable that there was to be some exchange of words.

"Anthony, what I am about to say, I do not say it lightly," Mr. Watson said. "You are the finest pupil who has ever come through the gate of Kingsmill Secondary."

"Thank you, sir."

"I second that, and I say this as a former student, a teacher, and a member of your committee," Mr. Baidoo agreed.

"Wish I could say the same for you," Anthony mumbled to himself.

"What was that?" Mr. Baidoo asked.

"Oh, I just said I could say the same for you," Anthony said, smiling.

"Oh, don't be modest. I could never fill the boots you walk in," Mr. Baidoo said, smiling back at him. If he could read Anthony's mind, Anthony knew he would not be so happy. The platform, the chairs, the entire setting was wonderfully in place and as long as Anthony could make his statement, then all was well.

Four o'clock came and the parents, students, and the general public were in their seats with a full assembly hall. Mr. Jones was the center of attraction on the platform. Her turquoise linen dress with the flowery bow to her neck was simple, but outstanding. Devon was a new face and he was poised to give a talk, but first Anthony stood to the front of the audience. "My most Distinguished Headmaster, Mr Watson, I want to say thank you for believing in me and the group from the start," he started. "Mrs. Jones, Devon Brown, and Gene Farrel, I want to say thank you, from the bottom of my heart," he said. The look on Mr. Baidoo's face was priceless. Mr. Watson tried to touch him, but he could not reach. He had to resort to whispering, but his microphone picked up his voice.

"You have missed out Mr. Baidoo," he said.

"Oh, no, I have not forgotten Mr. Baidoo, it was

intentional," Anthony said. "This man, Mr. Baidoo, is one of the bravest men on this earth," he said, the sarcasm evident in his voice. Mr. Baidoo picked up on it, and clocked everything once Gene was acknowledged instead of himself. He chose to sit calmly as if nothing was wrong. "He is brave because although he knows in his heart that he truly does not understand or care about our aims or our ethics, he still sits on the committee, he still works his guys to the floor for the club that is, in fact, his biggest enemy," Anthony said. Mr. Baidoo knew that it was all over and as he turned his neck to the left of the stage, he saw two uniformed police officers approaching him. There were also two coming from the right, and another three coming down the aisles made by the chairs. He was busted. They reached him, and the lead officer spoke.

"Sir, please, come with us down to the station," the officer said in full view of the public. Because of Mr. Baidoo's microphone, the whole audience heard them. A hush swept across the room, but it didn't last long.

"You pedophile, I hope you rot in hell!" Gene yelled out, her voice resounding throughout the hall thanks to the microphone. Anthony quickly rushed to her side and comforted her, just as Mr. Baidoo was led away.

"I'm sorry that it was done this way, but your courage will be remembered forever," Anthony whispered into her ears. She was consoled by Anthony, and tried to regain her composure. Outside, she did. Inside, she was torn apart, but she refused to let that show. "Come on, Gene, pick yourself up, dust yourself off, and start a fresh life," Anthony said. He took her hand. "Remember, life will always knock us down, but we can choose to pick ourselves up again," he told her. "He is gone now, so pick yourself up and do this for the others," he added. She nodded in agreement, and stood the podium. She took a deep breath, and then she described the Jekyll and Hyde life of Mr. Baidoo. After she had done, Devon stood up and described a similar story. They both showed the validity and need for the charity. The justifications were so clear that its need was no longer seen as a confinement to the school. A local business man, a land developer, stood up and offered his support as well as a building and land to the cause. He offered them as a gift, and so the official headquarters of Young People Against Abuse was found. Mrs. Jones stood up, amazed.

"You're not serious, are you?" she asked, cautiously.

"I am most serious. The building and land is currently sitting in Springfield doing nothing, and the charity has need of such a place. Since it is a worthy cause, I am happy to offer it to you," the man, Mr. Christopher Harmon, said. He was unknown to many people, but that wasn't important to Anthony. He was over the moon. "I will speak with my lawyer today, and get the land and deeds signed over to the charity," he said. "It won't be much, but let us talk about this some more some other time when time is kind to us," he finished.

When everything was finished at six o'clock, Mr. Watson and Anthony stood with Mr. Harmon and signed the paperwork, transferring ownership of the land and building over to the charity. Mr. Watson had agreed to represent Anthony and the club since he was an adult. He also made sure everything was in order. The future looked so bright for Anthony, but the drama was something he went looking for. He did not care too much how much to undertake as his spirit was awoken and hungry to fight for his peace of mind.

Chapter 22

Anthony was not a normal child, his mind was never settled. Perhaps, that was the reason his life was punctuated with drama and everything that was dysfunctional. He was happy with life, though. He thought that he was blessed to be able to transform those needs to helping others who had no idea how to transform negative emotions to positive actions. It was no wonder that Margaret stared at him in amazement. "You are one in a million. How do you do it, Anthony?" Margaret asked.

"Do what?" he replied.

"How do you suffer the way you do and still have the energy to fight your corner and then go on to fight other's corners?" she asked.

"Will power, OK, tell me something. There are myriads of people who will go out of their way to make others miserable, even suicidal. Where do they get the energy from, and why should their victims sit back and allow them to destroy us?" Anthony asked. Margaret watched, listened, and learned. "I believe that we, too, have the energy and the brains to fight back the smallest threat that faces us and it does not matter how small you are," Anthony concluded.

"Are you sure about that?" she asked.

"Let's face it, if I never had a terrible mother, then I would never have been the same. Remember that it is circumstances that changes people," Anthony said.

"Now that is food for thought," Margaret said before she left.

It was days of conversations like those that gave Anthony self awareness. He was oblivious to just how much communication was teaching himself about his traits and at the same time, healing sessions for himself. Sessions like those carried him through the rest of the week and before he knew it, it was Saturday, the day of reckoning.

For some reason, Anthony felt uneasy and scared. He packed his bags with just enough clothes to see him through the weekend. "Now, you just be careful," Margaret warned. Stanford was asleep, he had no idea when Anthony left the house. Anthony dragged his feet, it was the longest journey ever and, yet, it was only five miles. Anthony arrived at nine thirty a.m. at Jade's house. Jade was already at the gate, waiting for his arrival. Anthony's heartfelt heavy. She was someone he never wanted to see again, but it was a necessary task.

"Oh, my baby," Jade said with excitement. She tried to kiss him, but he moved his head away and she caught him on the chin. He was motionless, although at one point he was trembling. Jade realized his indifference, but she had put it down to his nerves. Besides, she did not care one bit as long as he was there, that was a good start for her to play her tricks on him. She was determined to win him over. "Anthony, please, make yourself comfortable. Marie is out with her dad, so it will just be you and I," she said. Anthony still looked motionless, but that bit of information was the thumbs up he needed.

"Remember, it is your home, too, have anything you like in the refrigerator, the kitchen, anything. I will be going to the supermarket and market to stock up, all just for you," she said. For the first time, she got a smile out of Anthony. It was as if he had hit the jackpot. Any minute she would be out of the house. Anthony rubbed the palms of his hands together, but he began to feel impatient. She could not get out fast enough as far as he was concerned. "See you later, Anthony," she screamed, followed by the slamming on the door.

Finally, he was alone and right away, he was alive. He got up from his room and quickly dashed to her bedroom. He wasted no time as he went through her drawers and then he got to the desired drawer, the one he was certain she kept her mail, important and private mail. He carefully sifted through the mail, sometimes, returning to previous ones. Twenty five minutes and still he was looking through the drawers, it was his second time looking. Jade, by that time, had collected all the items in her basket and she headed to the cashier to pay for her items. In her mind, the next stop would have been to the market, but as she took out the purse and opened it, she realized she had insufficient money.

She had to go home without stopping at the market. It was only a seven minute walk.

Anthony, in the meantime, found nothing. He still had the drawers opened with the ruffled belongings, clothes, stocking, underwear, everything out of place. Then, his eyes caught the one suitcase she kept by the side of her wardrobe. Quickly, he unzipped the suitcase and when he opened it, he saw another stack of mail. Like children seeing sweets for the first time, he went crazy, looking through the letters. It was as if he knew time was having the better of him. He was so preoccupied rummaging through the suitcase that he never heard Jade slamming the door.

His calculation of her return was twenty minutes out, and he would have been right if only she had gone to the market. Oblivious of her return, Anthony diligently continued his search and his handiwork finally paid off. He finally found what he was looking for. "I knew it, I knew it!" he screamed with satisfaction as he opened the letter. Little did he know, Jade heard his very words and most damning for her, the sound had come from her room. She knew that her game was over, but she decided not to end it without a fight, possibly returning to her old self. She already had worked out that he was 175 centimeters tall and eighty five kilograms in weight. She was no match for him, but an element of surprise might just do the trick, she thought.

In the interim, Anthony opened the letter. He was flabbergasted, to say the least. He could not believe what his eyes had seen. The letter was addressed to

Anthony and no one else. He began to read the letter. At the top of the page was a New Jersey address. As he read it, it was as if he could hear Alphonso's voice.

Dearest Anthony,

By the time you would have received this letter, I will be dead and gone. Remember how I told you that I have so much to tell you and that the right moment would come? Well, since I have only a few days left, this is the right moment.

I could go into detail into the history of your father's family and your mother's family, but that is not the purpose of this letter. It is to let you know the relevant trust and to let you know that your father loved you.

After Joseph learned that his father's death was murder intended for Jade's father, he felt cheated and upset with her family. Jade was no exception to his feelings of anger. It was unfortunate that she was pregnant at the time. Everything was going wrong, so he and his uncle Barry left for Canada. In hindsight, when they divulged their plans to me, I wish I had stopped them, but I, too, was hurt for the loss of my nephew, Jerome. While in Canada. Your father went to university, and for four years, he successfully studied to become a doctor. He then realized that there was no excuse to ignore the responsibilities of being a father, and so he decided to leave Canada after the five years to see you. He had some savings and I gave him some money. Everything he had was intended for you.

I was shocked to see him at my house the very next day. He looked so shaken, I had to ask him what the matter was. He told me that, at first, it was difficult to track down your mother. Luckily, he had your aunt Crystal's details, and she directed him to find her. Joseph then told me that they met and Jade wanted to renew the relationship, however, Joseph told her that it was impossible for him to love her in the same way again. She begged and then when he asked for his child, she told him that she had gotten an abortion.

He told her Crystal had told him he had a lovely son, and she said that Crystal was lying because she did not want to be the bearer of bad news. He then told me how he wept like a child. Joseph then left me and went to his room. An hour later, I decided to check up on your father in his room, and there I found him on the floor; I had never screamed so loudly in my life.

The doctor and autopsy report agreed that your father died from SADS, Sudden Arrhythmic Death Syndrome, an unexplained type of heart attack mostly affecting the young. But, I know and you now know, that it was your mother's actions that killed him. I am so glad that I could finally share the truth with you.

Remember, life will always be a challenge, and the hardest challenge of life is to live. Please, live a full and healthy life, for me and for your father.

Your Grand Uncle

Alfonso.

Jade knew that Anthony was totally unaware of her presence in the house, so she made sure to use the time to find something strong and solid to do the job. There was no turning back now. She saw a crowbar in the corner behind the door. She had forgotten that she had taken it to the house for her safety. She called it her man at the time. Anthony, in the meantime, gripped the letter to his chest. Now he wished he had never seen the letter, the pain was too deep. Jade, with the crowbar in both hands, crept to her room. The door was ajar, allowing her to view Anthony and his position. She wanted to get him off of his guard, that time not to bear him, but to kill him. She was in such a rage. Anthony was confused and there was only one way to reduce the pain, he thought. He had to call Margaret. The telephone was by the bedpost. He turned his back, reached for the receiver, and as he dialed the number, Jade was sure that he was off his guard.

"Hello?" Margaret answered the phone.

"I found the letter," he said, but he couldn't say another word as Jade pounced on him with a loud scream. She was aiming for his temple, but his impulse and reflexes had the better of her and the crowbar caught his shoulder instead. Margaret heard the scream and knew Anthony was in grave danger. Anthony was on the floor, holding his shoulder as he looked for an escape.

"So, the first letter was not good enough for you?" she shouted as she got closer to him, aiming the crowbar over his head. Anthony knew she was not well, if only he could distract her, he thought.

"Mom, I am your son, remember? This letter means nothing to me," he said. She would, however, have none of it as her hands fell with a mighty blow from the crowbar. It was his good reflex that had saved him. Anthony was just in time to move his head as the crowbar connected to the wooden floor instead. He was weak, but he managed to crawl on the floor. She took advantage of his slow pace and like a raging bull, she launched at him, she wanted him good. Jade jumped at him and she was on his back, but Anthony flung her to the ground. The crow bar was on the floor as Anthony tried to make his escape. She would have none of that. She threw the crow bar, but throw as she might, her strength was not enough. She only managed a yard's throw. Anthony was at the door. He had to slow her down. He slammed the door shut, and he had to think fast.

A box of clothes was all he saw by the side of the door, it was just as well to barge the door in. It was not enough to prevent her opening the door, but it slowed her down long enough. That was all he needed. She was also weaker than before and one minute of slowing her down was just as good. It gave him the escape he needed as he got up and for the love of his life, he never knew where he got the strength from, but he was determined to run toward the front door of the house. Running for his life, Anthony quickly raced toward the front door of the house with Jade trailing behind him. He opened the doors and ran down the steps just in time to meet a number of police. There were other police cars speeding around the corner.

They stopped, and he saw at least three other officers taking positions. Anthony knew that Margaret had called the police and because of whom it was and the danger he was in, they sped there right away. He felt safe and free at last. Jade was face to face with the police as Anthony looked on from a distance with the letter still gripped to his shoulder.

"Lady, put down the crowbar and put your hands in the air," the police ordered, drawing their guns as a precaution. Jade changed immediately from a self possessed maniac to the most misunderstood victim ever. It was the Jade Anthony was used to, a true Jeckyll and Hyde character, but at least he understood why. She started to cry as she was in total submission of the police officers. The police led her away and as they passed by Anthony, she paused, looking at him.

"I don't know why I do these things anymore," Jade said.

"I do. You are a sick woman, I believe it is Bipolar Disorder," he said to her. He had no hate, but genuine concerns for her. He had hoped that she saw his sincerity.

"You must hate me?" she asked.

"No, Mother, you will always be my mother. I am just glad I have found my closure. I hope you do, too, because I feel sorry for you," Anthony said.

With that, she was led away and Anthony stood clutching his closure, the letter still in his hands. It was like he had a fresh start with a bad history he chose to leave behind. Now, he had a bright future, one he hoped would be with Gene, Margaret, and Stanford.

One he could look forward to. No, one he did look forward to.

With Anthony's strong reputation and ironed character, it was easily forgotten that he was barely a teenager. The reality was now surfacing since his own Mother had so fiercely attacked him. It was not even the attack that had shaken his self esteem or his mature persona, but the reasoning behind his own Mother's attack. The vanity and materialism he had hoped would have been irrelevant to the love and protection of her only son, her own child. Even a wild bear would have understood that her own survival was secondary to the love of her own cubs. It was this that had exposed Anthony's vulnerability and he was totally devastated. He needed someone of his former persona who understood his hurt and pain to give him the same comfort and strength that he had given to so many, sadly, he was on his own. How he would manifest his vulnerability was now the one million dollar question.

Chapter 23

Things could never have gotten any worse for Anthony. Just when he thought that he had conquered his own fears and started to regain his own confidence, he was set back to where he had begun. The spiraling lights, whispering sounds, and watchful eyes were all still part of the scene.

"Hi, Anthony, I am from the New York Police department, but I am also linked to the children protection and counseling unit. My name is Nichole Patterson, but you can call me Nichole." She kindly befriended him. She did look the part with her mushroom, low cut hairstyle, and casual wear. Just a simple jeans with a nice striped cashmere sweater colored brown alternately mixed with grey and light blue. Anthony could not say a word, still lost for words.

"I am Margaret, he stays with me. He has been with us for a while now and.."

"That's interesting because I was under the impression that he was with Jade all along." Nichole paused.

"So, who are they?" she continued.

"My Grand uncle!" blurted Anthony.

"I understand that you have a sister?" inquired Nichole.

"Yes, she knows where to go in situations like these, you can say that she has a father." Anthony was starting to open up…just a little.

"He has had enough for the day, please, understand the sensitive case we are dealing with," Margaret humbly requested.

"Oh sure, but I will need to stop by your home in the near future. I would love to have your number?" asked Nichole.

Margaret reached into her handbag where she grabbed a pen and paper, and quickly scribbled the requested details.

"You can call me anytime," said Margaret as she passed the note to Nichole. It was admirable how protective Margaret was to Anthony, she had grown fond of him. The mutual response from Anthony was just as admirable, the type of behavior any protective officer would have wanted to see. Nichole, herself, admired that, although she knew of different occasions where it was very much a farce from both parties.

They began walking away from the scene, about fifty yards away when Nichole shouted at them.

"Please, wait, I will take you home. Please, enter the car," she offered as she pulled up closer to their bodies.

"Are you sure?" asked Margaret.

"Come in, I insist."

"How kind of you," said Margaret.

"Thank you." She would not stop, it was her usual

grateful attitude to anyone showing any form of kindness.

As they poised themselves to the back of the black Lada Niva car, Nichole saw the opportunity to get closer, at least one foot in the door; anything to break the ice.

"You know, I have been doing this job for fifteen years, and I must say that you are the bravest lad I have ever met," she said as she slowly cruised.

She could not break that ice because as he sat to the back of the car, he reflected with flashbacks of the cruelty he was exposed to. In his mind, he remembered how he was used even at eight years old repetitively to beg strangers, but he saw no shame in that as he thought he was doing the deed for his mother. It became a weekly routine to give him notes to beg shop keepers, most likely after befriending those same shop keepers. In that moment of thought, he realized that she had no qualms about using him because for her, that was what he represented; a beggar, less of a kind. He wondered more about the distinctions between her actions and her illness. He was convinced that her actions were totally separate from any illness she might have had.

The evil and forceful look that she would give him flashed across his mind and he knew that she had developed a hate, but a hate that conditioned by different situations.

Nichole glanced at him and realized how focused he was in his thoughts, and so she preferred to leave alone; at least for now.

For some reason, he shifted his focus, it was a more positive one. He wanted to remember the saints in his past, the ones who were in the midst of his hell. He remembered Mrs. Tomlinson, Gloria, and John. They were all adults. He thought they knew what he had been through so many times, and, yet, even they were helpless from doing a complete job of keeping him safe. It made him ponder about the many isolated and helpless children, some who have had to endure more than him. How many might have been killed because there was never an intervention to the fullest.

They were now along Park Lane and as he looked through the windows, he passed the Queens Public Library once more. It bought back fresh memories. Nichole could see him from the rear view mirror and saw the pensive and reflective mood of Anthony. She understood that silence was still golden.

The family was well known to the NYPD community and detective Armstrong had already briefed her on their goings on. She, however, wanted to hear more, and even so, hear it again from the horse's mouth. She was a very ambitious lady and since she had recently taken on the role as the Child Protection Officer, it was a promotion from working all those years under her superior who had just retired, and subsequently, she still had a lot to prove. NYPD Department was nothing to the New Jersey Department where she was stationed before, but to be attached to the Redfords was like catching the big fish and she was determined to make a name for herself. The next five minutes, you could cut a knife through the air. She had a hunch that something was wrong. She looked at Anthony once more through the rear view mirror, but he looked as though he was at peace with himself. Perhaps, that was because he was thinking about some of his achievements and still the many who were so positive in his life. Nichole had, however, looked further than his facial expressions. It was if she was reaching his soul. Who said the window to your soul was not your eyes? Well, Nichole was about to prove them wrong because as she intermittently gazed through the rear mirror, her eyes caught the cold, dry, and empty brown eyes of Anthony. From those eyes, she determined that something was up with him and she knew that he would lose it, and she knew that it would not be long. She decided that she would be at their tail for as long as it took.

She steered left from the road, Knutsford Boulevard, to a narrow lane leading to a their territory.

"Ok, we are almost there, a hundred yards in and then turn to the left," Directed Margaret.

"Ah, there it is, that big house to the end in front of this road. and that grey colored one is ours," Margaret further instructed Nichole.

"Nice house," said Nichole.

"You think so?"

"Don't be modest now, you know very well that it is quite a nice house you've got," replied Nichole.

She was only being polite, the house was nothing special, moderate at its best. Besides, the house being grilled throughout made it look more like a prison, but its architectural simplicity was its best attribute.

"Thank you very much being so kind," Margaret said as she waited for Anthony to help himself out.

Nichole smiled half heartedly waving her hands, she needed to stick to her plan and she was determined.

Margaret took the bunch of keys from her handbag and carefully she opened the lock to the grilled gate, leading to the car porch.

"Stan!" she shouted.

He slowly opened the bedroom door leading to the red tiled verandah and there he took his key and opened the grilled gate of the verandah. He was in his trademark brown sandal, still in his dotted pajamas. By now, Margaret and Anthony had entered and were now free to walk without the use of a key.

"So, I see that you are here again," he said.

"Not now, Stan, can't you tell that…"

"That what?" he asked.

"That he left the house to go where he was forbidden?" Stanford continued.

He was from the old school and with his stricture attitude, it was just how he was packaged, but it was just not the right time for all his motions. She pulled him aside and loudly whispered to him.

"Look, he is your blood and if ever he needs you more, now is the time. He doesn't need a second rejection!"

Anthony was in ear shot and heard every single word.

Nichole was, at that time, more determined to do as planned. She had earlier noticed the puffed up pocket of Anthony's jersey jumper when he walked away from her car. His hands in both pockets seemed unusually packed, and that in itself made her just a bit more paranoid. She had found the perfect spot without invading the private space of the corner house adjacent to the Redford's home. She chose to park under a Princeton Sentry tree, it had a girth of about 25 cm. Its inconspicuous green flowers made it the perfect parking spot with its green foliage spreading out just as she desired. She felt confident to carry through her plan.

"Armstrong!" she radioed.

"Roger that," he replied

"I shall be camping it out outside the Redford's, roger that?"

"What are you up to now?"

"Well, it might be nothing, but I would rather not regret losing the chance to possibly save a life," she replied.

"Sorry, but I have to say that you desperate rookies get worse, you never miss a chance, do you?"

"I will take that as a complement, but I am sure that I am on to something here,"she insisted.

"Ok, I will make a note of that, see you tomorrow afternoon, roger."

"Bye and thanks." She ended the conversation.

About the same time, Stan still would not have any of Margaret's argument, but he had begun to show some signs of backing down, at least until Anthony had gotten over the trauma which he never knew about.

"Come on, love.

I have made up your bed, and all is well," Margaret soothed Anthony. She was alone with him, but he would say not a word.

"I understand the shock you have been through, but sooner or later, you will have to talk, love, that is the only way to get it out of your system," she said.

Anthony looked at her and nodded to reassure her that he would. She did not look too convinced. For him, he was not his usual self and it burned her inside out.

"In your own time, love, in your own time.

Come, let us drink a hot cup of Horlicks," she suggested

"I am alright, I would rather going to bed now."

"Stop the nonsense, I am going to fix you a nice cup of warm Horlicks and I will also make some nice tuna sandwiches for you, your favorite," she said, but still he horizontally shook his head.

"You go to bed, but I ain't giving up on you. I shall take the hot drink and sandwiches to you."

Anthony walked to his room while Margaret put the kettle on. She got the 'I can't believe it's not butter,' another of Anthony's favorite from the refrigerator. She hummed to herself as she got the bread and tuna, which she crushed, adding the onions, mild pepper. The kettle was on, soon whistling as she multi tasked with a separate menu of chicken breast nuggets and mashed potato ready for Stan.

All seemed well, it was nothing unusual for her since the kitchen has always been her second home.

Nichole had been outside for an hour with the eye of an eagle and the ear of an elephant, but nothing happened Perhaps there was nothing to worry about. She shrugged, but was still, she wanted to give it some more time. She resorted to entertain herself as she believed that patience was a virtue. She got her crossword puzzle out.

"Nothing like this to beat time," she said to herself. At least a favorite question came up. One challenge followed another, and soon she became hooked. There was one question that she spent a while figuring out, the topic of interest was the battle of Hastings. She knew that there was a bridge in it, but she just could not get it out. It was only after using word association that she figured that the answer was Stamford Bridge.

She was comfortable where she was, unlike Anthony, who had been in the adjoining room of Stan and Margaret. He laid his body on the bed with his head placed on the pillow while his eyes gazed toward the ceiling. His eyes then shifted to his jumper, still puffed up with something, something sinister. He reached his feet to the ground and then went toward the wooden arm chair positioned at the bed foot. The jumper hung over the curved top arm chair. He reached for the same jumper, but he never bothered taking the jumper from the chair, instead, he took his hands and with his slender fingers, he felt for four plastic bottles, each filled with sixteen aspirins each of at least 250 mg dosage.

Beside the chair was a brown, curved up, polished mahogany stool. A full glass of water sat on top of the stool. Margaret, always the conscientious, had always left a glass of water because she knew how important water was to people, and having a glass at hand saved them the trouble of getting up and walking to the kitchen so late in the night.

Anthony took the bottles one by one, throwing the entire sixty four onto the bed and at random, he took up a heap in the palm of his hand, closing it to make a fist. At first he pondered for a while, his conscience nibbled at him, but in the end his demons had the better of him, and with the glass of water he gulped down what he managed to grasp all at once. At first he felt nauseated, but in his disoriented state he clutched a few more, and then realized he had drank all the water. Realizing that, he threw back the rest to wherever they landed.

He felt too ill and weak, and could not manage to replace the glass. He body slumped to the edge of the bed. Soon he turned, pushing his body marginally to the center of the bed. His body began to curl in a fetal position.

Nichole had completed her puzzle. She turned her wrist, exposing her watch for the time. It was six thirty p.m., and she had been waiting for some time, enough for her to doubt the need to stay any longer.

"I guess my instinct was wrong this time," she muttered to herself. She then threw the crossword puzzle book to the back of her car, turned the ignition, and her feet gently touched the accelerator. The car began to slowly move away. She had to pass the

Redford's gate in order to face the straight road for the exit. Toward the left was a cul-de-sac and she needed to turn in to maneuver the car toward the exit.

While she did that, Margaret had already prepared the tuna sandwiches. She had sliced the sandwiches in isosceles shapes. She took the whistling kettle from the stove and poured its content in the teapot. She had a lovely silver tea set and she only used that particular one on special occasions. On the silver tray, she meticulously placed the teapot, teacup, and milk pitcher to the outside with the saucer of sandwiches placed to the middle. She was satisfied with her efforts, so she held both ends of the elliptical tray's handle as she ventured toward Anthony's room.

Nichole, in the meantime, was near to pass their gate with shear disappointment. At the same time, she felt guilty because there was a part of her that wanted something to happen; it was all about her profile, something to put on her cv, just another stepping stone, but she thought how wrong that was. Her plan was to get to the office and write up the report on her day's duty. She was only three gates away and by that time, the adrenalin had gone from her. The curiosity, however, had not totally faded away. Just as her mad persona was about to return and she would have sped away, she heard from a distance a harrowing scream. She slowed down, wondered if she was hearing voices, and then accepted that it was her imagination playing on her again. The paranoia had kicked in once more, she decided, so she was ready to accelerate again, but that time, she knew it was not her. She heard that helpless scream once more, and then with a renewed strength she touched the brakes. The car made that screeching sound as she franticly reversed by several gates backwards. She made a sudden halt to the Redford's gate, and without any hesitation she jumped out of her car and ventured toward the gate and opened it.

"Let me in!" she shouted. Whatever it was, she knew it was serious and as a Child Protection Officer, she was trained in first aid, CPR, restraining rights, the lot. She knew the essence of time, and at no time should anyone assume that they had enough time, but at the same time it was imperative that she stayed calm.

Stanford hurriedly searched for the correct key to the grilled gate, but the anxious wrinkled and frail hands had the better of him. He passed it on to Nichole, and it was as if it were her own house because at one try, she had that grilled gate opened. Without a word, she directed her body to sounds of confusion and sobbing. Her pace slowed down as she approached the ajared door of Anthony's room.

The empty bottles and scattered tablets were the first to attract her attention. She failed to watch for her own safety as the sole of her feet narrowly missed being impaled by a large chunk of broken tea cup sitting upright with its two pointed edges. She instinctively moved her feet away as quickly as possible and the same time, moved swiftly to the aid of Anthony. The pills gained in numbers the closer she got to his right elbow. She checked for his pulse and was relieved that there was one.

"911, how can we help you?"

"There has been an accident, we think it was aspirin poisoning. We need an ambulance immediately," Nichole frantically replied.

"What is the state of the patient, ma'am?"

"He is unconscious, but there is a pulse and he is breathing."

"And, how old is he?"

"Thirteen," Stanford whispered to Nichole.

"Thirteen," she repeated to the operator. She went on to tell the operator the address in detail. She wanted everything to go right.

"OK, ma'am, someone is on the way. Please, do not attempt to do anything except gather as much information about the source of the overdose," the operator advised.

"OK, these are all the bottles it seems," Nichole said as she examined the dosage of each aspirins. Stan stood helpless, wanting to do something.

"Is there anything that we can do?" he asked.

"Yes, look everywhere, under the wardrobe, the bed, the dresser, anywhere for any loose aspirins," she asked.

The floor was clean by now and they were all on their knees, searching diligently.

"Here is one, this was under the wardrobe," Stanford said.

"I have found two under the bed," said Margaret as she handed them over to Nichole.

She then counted the amount retrieved, and it all added up to twenty three loose aspirins. Her quick calculations meant that Anthony had ingested thirty nine pills. That explained his unconsciousness and as she made closer observations, she could see the sweat around the sides of his hairline.

"Look what we have brought on ourselves," moaned Stanford.

"Enough now!" barked Margaret. It was the first time that she had shouted at Stanford. He had taken the hint well and said no more.

The emergency service was now present and soon, the two men entered the house.

"Here is all the information and evidence that the hospital might find useful," said Nichole.

Anthony was placed on the emergency stretcher and then rushed off to the hospital, arriving in six minutes. Anthony was already fitted with an oxygen mask and an IV drip. It was clear that he was dehydrated.

Dr. Martin was on the scene with the nurse in the patient's cubicle.

"This is a case of aspirin poisoning," he said.

"As soon as the results of his blood test return, I must know immediately. The last thing I want is the salicylate being released any further, causing greater damage that may have already have been caused to his organs."

"Yes, sir, anything else?" inquired the nurse.

"Monitor the activated charcoal given to him, he might need more," Dr. Martin directed.

"Will that be enough to reduce the level of salicylate, sir?" she asked.

"We caught him in time. This one won't need to be on a dialysis, just make sure that he is getting sufficient IV fluids," he advised before leaving.

Anthony looked much better. The doctor's treatment worked wonderfully well, but Anthony was admitted. It was necessary for the medics to rid the aspirin from his body, and it was later decided that other interest groups such as counseling department, amongst others, were advised to see him.

Anthony seemed weak, but he was conscious of his surroundings by eight p.m. Already, he had visitors. Stanford and Margaret had already seen him, left his clothes, and everything they thought he would need. What Anthony did not know was that like a wild fire, the word had spread about his misadventure.

Nadine and Crystal had come by his bedside as he slept, but they did not wake him. They watched him for about ten minutes.

"He definitely did not deserve this," whispered Crystal.

"If I knew then what I know now, I would have done a lot more to prevent that relationship," Nadine replied.

"There is no way anyone would have known that this would have been the outcome," replied Crystal.

"Besides, the outcome hasn't been that bad. He is a strong boy and what he has achieved so far, none of us have achieved that much. I am sure that he will pull through and make us proud," Crystal said. They then quietly left the room, looking back at his tender face.

It was not the most comfortable night for Anthony as his consciousness becomes more apparent. He was looking around in the strange surroundings, but the voice of other children shouting nurse did not sit too comfortably with him. The night could not wear off quickly enough. He laid on his back and for that entire night, he was in the reflective mood. He was, strangely enough, very aware of what he had done and regretted it. He started to realize how selfish it had made him, especially if God was not on his side. The people that he would have left behind in pain, his friends and family, meant a lot to him, and so he felt further guilty about the mess he might have put them through. Luckily for him, the night had turned to day, and the sunshine was blazing in his path.

"Hi, I am Karlene Hitch, your nurse for the day, and I can see here that your name is Anthony," she said with a warm smile. It lightened up his day.

She worked in a whiz as she updated his notes, and his IV drip. His medication was followed up and like a pro, she made up his bed as she dropped one liners of jokes, sometimes having him in stitches. Soon, she was gone, but not for long whilst he had other visitors. Everyone was about to see just how popular he was.

At about nine am, his first visitor was someone he had not seen for a long time, it was a pleasant surprise for Anthony.

"Oh my God!" the familiar voice screamed with delight. Children nearby became curious. It was Gene.

"Here, I got you a well wish card," she said, giving it to him to read. He read the card and then smiled.

"Thank you, Gene," he said with admiration.

"No, I should be saying thank you," she replied.

"What for?" He looked puzzled.

"Don't be like that, you know what you did for me," she quipped.

"Gene, I will not take the credit for that.

You were a brave girl, and so should all girls who have faced the same like you."

Gene had a tear in her eyes.

"Sorry, I do not want to speak about it anymore, but you gave me the courage to speak out, so thank you," she said as she sniffed her nose. What Anthony did not realize was that Gene was just the start. It was all an orchestrated visit by many more, so when he saw Devon enter the room, he was never the wiser.

"This is a coincidence, Devon, you have come to see me at the same time as Gene."

Devon had grown much taller and even his voice had broken with puberty kicking in. Devon also could not contain himself. He, too, had tears streaking down his chin.

"Anthony, I now have a voice, and it was all to you and my living God. Thank you very much," he said. It was a touching moment because you could actually feel the sincerity coming from the trembling voice of Devon.

Anthony was lost for words, and he was confused because his actions that had place him in the hospital was not what they had come about. He expected them to more or less chastise him as a hypocrite, but they were there to honor and support him. It was the type of network he thought should have existed between young people who were abused. A support to say that they were not alone, and for them to realize that it was not their fault. When Anthony saw Mrs. Brown enter and hug him with a big smile, he knew that it was a lot more than what he had thought. Then entered a man glowing with pride and before he could say a word. Anthony's eyes beamed, and it was as if he were not ill at all.

"Stewy," he shouted with a joy not many could relate to.

"You did not just help the kids of your generation, but even of my own. My entire family is grateful to you," Mr. Steward said as he went to give Anthony a great hug.

Anthony was overwhelmed. He did not know that there were so many who had loved and cared so much for him. The room was getting packed and even the other kids in their varied sick state had become a part of what seemed a big celebration. That, however, did not stop Mrs. Merchel from dropping in. She was all over him, telling her that she should have been his inspiration, but it was the other way round. Anthony had forgotten that he was so depressed not long ago. He was fully submerged in the love, enjoying every bit of it. That, however, was not all. Barry J had made his entrance and Anthony was not so sure whether he should look or close his eyes. His hero was also in the house.

"Should we do it now then?" a voice said.

"Anthony, I would like for you to look outside and see what is out there," Barry J said as they pulled his bed closer to the window. He was on the seventh floor.

Anthony was in position to get a great view, but what he saw was the best of all. He could not believe his eyes when he saw the crowd. They were all there for him. He noticed the banner reading, *Young People Against Abuse is all because of you, Anthony*. Another banner read, *We have a voice, you have a voice, use it!* He was gob smacked, to say the least. Then he saw the biggest banner reading, *WE HAVE FORMED A SUPPORT NETWORK WITH OUR OWN NEWSPAPER, ALL DONE BY CHILDREN. THANKS. ANTHONY*.

Anthony became speechless and very emotional. Tears trickled from his eyes. No one would understand the meaning behind those tears because in the midst of the moment, Anthony tried to put in perspective his main issue, and that was his inability to let go of the hurt and pain he endured, although his mother could have done worse. She could have run away, she could have sent him to be adopted, she could have even killed him as she had threatened. Then, the penny had dropped. All he wanted from her was the unconditional love every child craved from their parents. For him, the knife had figuratively been plunged deeper into him when he realized that his mother's love was conditional on the presence of his father, the amount of money she had, the idea she had that she only bred him for her own future should he be successful or gather wealth from an inheritance, or for someone to look after her when she got old. However, all that had no meaning anymore when he saw the love in front of him. His perspective had changed. It was all about empowering others like himself, and where there was room, to forgive; forgive, forgive, forgive.

Lightning Source UK Ltd.
Milton Keynes UK
UKOW050713171011

180435UK00001B/2/P